PRAISE FOR *NOT CON*

"In *Not Contagious—Only Cancer*, Kyong Ah Choi can read body fluids with the skill of a trained coroner. A nurse's aide in a Skilled Nursing Facility, Kyong Ah tends to every need of her dying patients: decoding their grunts, changing their soiled diapers, and negotiating for their favorite foods. Overworked, underpaid, and without benefits, she is a champion of life, mixing cigarettes, Korean food, and folk medicine to care for others and for herself. In this lively, bittersweet and comic novel, writer Miriam Ching Yoon Louie plunges us into the breathless momentum of Kyong Ah's world as she negotiates uneven relationships with her three children, wards off the ghost of her cheating ex-husband, and schemes to manage her illness compromised by systems and insufficient medical care. The dialogue pops with utterances, beneath the breath rumbles, and secret messages to the dead. *Not Contagious— Only Cancer* drives relentlessly from beginning to end, bringing a satisfying mash-up of pain, love, concern, amusement and compassion. Each of the small chapters drops a seed of wisdom and insight that coalesces into an instructional guide on self-care that allows hope for life and honor for death."

—Elmaz Abinader, author of *This House, My Bones*

Not Contagious—

Only Cancer

Wishing you strength & joy & ♡

[signature] Ching Yoon Louie

Also by Miriam Ching Yoon Louie

Sweatshop Warriors: Immigrant Women Workers Take on the Global Factory
Women's Education in the Global Economy (with Linda Burnham)
Ranting Tiger—Thundering Bunny: Words & Art Together
(Poetry with Nguyen Louie)
XicKorea (Poetry with Beth Ching and Arnoldo García)

Not Contagious—
Only Cancer

Miriam Ching Yoon Louie

Illustrations by Nguyen Louie

Rabbit Roar | Oakland | 2016

Published by Rabbit Roar
4900 Shattuck Avenue #3682, Oakland, California 94609, U.S.A.
rabbitroar.com

Cover art "Vermilion Wings Rising" and book illustrations "White Knights," "Cancer Goddess," "Dope Ddeok," "Tumor," and "Wings Rising," copyright © 2016 by Nguyen Louie

Book design by Jai Arun Ravine
Author photographs © by Belvin Louie

Publisher's Cataloging-in-Publication

    Louie, Miriam Ching Yoon, author.
      Not contagious--only cancer / Miriam Ching Yoon Louie ;
    illustrations by Nguyen Louie.
      pages cm
      ISBN 978-1-943301-00-3

      1. Nurses' aides--Fiction. 2. Cancer--Patients--
    Fiction. 3. Medicaid beneficiaries--Fiction.
    4. Immigrants--United States. 5. Koreans--United States.
    6. Oakland (Calif.)--Fiction. 7. Psychological fiction.
    8. Medical fiction. I. Title.

    PS3612.O788N68 2016   813'.6
          QBI15-600192

Library of Congress Control Number: 2015956990

Printed in the United States of America
10 9 8 7 6 5 4 3 2 1

Printed on paper that is both acid-free and totally chlorine-free (TCF)

For
Cancer Warriors
Nursing & Homecare Aides
& Caretakers All
strong be your lungs

hearts

spirits

For
Minnie Omma & Herbert Baba
joyful be your road

CONTENTS

I. DENIAL: *White Knights*

1. Ins&Outs	3
2. Caller	12
3. Salty	19
4. Strings	26
5. Lounge	32
6. Prodigal	38
7. Asiatics	43
8. Culture	53
9. Sponges	60

II. ANGER: *Cancer Goddess*

10. MediBeggars	71
11. B-Word	78
12. Gametime	84
13. Home	92
14. Guilty	99
15. Rebels	106
16. S&M	113
17. Emo	118
18. Drill	122

III. BARGAINING: *Dope*

19. Brinksmen	133
20. Hubble	140
21. Painkillers	147
22. Odds	156
23. Carded	164
24. Edibles	172
25. Trial	179
26. Favorites	186
27. Danger	193

IV. DEPRESSION: *Tumor*

28. Flame	203
29. Pulse	209
30. Bail	215
31. Clot	222
32. Haul	230
33. C-Word	237
34. No!	245
35. Peasants	252
36. Graverobbers	258

V. ACCEPTANCE: *Wings*

37. Rock-Paper-Scissors	269
38. Snuff	274
39. Cudgels	281
40. Platinum	289
41. Shave	295
42. Fever	301
43. Practice	309
44. Re-Up	316
45. Gift	325
Glossary	337
Acknowledgments	343
About	347

ILLUSTRATIONS

Cover

    Vermilion Wings Rising

Parts

    1. White Knights   1

    2. Cancer Goddess   69

    3. Dope Ddeok   131

    4. Tumor   201

    5. Wings Rising   267

I. DENIAL: *White Knights*

*"What you waiting for, Granddaughter?
Oxcart to doctor?"*
—Halmoni

1. INS&OUTS

After toileting, washing and readying two dozen Golden West Rest and Care patients for breakfast, Kyong Ah Choi exhaled. *Almost done.* She patted her cigarette pocket, coughed, and raised her fist to knock.

"*Kuurrh!*" A guttural, distinctly Korean cocktail of phlegm, blood, and fury trilled on the other side of the door.

Kyong Ah rushed in. "No, no, no!"

"*Kuurrh!*" Blood flecked the new admit's fingers. A tangle of soiled, unspooled bandages festooned his lap like a freshly violated mummy's. His throat surgery incision frothed as he clawed his sutures.

"Stop, you're making it worse!" Kyong Ah pulled his hands down, reading his wristband. "Mistah Won Song Bak?" She switched to Korean. "Are you one of our country's people? No, don't touch!"

Aide and patient grappled, he, weightlifter strong, and she, people-hefter experienced. She'd wrestled too many patients hell-bent on detonating superhero powers before their final surrender. Panting, she bound his wrists with the spent dressing.

"Want nurses to put you in restraints twenty-four seven?" She glanced over her shoulder and whispered conspiratorially. "Or put you under? Because if you wreck your surgery, they'll have to send you back to hospital. More returns, more problems, more pain."

"Kuurrh!" Froth.

The crow's feet around Kyong Ah's eyes and mouth deepened, making her look tavern madam mean. "I'll untie you only if you swear not to touch your neck. Promise? Don't talk. Squeeze my hand once for *yes*, and twice for *no*." She placed his fingers around her fist.

"Kuurrh!" The forklift operator trilled in the only sound the docs had not sliced out.

"Promise?"

Squeeze.

Kyong Ah winced; his bound paws were perfect for twisting fruit—or a small animal's head in half. Here he was caged with Golden West oldsters. Hidden away in Oakland's New Chinatown amidst Vietnamese *phở* and *bánh mì* joints. *Taquerías* and nail salons. Bars and auto body shops.

Her nostrils twitched. *Stale smoke; a fellow fiend.* Her cliff-high cheekbones sharpened. Her right brow spiked above the eye that floated larger and higher than its shy mate. The unevenness might be mistaken for Bell's palsy. In fact, Dead Husband's fists were the surgical instruments that had reset her face. At times the misalignment strengthened Kyong Ah's *nunchi* mind-reader ability and allowed her to see wounds patients held inside. Like the childhood-embedded fear of showing vulnerability she suspected would limit this man's visitors.

"Okay, let's fix your dressing. Don't move or talk." Kyong Ah raced to the supply cabinet for disinfectant and dressing. On the way back she ran into fellow aide Leng Fong, feeding liquefied breakfast to patients lining the hall's seats. The air smelled of oatmeal and lint. White bread and Pine Sol.

"Still no backup from Registry?"

"You kidding? Just you and me again." Leng's potscrubber perm was already separating into clumps. The five-foot-tall Chinese aide wore a dinosaur print scrub top she had sewn from a remnant of the pajamas she'd whipped up for Dewey, her youngest grandson.

"I got to replace dressing new cancer admit tore off." When their cheap-ass boss failed to hire enough nurses and on-call docs to properly service patients, aides had to violate regulations and border cross into RN Nation.

"Where's Missus Santos?"

"*Aiguh!* Save Missus Santos' breakfast. I'll bring her out right after I finish Mistah Bak."

Kyong Ah returned, donned gloves and carefully cleaned Mr. Bak's wound before applying dressing. He gnashed his teeth but shed no tears, like a tiger refusing to cry. He looked vaguely familiar. *One of Dead Husband's Viet War buddies? Too young. Gulf I?* His docs had dug Cancer Goddess' grave deep and wide. Kyong Ah tapped his sugar drip and gave him a hard look. "Don't touch and you'll go home faster. Understand?"

Squeeze. He crushed Kyong Ah's hand as if she'd thrust an arrow through his neck; the taste of bone, birch, and feathers flooded her mouth. When he didn't struggle or pull off the dressing, she untied his bandage restraints and stuffed them into a hazmat bag. He grabbed her wrist, pointed to the drawer and made puppy love eyes at the compatriot he mistook for a nurse. Who might have been a looker once. Before working in this depressing dump.

Is he coming on to me? The five-foot-three-inch aide used to have a curvy figure and full chest that summoned appreciative male commentary. She tucked greying strands behind her ears and sucked in the small paunch she'd woken up with one morning a few suns ago.

"Need something?" Kyong Ah opened the drawer. A black plastic comb. Matches from Seoul Gomtang Restaurant. Half an empty pack of Kools. Her lips flatlined. She relaxed her paunch and handed him the comb.

"Kuurrh!" Mr. Bak drew two fingers to his lips. Inhaled secondhand smoke from her scrubs. Pressed his palms together in prayer.

"You must get doctor's permission first. And smoke outside. Sorry. That's the rules."

He folded his arms and glared, his eyes a rustier shade of pissed.

She closed the drawer, after sneaking some of his contraband up her arm and down into her harm reduction pants pocket. *Poor man. He'll soon be in withdrawal on top of trying to heal what's left of his squawk box.* A red tooth bit through his new dressing; Tobacco God must be exacting tribute for treading his land.

"Please rest."

Almost Smokers Lounge time.

She knocked and entered Mrs. Santos' room. "Sorry I'm late, Missus."

"Poo. Poo. Poo." The stroke patient's Coke-bottle-

thick glasses magnified her rheumy eyes. Shit and disinfectant assaulted the aide's senses; she sipped smaller
breaths.

"Missus S, next time how about buzz us before you
have to go? We come right away."

"Poo. Poo. Poo." Mrs. Santos' wrinkled lips quivered;
choppers peeped from a fizz bowl on the bed stand. The
small gold cross she wore twinkled like the eyes of the pre-
schoolers at the children's center in the Fruitvale District
where she worked. The early birds were probably already
swinging from monkey bars, slippery with morning dew.

Aide patted patient's liver-spotted hand and bent
closer. "Sometimes you don't know until too late, right?"
She lifted the bed sheet; her nose hairs napped up. Mustard sauce haloed around the granny's hips.

"Poo. Poo. Poo." A tide pool brimmed inside Mrs.
Santos' red-rimmed eyes. Urchin anxiety. Clam fear.
Mussel memory.

Ssibal! *Why isn't she wearing diaper? What's wrong with
Graveyard?*

Kyong Ah punched fists into baby breeder hips
bequeathed by her horse-riding ancestors. "Sorry, Missus.
We got to lose that panty." Kyong Ah snapped on a fresh
pair of gloves. Tucked a towel-cum-apron under the elastic waistband of her scrubs. Grabbed fistfuls of wet paper
towels and wipes from the bathroom for the mop-up
operation.

"Poo. Poo. Poo." Mrs. Santos was really a "Miss."
She'd taken care of her widowed farmworker father for so
long, she'd lost the chance to marry. Now she had no kids
to watch over her and translate her monosyllables into

sentences.

Kyong Ah rolled down the weepy granny's soiled balloon drawers. Swallowing roiling stomach acid, the aide mopped the poop soup from her bottom. Diapered and dressed Mrs. S in a marigold print top and in pull-on garden green pants.

Helping patients with their Activities of Daily Living or ADLs was the queendom where Kyong Ah and the aides reigned supreme. They cheered oldsters through meals and baths. Dressed and ambulated cranky limbs. Tracked daily Ins&Outs, especially Pee&Poo dramas, to help seniors push their walkers across Life's final speed bumps.

"Remember? Stand. Swing. Sit. Ready?" Kyong Ah helped Mrs. S rock forward, pivot, and sit in her wheelchair. Step by step. Like her son Mickey had taught his little sis how to ride a bike. Before he turned into a boozer. And Sally into a lesbian doing only Kwan Seum Mercy Goddess knows what at a sex toy shop down on San Pablo Avenue. Kyong Ah pressed the wounds her kids had drilled in her chest. She fastened Mrs. Santos' seatbelt and adjusted the footrests.

"So. So. So." The granny's eyes glistened with salt from an ocean of words that once swam her throat. Her lilting soprano had introduced legions of Oakland tots to "Itsy Bitsy Spider" and "You Are My Sunshine." Now only scared syllables escaped her droopy mouth.

"So. So. So."

Kyong Ah tucked the granny's hair behind her ears, studying her twitchy lips. "You mean so-rry? Thank you for saying that. But no biggie deal about your accident. Everybody got to poo, right? If you can't poo, *then* you make me to worry."

Aide wheeled patient out into the hall and fed her breakfast. Then Kyong Ah and Leng wheeled Mrs. Santos and the first set of charges to Winny and the physical therapists. Past patients waddling and cooing like pigeons. Past bulletin boards messy with their crayon rehab masterpieces. Past the wall Boss had inexplicably ordered Custodial to paint upset-stomach pink.

That done, the aides split up to tackle the bedridden. Using the magic of sheets, pillows, and physics, Kyong Ah rotated patients to prevent their bodies from getting sores and breaking down. She gave sponge baths and emptied waste before checking back on her countryman who was asleep, thanks to Kwan Seum Bodhisattva who lost her eyes to see the sounds of the world's suffering. A red tooth bit through Mr. Bak's snug dressing.

Kyong Ah was dying for a smoke, maybe one of the ripped-off Kools snuggling with her Camels. She grunted. *Hard work first, then reward.* She returned to Mrs. Santos' room and studied the color and consistency of the feces on the soiled undies. Granny used to say Kyong Ah could smell a mouse farting in a hemp rice bag two villages away. Though decades of smoking had dulled her sniffer's potency, she could still Sherlock out shifts in oldsters' effluvia, including last night's excess onions and fear.

Back home, troubled women could consult fortune-tellers to read face, palm, or the eight characters of birth time to divine a wrestle hold to slow Fate. Golden West had turned Kyong Ah into a poopteller reading fortune through the shape, color, and frequency of oldsters' *ddong.* She helped them eliminate poisons faithful as daily meditation so they could heal, less backed up with pain. As Mercy Goddess' handmaiden, she was her nose-in-the-air psychologist daughter Yumi's equal. If only those sausages and snakes, bullets and mustards didn't smell like, well, poop.

Kyong Ah scrubbed down the rubber mattress cover. Opened windows to free the funk. Bundled the soiled bedding and clothing in separate labeled bags and dropped them down the hazmat chute. Winded, she sat down. Hard as work was on her back and lungs, she did not envy Laundry or Custodial. As she made entries in her ADL notebook, Kyong Ah's big eye blinked at the adjacent bed where two nights ago Mrs. Santos' roommate, Eugenia Brown, had surrendered to stomach cancer bandits. Poor Mrs. Santos must have witnessed it all. A final shriek. Orthopedic soles stampeding linoleum. Heave-ho of staff bagging the corpse. Death rattle of elevator doors.

Kyong Ah's eyes widened; what if Mrs. Santos' accident wasn't caused by Graveyard's diapering flub? What if the granny had pulled on her own underwear to flee this place? Now *that* would be an act of spunk, whether she was ready or not. Like when Kyong Ah's knucklehead grandson Evan front-ended his father's car at age nine. Only Mrs. S was waging her War of Independence at Life's backend.

Kyong Ah coughed up phlegm, thick with smoker's guilt. She spit it in a tissue, washed her hands and corrected her poo entry.

—*Don't know if someone forget to put diaper on last night or if Mrs. S try to dress self*

—*She try to say sorry*

Kyong Ah chewed her thick lower lip. Now that was the

trick wasn't it? To exit gracefully before you lost your voice and strangers had to clean up your shit.

2. CALLER

"Get off, you're choking me!" Kyong Ah fought to redden her air sacs with oxygen and wake up.

Wolf pinned her down; its razor fur reeked of Dead Husband's pomade. "Ungrateful wench. After I've come all this way."

"From Evergreen Cemetery just over the hill? Your dead whores sick of you, kaesaekki-yah?"

"Feisty tonight, eh, Wife? You know how that excites me. How about a hump for the road? Don't deny me your delicious melons." Jae Pil licked the earlobe that used to unlock a delicious network of orifices.

"Kkeojeo! Screw you, Jae Pil!"

"Exactly. Open your legs. Let me in."

Kyong Ah whimpered. But she did want him; it'd been eons since she'd had sex with anyone besides herself. The smell of his hair and skin on hers dispelled lonely nights spent tossing on her manless bed. Desire and dread spidered her lungs.

"Get off, Jae Pil! Don't give me sex diseases you caught from your graveyard hussies!" Her womb winced from an old wound—some whore's gonorrhea he'd implanted when she was pregnant with Sally. Kyong Ah had washed down each penicillin pill with tears, fearing their baby would be born missing limbs or lobes. Instead Sally had emerged after a long labor, big, kicking feet first.

"Sex disease? You're so crazy you make me crazy, too." Jae Pil feigned ignorance, not admitting that his afterlife punishment included an eternal burning itch. He ravaged her breasts. Tongued a road down her belly and abdomen. Circled her bud. Entered her womb.

She gasped as pleasure climbed her scarred walls; persimmon tree ovaries plumped. Ecstasy surged over kidneys and tummy and crashed in her heart. Then Wolf sank fangs into her lungs—the vine-lashed mud hut where Grief lived.

Predator howled; prey gasped. Her skin purpled as he drank her breath and ki life force. Blood whirled backward. Left Lung collapsed; Right plumped with adrenaline. Mouth clacked coffin dust.

Beast is fake. No can breathe is real. Wake up!

She shoved him off. Her eyelids cracked open. Bless you, Kwan Seum Bosal! Gasping, she turned on the lamp. Where was the pillow helper she'd propped up to open her wheezy airways as she did for oldsters?

"Ssibal!" The beast she'd pushed off was none other than said pillow.

You idiot! Wrestling feathers and humping a ghost. Trying to suffocate yourself? Like poor Yoneda San, while he had the brain and brawn to do it?

Before Mr. Yoneda checked into Golden West skilled nursing, Kyong Ah had harbored a grudge against anyone with the slightest Japanese accent for enslaving her people. Stealing lumber and land. Minerals and women.

But she had grown to admire Mr. Yoneda's quiet dignity, especially after discovering he'd served time in a Beautiful Country concentration camp during WWII. A gardener whose name meant "rice paddy" stuck in the desert. Can you imagine?

"Is that the *kyong* that means *sutra*? How lovely," Mr. Yoneda had said one day, smiling so that only the teeth he had left showed as he offered her a forest green *mochi* flavored with *ssuk*. His doting daughter brought him beautiful packages from Japantown, wrapped in white paper crisp as a freshly made bed. He'd guessed that the mugwort flecked ones were Kyong Ah's favorites, one pleasure their people shared in common. And he knew to offer it to her three times before she politely accepted.

But that was before he started vomiting blood again.

Kyong Ah had found him without a pulse, yet hugging his pillow. She had cleaned him up while her boss, Pockmark Whang, called Mr. Yoneda's daughter with the bad news. Kyong Ah smoothed wrinkles from his sky blue gown and tortured brown face. Even as Death's mask settled, he looked handsome, his brows thick, his sculpted arms and shoulders muscled. She happened to be wearing the iris print scrubs that used to lift his spirits, whether because the flowers reminded him of his wife, or because he liked having Kyong Ah around, she didn't know.

"Travel safely, Yoneda San," she had said, "to join your wife on other side. Don't worry, we tell your children you died peaceful in your sleep. That you felt no pain."

Like we tell everybody.

Though sad for Mr. Yoneda, Kyong Ah was awestruck at how he'd managed to Kevorkian himself. He'd apparently learned a few things growing and pruning the greenness of life. Before Yoneda San she never would have believed a pillow suicide possible. Especially after having been begged by dozens of oldsters for help after they'd failed to execute death by feathers. The poor things discovered that as soon as they stopped breathing, they'd inadvertently un-hug their would-be assassins and hungrily gobble air.

She'd shaken her head *No* to their pleas. Rubbed the papery wrinkles on the backs of their hands. Kissed them on their foreheads. Tricked them into sharing a childhood memory. Sat with them until their minds wandered off to a safe park bench.

Now, in the stifling Indian summer night, Kyong Ah shoved Pillow Assassin away. She turned on the lamp and strained to remember if Mr. Yoneda had appeared in her dream before Dead Husband's ghost jumped her. But the careful gardener had left behind no twig his caretaker could grasp.

That was the trick, wasn't it? To live as long as you could, but not get too greedy and miss your chance for a dignified death. Then the only feelings you'd have left were churning morphine stomach and your kids' tears dripping on your potato face. *No way, Joe-say.* Not after all the pitiful exits she'd witnessed at Golden West.

Kyong Ah coughed into a tissue and patted her chest; goblins kicked her air sacs with pointy boots. She should quit. Like the tarred tumor poster in the washroom warned. Like her keep-smoking-and-I-won't-visit-you-in-the-Cancer-Ward daughter Yumi nagged. But Kyong Ah didn't drink or drug. And she no longer had sex. Well, except just now with a gigolo ghost. She couldn't remember how long it'd been since she'd broken it off with Felix

Gao, the last love interest of any significance. A paramedic fifteen years her junior with strong limbs and a naughty chuckle. They'd flirted for two years and slept together for another two. But he had mother issues and she was long done nursing babies.

White Knights are all you've got to blunt the knife of loneliness. Pathetic.

Kyong Ah felt her way down the hall to the bathroom, the walls thick with countless coats of paint to seal the exit of each previous tenant. She placed a White Knight between her lips, striking a match and inhaling the heady scent Fire released when it first discovered humanity. Her thirsty lungs drank delight, dispatching nicotine runners to wherever want gathered. Joy and the rhythmic marking of time returned to her chest.

One of your damn floozies summoned you, Jae Pil. Leave me alone.

Kyong Ah started coughing, so hard she had to rest the knight on the sink. She spit thickly into toilet paper. Patted her chest until it calmed. Relit Whitey, drawing his lovely smoke down her air and water channels and purging fear and Dead Husband's visit from her lungs. She checked the Ins&Outs in her sputum.

A clot of virgin red swimming in sludge. Impossibly flecked with swamp green.

She sniffed, Sherlocking out bits of tonight's spicy crab stew. Blood watered the weed patch worry lurking between her ribs. No way; the red must be from screaming at Wolf to get off and stop deviling her dreams. A strong, healthy impulse. Kyong Ah closed her eyes as waves broke on the shores of Dolsando, the Rock Mountain Island that lay at the end of the road Granny and she had taken when they fled from Hwanghae Province during the Korean War. Before they made a new life selling fish. Before she met Jae Pil on a Peace Market assembly line in Seoul. Before he returned from mercenary service in Vietnam. Before he finagled immigration papers with help from GI Joe contacts. Before they fled to Beautiful Country with Yumi in hand and Minsoo in belly.

Now a bracing ocean wind raised chicken flesh on Kyong Ah's arm.

"Enjoy your freedom, Granddaughter. I forbid you to dream about that useless bum. That no-good cheater. That bastard son-of-a-bastard."

"Halmoni, I think kids want me to be buried next to him. Especially Yumi."

"What happened to their brains? Well, Yumi I can understand. He favored her. Before his army of whores drained away his vital essence. Aiguh! *Why are we talking about HIM again?"* Halmoni *twisted the chignon tight at her neck nape, securing it with a bone hairpin. She wore a white Hanbok Korean-style cotton dress of gathered skirt and short jacket bound with a tie.* *"He's dead. Good riddance! Better not see him on this side when I'm carrying my fish gutting knife."*

Grandmother growled; granddaughter coughed.

Which must have unblocked a ki channel; the Christmas colors in Kyong Ah's spit had to be from the *ssuk* leaves and red peppers she'd tossed in tonight's stew.

She smiled, remembering Mr. Yoneda's mugwort rice-cake gifts.

What a nice man. Bet he didn't beat and cheat on his wife.

Kyong Ah crumpled the soiled tissue and flushed it

away. She returned to bed and fluffed her pillow partner. Its dreamy feathers cradled her head.

Yoneda San, please share your mercy pillow secret with me someday.

3. SALTY

Kyong Ah wheeled Mrs. Santos out into the hall for breakfast. The place smelled of last night's boiled chicken bones.

"How about sit next to Mistah Rheegasepee?" She pivoted Mrs. Santos into a chair with an attached desk, retired from Oakland Unified School District. Instead of students and books the OUSD seats now held oldsters and meal trays.

The eighty-three-year-old Navy vet rapped his spoon against his cast. "What the hell? Oatmeal and *jook* por breakpast again? What's the matter with you people? Acting like we've all lost our teeth and taste bumps." White hair swirled around his head as if he'd battled a thorn bush last night.

Kyong Ah's eyes narrowed. "No yelling please, Mistah Rheegasepee. Not good for blood pressure. Don't upset Missus Santos." She made a mental note to take a hair-brush to him before lunch. The hall smelled of whiskers and spent plastic gloves.

"La. La. La," said Mrs. S, her eyes as watery as the rice gruel.

"Hey, Ate. Don't you want *bagoong* in your *jook?*"

"La. La. La."

"See, she wants *bagoong*." Mr. Legaspi roostered his chest like Hacker, his beloved fighting cock, rest in peace.

Kyong Ah's right brow spiked, tugging her eyelid up to ferret out trickery. That was the trade-off, wasn't it? While able patients like Mr. L could perform more ADLs, they could also raise a higher roof on devilment.

"You said 'la,' right, Missus?" *Not ba. Not goong.* But the granny pinched her beak tight against Kyong Ah's spoon. "How about milk protein for stay strong? Mistah Rheegasepee, your breakfast getting cold."

"Half your staff is Pilipino." He crowed louder. "Tell our countrymen we want *bagoong*—now!"

"La. La. La." Mrs. Santos' head lurched forward. Old-sters looked up, spoons frozen mid-air. Though weak of body or mind, they relished spectating a good fight. Whether on their favorite afternoon Korean, Chinese, or Telemundo soap, or the Seniors vs. Staff Wrestling Federation.

Up and down the hall the aides picked up the red meat scent of rebellion. Leng Fong's eyebrows vee'd like a temple guardian's. Luz Montenegro's wavy hair crackled with electricity. Remy Ramos' nostrils flared. Kyong Ah Choi's cheeks turned autumn pepper red; she was seized by the urge to cock the spoon and flip *jook* against the back of Mr. L's throat the next time he opened his beak. There was, however, the pesky problem of paying her rent.

"How about eat breakfast first and then we see what we can do?"

"No, you get my *bagoong* pirst and then we see." His

ivory tufts curled into carabao horns.

Kyong Ah inhaled deeply for patience, triggering a nasty cough. Mr. Legaspi covered his nose. Mrs. Santos leaned away.

"Sorry. Not contagious. Only allergies." Kyong Ah coughed, squirting sanitizer from the wall dispenser, on her hands.

"Ba! Goong! Ba! Goong!" Mr. L pounded his drum mallet fist. Gruel jiggled; milk shimmied. Adrenaline surged through his body. Like when he used to release Hacker into the ring.

"Ga! Ga! Ga!" Syllables sloshed inside Mrs. Santos' mouth, salty with memory.

Kyong Ah stepped before the mutineer. She stopped short of laying hands on him lest it escalate his behavior. Though his broken ankle would slow him down, depending on its range of motion, the cast on his bum arm could hurt. And only Kwan Seum Bosal knew how many lug nuts that roll off his roof had loosened in his noggin. Instead, she spoke in the low voice that used to make her kids run for cover.

"Quiet down and we talk like nice people. You are vet so you understand. You give me respect, I give you respect. First, tell me what means bagoon."

"Not *bagoon*. *Bagoong*." Mr. L's bulging eyes searched Kyong Ah's. She narrowed hers so he couldn't detect weakness. He scratched the nut brown skin above his cast. "It's salted shrimp for God's sake. Spice of life. Raises the dead quicker than Lazarus."

Kyong Ah's mouth flooded. "Why you not say so? In Korean we call it *jeot*. You know kimchi?"

"Of course. My arm is broke, not my brain."

"Anyway, we stuff *jeot* and raw oysters inside cabbage leaves for best flavor."

"Isn't that what I just said?"

"But *bagoong* must be bad for people on low-salt diet." She readied her trump flower card. "And your daughter Anita said 'only low-salt food for my dad.'" *Thump!*

"Not true. When did she say that?" Legaspi's horns drooped at mention of the traitor who had stuck him in this saltless hellhole. Who'd made him swear off cock fights after Hacker got hacked. "What's the goddamn use of living if you can't eat *bagoong*?"

"What about other patients on no-salt diet who smell your *bagoong* but can't eat? That's mean."

"Ridiculous! Why make everyone suffer because a couple rotten apples can't cut it? Your overcooked crap's making everybody pasty. I'm turning white as this goddamn cast. I want my *bagoong* and I want it now!"

The split second Mr. L's fist sent his tray into the air, Kyong Ah released Mrs. Santos' spoon and caught it.

"Ga. Ga. Ga."

"*Kuurrh!*" Kyong Ah trilled, glaring at him. She turned and patted Mrs. Santos' hand, frail as a sparrow feather. Wondering what the *halmoni* made of the shrimp ruckus.

"How about you write Pock—I mean Mistah Whang— our boss, about shrimps. If he and docs agree, maybe Kitchen can do."

"Get me paper and a pen. Mr. Pock Whang you say?"

Kyong Ah paled. "No, Mistah Lincoln Whang."

The hellion scratched his chin stubble. "If I'm going to all this trouble, you better believe I'm asking for more than some shrimpy shrimps."

Frank Sinatra's "My Way" vibratoed in the back of Kyong Ah's skull. Old Blue Eyes' song must enjoy the same kingly status in Pilipino karaoke bars that it did in Korean *noraebang.*

"Korean, eh? I thought you were different. You from Pusan?"

"No, farther west. South Sea, not East Sea. Near Yeosu." She didn't mention her real hometown in what was now North Korea. As an outsider refugee kid, she'd had her birthplace beaten out of her long ago. "I get paper and pen after you finish breakfast."

"Your eyes are slanted longer than Chinese. More mysterious." He flashed a crocodile grin; she scowled.

This ddong *talker must have charmed his way under skirts in many ports. Don't be fooled by his cast and ankle brace. Mere speed bumps.*

"Us non-Chinese don't want *jook* por breakpast and over-boiled bok choy por dinner every damn day. How about *pancit* por a change?" He winked, sliding his hand over hers. "Or kimchi."

Scowling, she snatched her hand away. But Mr. L had a point. They served *jook* each day, faithful as a morning prayer. The miracle grain of the ancestors kept the sick and toothless, the old and young, alive through Life's most dangerous passages. Yet *jook* was only meant to act as a palette for nature's colors; who wanted to eat a blank canvas day after day? At home Kyong Ah seasoned *jook* with clams and flavors of ocean childhood memory. The gruel Leng shared with her during lunch swam with ground pork, black jelly chunks of thousand-year-old eggs and fried peanuts. While corn sustenance girded Luz's homemade *tamales* and Remy's *pupusas*, both were also spiced with treasure fillings.

He's from ocean country, too. Must be hard to give up Pilipino jeot *and hometown spice.*

"Ga. Ga. Ga" Mrs. Santos tried to push the sounds forward with her tongue.

"Right." Kyong Ah tipped a glass of milk to Mrs. Santos' mouth and then closed the granny's fingers around her napkin, raising it to her lips and blotting. Kyong Ah guided Mrs. Santos' good hand around the spoon and up to her mouth a few times each meal to keep muscle memory alive. But Mr. Legaspi's antics had gobbled up her attention.

"Great job, Missus S!" Kyong Ah picked up Mrs. S' tray and Mr. L's unfinished one.

"Wait!" Mr. L grabbed the bowl of *jook* with his good hand and one-shot'd it, before snatching the toast.

"Ba. Ba. Ba!" Mrs. Santos' eyes brimmed with salt when her sea slug tongue tossed up the right sound. Mention of the pungent brew she had used to flavor stews and garlic fried rice watered her mouth with joy. She prayed her noisy countryman would win the thumbs up. The magic sauce might tickle movement in the wooden half of her body.

Mr. L grinned like a bearcat. "That's right! *BAgoong.* We're pinally going to get some real pood."

Kyong Ah's BS-o-meter flatlined as she loaded the cart. Pockmark would punish her if he found out she had anything to do with Mr. L's plan. But the vet *ddong* stirrer had boxed her in. Anyway, it served Pockmark right for taking away the complaint box and leaving staff to field the flack.

Mr. L's mouth hectored her down the hall. "Hurry up with that paper. Going to take a long time, writing with my left hand and all."

She spun around. "Remember what I say about respect? What about magic word?"

"Please." He rapped on his cast and grinned. "Now hurry up and get my stuff—Korea."

The aide growled. "Korea?"

4. STRINGS

Pick up, Omma. Yumi squared her jaw; her finely penciled brows arched severely. She twisted knots in her long floaty skirt. Tugged at her fitted lace-trimmed blouse. Scuffed her red ballet slippers beneath the desk.

Pick up, Omma. Time's running out. She'd walked countless clients through phobias and avoidance. But what about tackling her own? She had yet to tell Omma she was about to hop a plane to pick up a new baby. Might as well swap out her Psy.D shingle for one that said "Doctor of Hypocrites. School of Hot Air." She hung up and dialed again.

Pick up, Omma, pick up. Don't make me drop the adoption bomb in your message box. She'd stopped depending on Omma long ago, babysitting in middle school to pay for violin lessons and new clothes, and working her way through college and grad school. Drawn to counseling because of her screwed-up family, Yumi had a talent for helping others overcome trauma. She'd won recognition from boisterous community groups for her conflict resolution skills. Yet Omma denied giving her even a thimbleful of respect. Yumi turned up the meditation music that calmed patients. Hung up. Speed dialed her mother again.

Pick up, Omma. Or we'll show up on your doorstep. The message beep sounded and Yumi spoke in Korean, as they did when it was just the two of them. "Omma, I'm leaving for Korea tonight. Call me." Yumi hung up and called again. Hung up and called again.

"Yumi? I just got in from work. What's wrong?"

"Are you saying I only call when something's wrong?" Yumi slipped into her *ppalli ppalli* hurry hurry VIP voice. It clashed with the ocean wave and violin mood music emoting through her counseling office. "Thanks a lot, Omma. I love you, too."

"Whatever. I had hard day. Let's not fight."

Yumi pulled her thick ponytail tight. "Did you hear my message?"

"No. *Aiguh!* Is Agi leaving you? Three strikes you're out. . . . Yumi-yah, are you there?"

"Why do you always doubt me? Of course, we're not breaking up." Yumi's face hardened into a brick. A vein spasmed in her neck. "We're adopting a baby from Korea. We're leaving tonight to pick her up."

"Baby? What are you, forty-seven? Almost half a century. Do you even still bleed?"

Yumi screeched over the violins. "Yes, not that it's any of your business. After all these years of pestering me for grandkids, I thought you'd be thrilled." Yumi massaged her screaming temples. She freed her hair from its band. The musky scent of Father's aftershave filled the room. Yumi's eyes burned.

"If Apa was still alive, he'd be happy for me."

"Apa? *Kuurrh.*" Kyong Ah struck her chest; like the

barrel drum used to rally peasants against invaders. "Didn't you notice I stopped asking about grandkids years ago? Old women can't make babies for good reason. Too old to nurse. Too slow to chase. Too weak to carry."

"Stupid me. Why did I expect you to understand?" Yumi tore off a hangnail; the sting soothed her.

"I do understand, Yumi-yah." Kyong Ah cleared her throat. "But you know the cursed luck women in this family have with men. You had too many men and your sister too few. Agi is your third husband. Are you sure he's the last? At your age, can you raise a child by yourself?"

Yumi sucked her bleeding finger. "Don't jinx my marriage. Never liked Agi, did you?"

"Out of all your husbands, I like Agi best. Although he'd look younger if he shaved. But I treated all your husbands nice. Raising kids is super tough even for young women. Listen, I learned hard way. Yumi, you still there?"

As she advised clients, Yumi drew a deep breath before responding. But the coping tactic only fed fresh oxygen to the fire. "It's your fault on I'm on my third husband. You gave me no positive role model for healthy relationships. You could have made it work instead of destroying Apa. He loved you so much."

There, you've finally said it. For yourself. For Apa. Rest in peace.

"Role model? Whatever. Fine, blame me. I was hundred percent wrong and he was hundred percent right." Kyong Ah sniffed. "Always the mother's fault. That what they taught you in psychology school? Feel better?"

Yumi talked like she was sucking razors. "Stop putting words in my mouth. I'm not saying Apa didn't make mistakes. But you were the stronger one. Now my daughter will never know her *halaboji.* Do you understand how that makes me feel?"

That's right; let it out, Dr. Min. Yumi plucked tissues from the box her patients used to mop up sorrow.

"*Aiguh!* You're adopting a girl?" Kyong Ah fell silent.

"Omma, are you there? Answer me." Yumi felt Apa's appreciative hand on her shoulder. The poor man had been outgunned by Omma. A one woman firing squad.

If Yumi's phone had more signal bars, she might have heard her mother muttering, "*No one dances with you and leaves unbloodied, Daughter. I know every word I utter is a bullet handed to you. Go ahead. More you attack, less you'll know. I have nothing to prove. You came out of me, not me out of you.*"

Yumi barked. "What? What?"

"Nothing."

Yumi dug her fingernails into her palms, afraid that Omma would deny the new granddaughter New Year's money as she had upon learning Evan used his for drugs.

Yumi exhaled slowly and unclenched her fists. No matter how screwed up her and Omma's relationship was, the new baby needed a *halmoni.* "We leave for Seoul this Friday to pick up our baby. Pray everything works out for us, Omma."

Kyong Ah sucked her teeth. "You swore you never wanted kids. Why now?"

A violin whined. "I don't know. First I had to build my career. Then the husband chemistry was off. Then I was afraid to bring a baby into this screwed-up world. Look at how Evan turned out."

Kyong Ah sighed loudly. "Yumi-yah, think about where you'll be twenty years from now. College will cost billions of dollars. It's not too late to change your mind. And what will Agi tell his other kids?"

Yumi's voice tightened. "He'll keep sending child support. I'm only asking you to do what you did for Evan."

"That was lifetime ago. This old body is too weak to carry baby on my back and suck snot out of their nose when they get sick."

"What? You're strong as a wrestler and lift people twice your size at work. You're not going to discriminate against our baby because she's adopted, are you?" Yumi's throat hummed with a squadron of hornets.

"*Yaah,* soup's boiling over. Got to go. Safe journey and good luck to you, Agi and your new baby. *Annyeong.*"

Yumi leapt to her feet. "Omma, stop playing your passive-aggressive ga. . . ."

Kyong Ah quickly hung up.

"Omma, Omma!" Yumi hurled the phone, shattering the framed doctor of psychology certificate that mocked her from the wall of awards. She punched the CD player, silencing the insipid harps and whiny strings. She rushed to the table of plastic dinosaurs kids played with during family counseling sessions, but stopped before upending it.

Ready for motherhood are we, Dr. Min?

Yumi took a deep breath. And another. And another. This time the tactic slowed her heart rate. She picked up her diploma. Emptied the broken glass from the frame into the trash, nicking her forefinger in the process. She sucked a glass sliver out of her finger and spat it out among the others.

Told Omma about adoption. Told Omma about her mistakes with Apa. Threw tantrum. Plus two, minus one. You're ahead for today, Dr. Min.

Yumi smiled bitterly. She hung up the diploma in its glassless frame, then tossed the trash into the dumpster behind the building. She remembered the soothing rise of the mountains on the north end of Seoul, where she and her parents had picnicked in happier days. Maybe she and Agi could take a short hike there with the baby.

Yumi's eyes filled as she remembered Apa lifting her on his shoulders, pointing out Han River boats fluttering with seagull hats. She must have been four years old when she had him all to herself, before Mickey and Sally came along. Before Omma drove him away. Before Yumi grew up and suffered depressions after each breakup with a "bad boy" remodeling project. For a long time she'd feared ending up lonely and brittle as Omma, unqualified to counsel clients on relationship challenges. Thank God she'd caught Aguinaldo's eye at her friend Celestina's party.

Yumi wiped away tears.

Wait for us, Daughter. Omma and Tatay are almost there.

5. LOUNGE

The same full moon that had unleashed Dead Husband on Kyong Ah several nights ago must have fevered Oakland ERs, too; by lunch Third Floor had processed three hip fractures, four heart attacks, three strokes and a broken back. The aides were so busy they lost the space between their eyes and noses, as Halmoni used to say during kimchi pickling season.

Not until late afternoon did Kyong Ah escape downstairs, striding past Custodial, Laundry, and the garage to reach Smokers Lounge. Where Boy García from First Floor and Dong Song from Kitchen were playing poker at the giant cable spool table.

Boy's cigarette rested lazily on his fleshy lip. His shag needed taming. Scrub sleeves pinched his thick biceps, which the aides summoned to heft morbidly obese patients. The former union leader had traded toting fire hoses and victims in Manila for hefting not-so-ambulatory oldsters after his nurse sister begged him to join her in the US, and avoid getting hurt by government goons.

Matchstick-thin Dong puffed his cigarette, steady as a Chevron refinery smokestack over in Richmond. He wore his perpetual scowl and an apron blotchy with mystery meat sauce. He was hell-bent on breaking the losing streak dogging him since the Red Hawk Casino tour he'd caught from Park Liquors on Ninth and Franklin last payday.

"Who's winning?" Kyong Ah scooted forward on a sun-chalked plastic chair.

"I am, of course," said Boy, mirth dancing inside his round brown eyes. "For a Chinese *jai*, Dong sucks at math."

"Go ahead, count all you chickens." Dong snapped his hairnet. "Before I beat you ass. Deal you in, Kyong?"

"No, I just want to sit. And do nothing." She hungrily lit a White Knight. The ache in her temples dissolved as smoke descended into her lungs like a cleansing spirit. Alveoli bloomed. Bronchioles glistened. Today Lounge was upwind from the dumpsters and some citizen had pushed the vicious blackberry vines over the cinderblock fence to the neighbors' side. Kyong Ah drew a deep drag, embracing Tobacco God's calming smoke before slowly releasing.

For a moment, all was right on this hazy patch of Oakland.

"Straight!" Dong fanned his cards, grinning at Fu, the Luck God's return with his winged hat and scepter.

Dong's yellowing teeth made Kyong Ah suck her own. She shouldn't smoke when she didn't have a dentist. But then she wouldn't be able to bear hump-crushing days like today.

"Flush!" Boy slapped down his hand; an ash clump fell.

"*Diu nei!*" Dong thrust his thumb between his ring and middle fingers.

"Yeah, fuck you, too," said Boy. "Eight new admits.

See that monster moon the other night? Never fails."

Kyong Ah inhaled. "We got ten out, ten in. Moon gives oldsters excess energy vibration. Then they hurt self. And we got throat cancer patient who don't look so hot," said Kyong Ah, using aide-speak for *he's shuttling between us and the morgue.*

"Throat?" said Boy pensively, a thick cloud hovering over his buffalo shag.

"Because of cigalette?" said Dong, smoke curling into a question mark above him.

"Maybe," said Kyong Ah. The jack-o-lantern grin of a scar leaking through Mr. Bak's neck dressing had choked off her questioning.

The three eyed each other nervously. Sighed. Shrugged. Continued puffing.

Boy re-ordered his hand. "You hear anything about a Covehaven offer to take this dump off Pockmark's hands?"

"Pockmark say that?" Kyong Ah lit another cigarette and drew an anxiety-suppressing drag. She tucked her hair behind her ears and sighed. *When am I going to make time for haircut?*

"That *chauhai* not say shit until too late," said Dong, his long bean body taut. "He's total *gauseelou.*"

"Right, dogshit bastard." Kyong Ah inhaled. "What that mean for us?

Boy blew out the opposite side of his mouth from his cigarette. "That we're fucked. My cousin Tez works for them in Fremont. Slave pay, jack benefits." He swore under his breath; he needed to get off his butt, go to nursing school and bring his family over from the Philippines. But all that took money and time he didn't have.

Kyong Ah snorted. "Slave pay? How that different from Pockmark?"

"They're big and corporate. Make you work off a meth clock." Boy leapt up and swung his arms like a varsity cheerleader, scattering ash. "Every minute make 1.69 beds. Serve .34 meals. Clean 9.3 bedpans." He plopped down and brushed ash from his scrubs. "Think I'm joking? Bye mom-and-pop places that grew out of people taking care of family members. With all the baby boomers falling down and stroking out, we're just another goldfish for Covehaven to swallow."

Kyong Ah tapped White Knight into the Harrah's Casino Irish-green ashtray some Lounger had snagged. "So what can we do?"

Boy frowned at his hand; he thrust his chin at Dong for another card. "How about sending a couple people on a fact-finding mission to get information from Pockmark?"

"Fact find?" Dong's scowl squirreled deeper. "There you go talking that union *masee*. Isn't that how you got kick out of Pilipeen? I need this job, man. No matter how shit." Dong scratched the stump of the finger a factory machine in the Dongguan Special Enterprise Zone had devoured.

"Where's your self-respect, dude? Stop being a pussy. They won't throw you and your family in jail like China or the P.I. Anyways, the team needs a Chinese guy to meet with our slick-ass Chinese boss." Boy's heart rate surged as it did before a fresh battle.

Dong switched out three cards. "Not this *jai*." He scratched his stump, remembering the government union in Dongguan.

Talk about pussies. Those chauhai *chickenshits.*

Kyong Ah's detect-o-meter spiked. "What? Don't look at me. I need this job, too. Anyway, what is *bagoong*, Boy? My patient wants in his *jook*. He's raising hell to Pockmark."

Boy licked his thick lips. "Fermented shrimp, anchovy or fish paste. My grandparents used to brew it once a year. Call us city kids to go home to Cebu and help. We'd leave smelling like a woman's . . . , well."

"*Chauhai?*" Dong grinned, remembering the cute bartender he and the other no-luck loser customers had been flirting with at Bow Bow Bar last night. She smelled like night jasmine, cigarette smoke and Toisan whiskey.

Boy wiggled his brows. "Let's just say that stuff's pungent."

"Sound like our *haam ha*," said Dong. "Super tasty steamed with ground pork and ginger. Or chicken fried rice. I already know Pockmark's answer—NO!"

"Flush again!"

Dong leapt up. *"Nei ge mama ge chauhai!"*

Kyong Ah laughed and started coughing. Which spread to Boy and Dong. Boy's rolled with phlegm; Dong's hacked like a cat choking on a hairball. Their distress somehow made Kyong Ah feel better; hers sounded less molasses-like than Boy's and thumped several decibels softer than Dong's.

Boy struck his sternum three times to bring his to heel. Dong fired up another cancer stick to smoke his out.

"Full house. Eat my dust!" Dong hoiked and spit a luggie against the cinderblock wall; it slimed down like a banana slug.

"Gross! You better not have TB, foo," said Boy.

Kyong Ah spit into a tissue, folded and pocketed it. Should she ask co-conspirators about the red in her sputum the other night? The trio shared pariah puffer status as healthcare providers persisting in risky behavior while caretaking dying addicts chained to oxygen tanks.

No. She wasn't ready for gossip to walk Golden West's halls like menstrual blood on the backside of a schoolgirl's skirt. Anyway, Leng would make a better confidante, even as a non-smoker. Practical, she knew how to fix problems without arousing the boss' attention. Skills she'd learned back home surviving Kuomintang and Chinese Communist Party rulers' Wheel of Fortune.

"Got to get back to work."

"Me, too," said Boy, stubbing out his cigarette.

"Me, three," said Dong. "And Boy, don't do union stuffs. Or we get fired. "

"Stop being such a chickenshit, Dong. Where's my three bucks?"

6. PRODIGAL

"Wake up. Let me in, Omma." Mickey hammered on the door of his mom's apartment across the street from San Antonio Park. He fake grinned through the peephole, flaring the nose he'd broken falling down drunk way back when. He wore an army flak jacket and jeans. His hair jagged like road spikes. He held a gym bag hidden behind his back, lumpy with work overalls and sweats. Once he'd talked his way inside, he'd let Omma see. Her Korean rollup mattress, fluffy comforter and sleep were just inches away. He even missed the brick-hard Korean pillow embroidered with peonies and mandarin ducks that his square head had begun to soften up during his last stint. Korean pillows. Cushion throwbacks to when warriors used rocks to rest their noggins after a bloody day on the battlefield. Just what he needed tonight.

His omma hissed through the door. "*Ssibal,* Minsoo. Why are you bothering me at this hour? What fool let you and how many mass murderers in downstairs? What are you hiding behind your back? That damn overnight bag? You can't stay."

"*Yaah,* Omma. Don't make me stand out here all night

like a beggar. Can I at least come in for a minute?"

"Why aren't you sleeping in your own bed?"

He snorted. "Charleena kicked me out. Long story. Not my fault."

Kyong Ah pulled him inside. "Shh, don't wake up neighbors."

"Thanks, Omma." Mickey hugged and swept her along into the living room, tossing his bag in a corner.

"No, no, pick that up. You not hear me? I said you can't stay."

"Omma, it's almost 3 a.m. I've got nowhere else to go."

"I bet Wayside Motel got night clerk. You go there now."

"That's coldblooded, Omma. Bedbugs on top of everything else? Have some pity. I'll be gone before you know it."

"That's what you said when last girlfriend kick you out and you stay for six months. Eat my food. Blast your music and movies. Piss off my neighbors. And make my landlord almost kick me out."

"Just give me a couple days to get back on my feet." Planting a messy kiss on her cheek, Mickey fluffed up the pink floral comforter like old times. "On top of it all, my f-ing boss gave away my job to his f-ing nephew. I think that shit's illegal."

Kyong Ah grunted; her BS-o-meter arced. "You go home, say sorry to girlfriend. Get down on knees if you have to."

"Charleena's been on the rag for months. Probably got early menopause. Thinks I've been fooling around with her best friend. Who has bulimia or some mess and isn't even my type. Everybody knows I like my women with meat on their bones. And Charleena's the one who told the toothpick to come to our shop to get her fender fixed."

Omma's lips flatlined. "Toothpick? Always excuses. Just like your *apa*. Swallow flying from woman to woman. Chasing skirt when you already got one wrapped around you. You wake me up for this bullshits? Get out!"

Mickey's nose flared. "That hurts, Omma. I am NOT like Apa. I never raised my hand against you—or any woman."

I stopped Apa from using you as a punching bag.

Scoring Mickey an indeterminate number of free passes with Omma. He just wasn't sure how many he had left. He chewed his lumpy lip.

"You go stay with your son. Male bondage."

"Ha, you're so funny, Omma. You know me and Evan can't be under the same roof without getting into fisti-cuffs. Okay, okay. I'll just be here a night or two. Don't you love me?"

Kyong Ah growled. "*Ssibal!* Two nights only. And don't eat stuff in blue container in fridge. That's my lunch."

"Thanks, Omma. You won't regret this." He grinned the grin that used to melt the iciest heart, but tonight had only infuriated Charleena.

"Right. Or else this time I kill you, Minsoo. No TV. No radio. Lights out. I got to go to work soon. And you better find new job tomorrow—no, today."

"Got it. You're the boss." Mickey stripped down to his shorts and got under the comforter. It'd take Charleena longer to cool off than the two nights he'd just promised

Omma. But like the AA bumper sticker on his fender said, "One day at a time."

Kyong Ah shuffled back to bed as Mickey began to snore.

At first light, Kyong Ah woke up gasping. She pushed Pillow Monster from her face. Groped her way to the bathroom. Bumped her knee on a table.

Better not fall and break your bones, old hag. Once you kick Minsoo out, you'll have no one to find you until stink crawls under your door.

She fumbled on the light, squinting at her palm. A clot swam in the snot. Like a bite of Dead Husband's liver. Mr. Bak's throat scar grinned rusty behind her third eye.

Can't catch cancer from patients. Nobody to blame but yourself. She was about to flush and forget when she heard waves lapping against a boat bottom. Inside, Granny stood with her stout legs spread wide for balance over a fishing net teeming with captives. She grabbed a mackerel and gutted it with two twists of her knife.

"When blood talks, you must listen, Granddaughter."

Kyong Ah held aloft her gunky hand like a throne of snot on the way to the kitchen. She slid the specimen into an empty beanpaste jar and stuck it in the fridge behind the kimchi until she could figure out what to do. Returning to the bathroom, she pulled down the seat cover.

"Just one more dambae, Halmoni."

"Don't!" Halmoni bellowed like when she used to scare sharks away.

Mickey groaned loudly from the living room. "*Yaah*, what'd you say, Omma? What time is it?"

Kyong Ah shouted through the bathroom door. "Nothing. You're dreaming. Go back to sleep."

Kyong Ah's trembling fingers lit a White Knight. To dissolve fear and summon courage. The way Halmoni used to burn rice paper to turn prayers into sky. The way beloved General "Mung Bean" Jeon and his Tonghak Eastern Learning movement rebels torched slave papers. Before foreign gunboats overwhelmed Korea's shores. Before executioners strangled peasant dreams with thick rope.

Because everyone knows: where there's smoke there's desire. And before healing comes fire.

7. ASIATICS

A toothless groan rumbled down the hall as the aides distributed the breakfast trays. Same oatmeal, *jook* and watery cabbage as the day before. Even the Jell-O was yesterday's green, a clear violation of Golden West's unwritten rule: Monday Red, Tuesday Yellow, Wednesday Green, Thursday Orange, Friday Purple, Saturday Pink and Sunday Joker's Wild. Kyong Ah shook her head. This must be Pockmark's answer to Mr. Legaspi: "Shut up or we'll make it worse."

"Green again—and no *bagoong*? What the hell?" Mr. L struck his table; the gelatin wiggled like a hula-girl dashboard ornament.

"Ba. Ba. Ba," said Missus Santos, the "goong" trying to climb the stairs of her throat.

"Exactly, Ate. Tell them you're not eating until you get your *bagoong*."

Kyong Ah's eyes narrowed. "Don't say that. She must have food to get strong. You, too."

"Don't tell me what to say. This is a pree country."

Kyong Ah's eye socket throbbed, promising a migraine. "Anyways, what Mistah Whang say about *bagoong*?"

"He's stalling." Mr. L handed her a line written on an upset-stomach-pink phone message slip from Lincoln Whang:

Re your request, we will inform you of our decision in two weeks.

"Bullsheet! This isn't Israel-Palestine war. All he has to say is, 'yes sir, customer is always right.' And float shrimps in my *jook*." *Puhlap. Puhlap.* Mr. L's spoon slapped the oatmeal and set Kyong Ah's teeth on edge.

Hope of avoiding a headache dribbled away like gruel. "You tell Mistah Whang what is *bagoong*?"

"Of course. And I added *pancit, lumpia, adobo, pinakbet, bibingka* and *leche flan* to the list." Mr. L licked his lips; his hair curled carabao horn happy.

Mrs. Santos lit up like a slot machine. "Bing. Bing. Bing."

"That right, Ate, *bibingka*. When it's my turn to sing karaoke, you'd better believe I'm going for the gold."

Kyong Ah could see Pockmark sputtering over the list and suppressed a chuckle. "If anything high in salt or sugar, he going to say no."

"Already thought of that. Told him *bagoong* was 'seasoned' shrimp or fish. But if they can send guys to the moon and spy on Mars, why can't they create low-salt *pancit*?"

"*Pancit*?"

"You know, noodles fried with garlic and chicken or pork. Por us *manongs* who built this damn country." Mr. L thrust out his chest in honor of countrymen from Hawaiian plantations to Alaskan canneries to Delano grape fields who'd dared stand up to the bosses.

"What means man hogs?"

"No, *manongs*. You know, pioneers. Like me and Big Sister here. The ones paying your salaries."

Kyong Ah refrained from saying, "Aren't you on Medicare?" But why be jealous of the lucky son of a gun? If only the blood in her spit would disappear like a bad husband for three years, she'd be eligible, too. It wasn't this old rooster's fault that she and her co-workers had no health coverage.

Two weeks? Pockmark must be counting on Mr. L being out of everyone's hair by then. Who knew what the vet's conception of time was after his roof roll? One thing was certain; he had the patience of a two-year-old.

Bad boy joy danced in Mr. L's eyes. "Kept your name out of it. I'm no snitch. Us Asiatics got to stick together. Especially us Asiatics who aren't Chinese."

Kyong Ah lifted the milk to Mrs. Santos' lips, unsure whether she wanted to hear what came next. "You talk so much your food cold. Drink juice before I take your tray."

"Wait, wait." Mr. L chugged his *jook*, then milk and juice. He skewered the Jell-O and lowered his voice conspiratorially. "Don't get me wrong. I like Chinese food much as the next person. But that's the only non-American food you serve. That's discrimination, Korea. We want more garlic, vinegar—and *bagoong!*" He pumped his good arm.

"Ba. Ba. Ba." Mrs. Santos clenched her beak against the Jell-O. Her aide didn't press the issue.

Leng helped Kyong Ah push tray carts into the service elevator. She wore Star Wars scrubs. Tonight, with the help of her trusty Juki, she'd whip up matching pajama pants for her middle grandson, Derek, the skateboarder who went through shoes as if they were made of paper sacks.

"What's wrong, Kyong? You eyes all red. Allergies?"

"Couldn't sleep last night. My son is making me crazy." Kyong Ah bit her lip.

Tell her about the blood in your spit.

"What? He clashing at you place again? You said no more." Leng prayed to Guanyin Mercy Goddess that her grandsons wouldn't turn out bad as Kyong Ah's loser son and grandson.

Kyong Ah's cheeks reddened. "Only today, well, maybe this week. But that's it. He make me crazy. When he's there I can't sleep. He and his problems too close to ignore."

"*Aiyah!* If let him stay, you going to need sleeping pills."

"I hate white man's drugs." Kyong Ah knuckled her big eye. "Maybe I can get herbs in Chinatown." The familiar smell of old roots, seeds, herbs, and antlers would sooth her.

"Good idea. And lychee syrup for you cough."

"Cough?"

"You sound bad today. Maybe pollens. Maybe too much cigalette." Leng's eyes rounded.

"Please Leng. No stop smoke talk today."

Leng grunted, untangling her perm with her fingers. "So what Mistah Laigaispi blab about? He got crush on you."

Kyong Ah grimaced. "No way, Joe-say. He just brag about letter he send to Pockmark."

"You mean one you help him write?"

"No, I didn't. His big mouth work all by self. But Pock-mark tell him wait two weeks for answer."

"To say 'no'? Booshit. Boss talking *fongpei* farts."

"*Eung.* Mistah Rheegasepee may be pain in *eongdeongi.* But he's right. Wednesday Jell-O again on Thursday? Give me break."

"Yeah, that's mess up."

"If staff don't care, why should patients? They're sick. Up to us to help them keep hope alive."

The aides pushed the carts on to Kitchen in the rear of First Floor. Bing and Jin opened giant cans of tomato as Dong and Tommy hefted cauldrons of water to the stove. Spaghetti again. The Italian version of Kyong Ah's *gooksoo* and Leng's chow mein. How hard could it be to hold the tomatoes and up the garlic for Mr. L's *pancit?*

"What happen you guys, Green Jell-O on Orange Day-*lah?*" Leng complained in English with Cantonese tonal inflection. "Same same Jell-O make patients confuse and piss off."

"Don't blame us. Suppliers screw up," said Bing, his paper hat fingerprinted with tomato sauce. "Those guys smoke too much glass."

"*Aiyah,* what's this?" Dong clenched his teeth. As if defusing a Bad Luck bomb, he gingerly removed the fork skewered in Mr. L's green Jell-O.

"Sorry," said Kyong Ah, for being too tired to notice the upright utensil inviting hungry ghosts to nosh. "Dong, you tell the guys about patient's *bagoong?* He wants other stuffs, too."

"As long as nutritious, taste good and easy to go down

and out hatch, we can do." Jin opened the bottom of the tomato cans and then crushed the cylinders under his boots for recycle. "Oh yeah, and not too expensive for Pockmark."

"Good to cook variety for patients, and us, too." Bing chopped hamburger clumps frying in a large wok, grease burn scars showing on the hand resting on his hip. "Too boring food breaks spirit. Then body give up."

Dong snapped his hairnet. "Yeah, but you know Pockmark's answer—'no—blah blah—no.' Boss got pole up his *seefut.*"

"Pockmark keep you tied up in Taichi Push Hands forever," said Tommy, weeping as he chopped onions and smashed garlic with a huge cleaver.

"Push Hands?" said Kyong Ah.

Tommy put down his knife, motioning Dong towards him. The two took opposing stances with hand blade edges meeting, pushing and pulling in circle eights. Tommy slid deeper into his stance. Dong's eyes widened as he lunged. Tommy caught the push and let it speed the velocity of their circle eights. A wave surged from Tommy's back heel and up through his body, tossing Dong into the counter. A steel bowl leapt down from overhead; Dong blocked it and beamed. "Hah!"

Leng clapped. "*Ho ho yeah!* At night, Tommy and wife run kung fu studio over on International. When you going to leave Kitchen and teach fulltime, Sifu?"

Tommy scratched his head modestly. He nodded to Kyong Ah. "Be careful with Pockmark. He fights dirty as a white-haired eunuch demon."

"Push Hands. Thanks." Maybe Pockmark's bobbing

and weaving could be stopped with a straightforward Tae-kwondo axe kick on the combover.

Forget it. Don't get caught up in your crazy patient's fight.

The aides returned to Third Floor.

"Ba. Ba. Ba." Mrs. Santos ruminated in the TV corral while watching a Chinese soap opera of old-time court intrigues.

"Right, Missus." Kyong Ah grinned, realizing that Mrs. Santos had taken two steps this morning; she said "ba" during Mr. L's *bagoong* rant and "bing" during his *bing*-something gimme list.

Attending squeaky wheel, don't overlook quiet one. Even if Squeaky stimulates Quiet's vocabs.

Kyong Ah knuckled her eye and scribbled on her note-pad.

—*Mrs. S try say* bagoong & bing *something*

—*She understands even if cannot talk good*

"Kuurrh!"

Kyong Ah rushed in and caught Mr. Bak, the throat cancer patient, randomly punching monitor buttons as if playing whack-a-mole.

"No! Stop!" She wrestled him away from the equipment. Blood bubbled through his neck dressing.

"*Yaah!* You're burning up. Wait, wait!" Kyong Ah ran into the hall. A crash sounded behind her.

"Help, Leng! Get nurse for Mistah Bak. He's got fever. And needs *seed therapy.*" Kyong Ah used the code words for sedative.

"Right!"

Kyong Ah rushed back to the room, tripping over top-pled equipment. She struggled to get a good hold on his arms but kept slipping. She couldn't stop coughing.

"*Kuurrh!*" He seethed.

"Not contagious. Only allergies." She panted. "Please calm down. So they don't send you back to hospital."

"*Kuurrh!*" Mr. Bak stopped abruptly and glared, his eyes full of hate. He shoved her away and tugged at his dressing, trying to stretch it over his head like a bloody necktie.

"Leng! Where are you? Get Boy!" Kyong Ah shouted hoarsely. Now she remembered where she'd seen him before—at Koreana Supermarket stocking rice bags and boxes of Matnani Kimchee. No wonder he was strong as a tiger. Just when she couldn't fight him a minute longer, Leng arrived breathless with Nurse Felicidad "Fely" Villalobos.

"Good grief! Stop!" said Fely. "Get back in bed. Hands off your throat. Don't contaminate your wound!" Fely's pixie haircut ended in a sharp point at her neck nape. Pockmark had gotten a good deal hiring her. She'd been a family doc back in the Philippines before fleeing a bad dictator and bum marriage.

"*Kuurrh!*"

Kyong Ah and Leng grabbed his arms, forcing him to sit down as Kyong Ah spoke in Korean. "Take it easy. Everything's going to be all right. We can call your family. No family? How about a friend?"

Finally an exhausted Mr. Bak let Fely take his temperature and administer acetaminophen and an antibiotic. She also slipped in a sedative. When he slowed down, Fely applied a new dressing, while the two aides supported his head and neck. When he began to snore, Kyong Ah and

Leng tiptoed away to nurse their bruises and attend other patients. But when his fever didn't break by late afternoon, Doc Chu, the on-call physician, wrote an order to send him back to his oncologists at Flatland Hospital.

Kyong Ah prepped him to leave, making one-way small talk until Gabe Quesada from Lifeguard Transport arrived. Gabe's tousled hair and sunny smile almost made you forget that white scar on his cheekbone, courtesy of a sit-down with police before he fled San Salvador. The EMT had learned to leap potholes under Time's gun. Remy said he was named after a saint and his partner Pierre LeNoir after another, good luck for the patients they transported.

Still mad and hung over from "seed therapy," Mr. Bak refused to squeeze Kyong Ah's hand and answer her questions. His eyes raged rusty as his neck.

If only he would cry, he'd feel better.

Gabe knelt. "Mr. Bak, you ready? Beautiful. Let's go nice and easy." Gabe pushed the wheelchair as Kyong Ah accompanied them. When the wheels struck the uneven elevator floor, something fell. Kyong Ah reached down and frowned.

"Cigarettes? Who gave them to you?"

"*Kuurrh!*" Mr. Bak's eyes begged. A fresh red tooth bit into the middle of his new dressing.

"Please don't talk and hurt throat."

"*Kuurrh!*" Mr. Bak grabbed her hand. *Squeeze. Squeeze. Help me, nurse compatriot!* He tried to stand.

Gabe put his hand on Mr. Bak's shoulders and gave Kyong Ah a look. "Take it easy, Sir. Let me hold that for you."

Kyong Ah bit her lip. *Poor guy. He'll never get his job*

back. Korean men without jobs are the meanest, most misera-
ble men. Cut him some slack.

"Okay, you win. Gabe here will hold them for you."
She bowed and gave the pack to Gabe. After palming half
and squirreling them down into her back pocket.

Downstairs Gabe fastened the wheelchair to the lift
and loaded Mr. Bak into the van. Kyong Ah smiled and
waved as they drove away and turned right into traffic.
Before the smile slid down into her chest pocket. Her
countryman was definitely on the hamster wheel between
recovery and sorrow. His protests may have hastened the
inevitable. Could he evade Cancer Goddess? She rubbed
the hand he'd squeezed thin over the past few days. She
refused to hazard a guess and jinx his luck.

Heal and go well, Countryman.

A cough devil dropped out of the cloudless sky forcing Kyong Ah to sit down on the curb. When the demon
released her, she checked her yield; a couple shades redder
than Mr. Bak's rusty throat scar grin.

Kyong Ah heard the squeak of Halmoni's rubber boots
as she hauled buckets of sea cucumbers, urchins, clams,
and mussels around the fish market and bellowed about
the freshness of her catch. She felt Halmoni's fish cudgel
silencer go upside her head.

What you waiting for, Granddaughter? Oxcart to doctor? Go
before you end up like our mute corpse of a countryman.

Kyong Ah fed Mr. Bak's cigarettes to the sewage drain,
keeping her own White Knights.

Just a couple walking sticks to steady myself, Halmoni. Like
the canes your Blind Couple Gods use to tap their way up heal-
ing mountains to secret springs.

8. CULTURE

Winded from bounding up the steps, Sally panted into her cell. "I'm outside your door, Omma. Not sleeping already, are you?"

"*Yaah,* Seungsoo-ah! It's late." Kyong Ah's cell was too blurry to read. She headed for the living room. The mattress and comforter were folded. Mickey's gym bag was still there, but joined by two more bags of belongings. *Where is he? Out chasing skirt?* Kyong Ah coughed thickly, hoiking into her hand. Holding the glob behind her back, she opened the door for her *maknae,* her youngest.

"Brought you a little treat." Sally pecked her mother's forehead and held a McDonald's bag aloft.

Kyong Ah frowned. "*Sesangeh,* what in the world! Why you shave your beautiful hair? So thick and black. I mean orange, no, blue."

"Blue? That was two years ago." Sally's lip curled like a toadstool, making the studs bunch up. Omma never dug her haircuts. Too bad. Shaving her skull felt like a spanking new start. Wearing black workman's pants and a muscle tee, Sally pulled off her boots and thrust her feet into the Sasquatch slippers Omma kept for her, Mickey, and Evan.

A phoenix tattoo unfurled its wings up her right arm; a thorn vine snaked across her shoulders.

Kyong Ah grimaced. "Tattoos make you look like Korean-Japanese *gangpae* hitman for Yakuza." She shrugged, "At least your face not tattooed like a slave. What happen your eyebrow? Infected?"

Sally touched her freshly punctured brow gingerly. "It's nothing." She shook the bag. "Hope you like fish burger."

"McFishy? Who knows how many different freezers it slept around in?"

"Sheesh, aren't you the one who always nagged us not to visit anyone empty-handed? Anyways, can I borrow your *yut* game?" Sally thrust her chin at the gym bag atop the folded mattress. "*Yaah,* Omma, you didn't let Mickey talk you into worming his way back in again? Thought you said no more. That he and Evan make you too crazy."

Heat climbed Kyong Ah's cheeks. "No, no, of course not. Stop nagging." She prayed Minsoo wouldn't walk through the door right then and expose her lies. But he'd be out soon. Maybe he'd found his next homecoming queen tonight.

Sally's eyes widened. "Hey, did you get a boyfriend? It's about freakin' time, Omma."

"*Yaah,* I'm too old for boyfriend." *Except for your* apa's *ghost.* "That's my friend Leng's bags. Just scrubs and stuffs she doesn't need anymore. *Yut* game, eh? Don't know if I still have. Look in hall closet. Want some spicy fish soup?" Kyong Ah left to scrape her blood laced sputum into the kitchen trash. She washed her hands and put the leftover soup on the stove and radish kimchi in a dish.

"If it's not too much trouble." Sally's stomach growled like the impatient tiger in the Korean bear woman creation tale. In the hall she mounted a stepping stool, armed with a yardstick. Everything bagged, boxed, and stacked deliberate as a rock wall. She inserted the stick under Christmas tree lights for a better look. "Shit!" Lights and teacups leapt into her arms as she fell. She landed on her *eongdeongi*, crunching a Christmas ornament. "Youch!" A pouch struck her head, loud as *nunchaku* sticks clobbering a foe. Sally rubbed the bump swelling on her brow. Set aside the teacups and lights. Opened the pouch and pumped her fist.

"You okay?" Kyong Ah shouted from the kitchen.

"Found the *yut*. More like it found my head."

"That's why you need hair, Seungsoo-ah. To protect brain." Kyong Ah wrapped ice in a kitchen towel and set it and the food down on the low rice table in front of Sally. "Where was it?"

The studs on Sally's face tightened as she held the ice against her head. "Should have known it was with the Christmas stuff since it's a New Year game. Um, that smells yummy." Sally handed the fish burger to Kyong Ah and kept the Big Mac for herself.

"What's that?" Kyong Ah thrust her chin at the broken heart tattooed on the web between Sally's thumb and forefinger; newly wounded, it wept. Kyong Ah prayed that at least a *jaji*-swinging man was the source of inspiration.

Babo-yah, *you know it was woman.*

"Why did you get another tattoo?"

"Oh, you know, for good luck." Sally cleared her throat. "Hey, this soup's kickin,' Omma. How come mine never tastes as good?"

"You use real dried anchovies for soup? Or powdered stuff that's half MSG?" Kyong Ah wiped her hands on her apron, shaking her head. "You look like giant three-year-old boy."

Sally's lip toadstooled as she rubbed her skull. "Don't knock it till you've tried it. Less hassle."

"I just wish you meet someone and get married. So I can die in peace, Seungsoo-ah." Mucous and worry clogged her chest. She suppressed a cough until she reached the bathroom. Where she hacked until the cough devils tired of trampolining her lungs.

Sally knocked. "Sounds awful. Better get it checked out." An occasional smoker, Sally didn't like to lecture. Consenting adults. That's what lubed the wheels at Good Ride where she worked.

"Not contagious. Only allergies." Kyong Ah emerged and they returned to the living room. "Make sure you got all pieces."

Sally emptied the bag and ran her fingers down the smooth side of each of the four half round, half flat sticks.

"That's chestnut wood. Makes beautiful drum sound. Hard to get nowadays. And silk board, too. Who you play with?"

"Friends," said Sally, not ready to divulge her plan to pilot *yut* as a bedroom board game for Good Ride. Queen-ita had bitched them out for not having enough "diversity" in the store and pics of people of color on their porn pack covers. Sally remembered the satisfying sound of *yut* sticks striking the wooden floor. If kids could tussle with it, why couldn't lovers?

"Remember how to play?"

"What I remember is Mickey cheating and clocking me upside the head when I won."

"You and Minsoo always fighting."

That's why Sally's this way. Her father and brother turned her off to men. And those VD pills you ate when she was trapped in your womb killed her girl hormones.

Sally picked a dried anchovy from between her teeth. "Glad you had two girls?"

"Your *onni* hates me." Acid roiled Kyong Ah's stomach.

"No, she doesn't." Sally swallowed a chili; her eyes bulged. "She just can't let go of Apa."

"But you did."

Sally shrugged, popping a red turnip cube into her mouth. "He wasn't around much by the time I showed up. Plus he never liked me. Not like he did Yumi." She jammed the stud on her tongue into the roof of her mouth. To out-pain the pain.

Kyong Ah's heart flew back to an evening long past when she had come home from work to Sally's baby face slick with snot and throat raw from crying untended. The apartment stank of sex and the rotting flower perfume of one of Jae Pil's whores. Kyong Ah pushed the startled bitch through the window so fast that dried-gourd-wielding Halmoni would have been proud. Before Husband grabbed her hair and brought them crashing down. As his screaming, bloody whore escaped.

Kyong Ah hoped Sally was too young to remember the dead flower whore. Or the lumpy butt one who favored leopard prints. Or the red dye job with the sultry voice. Or any of those other *kaesaekki* bitches.

Her detect-o-meter sharpened. "Your *onni* tell you about adopting baby from Korea?"

"*Eung.*"

"When?" Kyong Ah's eyes narrowed.

"Why, when'd she tell you?"

"Yesterday. Not even to my face. And grouchy, too. Don't you think she's too old to have baby?"

Sally crunched a pepper and fanned her mouth. "You know Yumi, Omma. Once she sets her mind to something—bam! More you tell her not to, more she digs in. Remind you of anyone?"

Kyong Ah sucked her teeth. "Your *apa.*"

"Right, it's all Apa's fault. Hey, you losing weight, Omma? And what's up with the Samsonite under your eyes?"

"You mean bags? Funny. *Your* face look like pincushion."

Sally's lips curled. Raspberry blotched her cheeks. She crossed her arms and scowled.

Kyong Ah sighed. "Don't get mad, Seungsoo-ah. You make fun of me first. I had bad day at work. Maybe boss sell Golden West and lay us all off. Let me see new tattoo."

"Like it? Could have gotten an orange red, but the blue red was tighter. Got to see some friends now, Omma. Sorry to visit so late. But you work mornings and me, nights." She tucked the *yut* into her pack and pecked Omma's sharp cheekbone.

Though a rhinestone stud scratched her cheek, Kyong Ah brightened. "So you're playing *yut* with your friend at this hour, eh? Bring them over for dinner, just give me time to prepare something tasty."

Sally sucked the stud on her tongue. She cursed herself for being too chicken to break through their "don't ask, don't tell" DMZ. But why subject Omma to disappointment and herself to loss of love?

"Got to go, Omma."

"Bye, Seungsoo-ah." Kyong Ah grabbed her daughter's large hand. "I love you."

Sally snatched away her hand. Omma *never* used the L word. And since the break-up with her girlfriend, Nesy, neither did Sally. She scratched her broke heart tat and picked up her motorcycle helmet. "Right, Omma. Promise me you'll check out that cough."

"Cough?" Kyong Ah hugged Sally and closed the door. She hoiked up blood. Downed lychee cough syrup and slept fitfully.

9. SPONGES

After avoiding the tumor poster in the washroom at work and flushing bloody spit down the mop closet sink, Kyong Ah headed for Flatland County Hospital's ER. She languished in the waiting room for several hours with Oakland's uninsured before getting buzzed inside. Only to join another purgatory line in the hallway-cum-gurney-parking-lot filled with the same ailing villagers as outside. Like the construction worker twisted into a painful question mark. The woman in a kale-green terrycloth bathrobe puking into a salad bowl decorated with cheery carrots. The kid in Spiderman pajamas with the swollen face and limbs, as if from a spider bite. The walrus of a man wheezing and half-delirious. The place smelled of gangrene and gunpowder. Kyong Ah's coughs riffed off the other beggars in a jazzy improv, making neighbors lean away in shifting patterns. Like OPD helicopter lights dancing across people's heads during a Festival-at-the-Lake riot.

"You from Registry?" A coffee-skinned nurse with a relaxed bouffant shook Kyong Ah's drowsy shoulder. "Break's over. See how swamped we are? Get off your butt and give me a hand."

"No, I'm patient." Kyong Ah whispered. "I need doc to tell me why I cough up blood."

The nurse peered over her glasses. "Not that nasty strain of TB going around, is it?" One of the first Black nurses to have been hired on at Flatland back in the late 1960s, Nurse Ricard wore a smile that mixed two parts sympathy and one part needle.

"Not TB. I smoke. A little." Shame climbed Kyong Ah's cheeks.

"Let's get your blood and X-ray work started. Sorry we have to do it here. But if you're lucky we'll get the results by the time you get a room. Arm, please." *Slam, bam, thank you ma'am*—like a war zone paramedic, the nurse filled two vials. "Follow the yellow line to our radiology unit around the corner and come right back when you're done."

"How much X-ray cost?"

The RN clucked her tongue. "That's not my department, praise God. No MediCal? Didn't Front Desk make you sign fine print on the way in? Then Back Desk will on the way out. If you've got blood in your sputum, it's worth every cent to get X-rayed pronto." She nodded like Kyong Ah did when she wanted oldsters to agree with her instructions. "You see how busy I am? Don't make me have to hustle you down there, Nurse."

"Thanks for promotion. But I just nursing aide."

"Then you know the drill. Scoot yourself to Radiology."

Kyong Ah wondered if the aides here got health benefits and if so, which hospital they bunked at when things got serious. She followed the yellow brick line around the corner to ER Radiology, where she shed her poppy print scrub top and donned a blue paper rectangle in the narrow dressing closet as instructed. A mackerel-faced techie zapped her. As she dressed, a nearby door slammed. Someone whistled.

"Check out the tumor on the left sponge. Three to six months tops. Yeah, take it and the rest to the docs."

Thick soled shoes squiggled against the linoleum. Kyong Ah's fingers snarled like peeled eels dancing in a vat of boiling fat, hopelessly tangling inside her top.

Tumor? Left sponge? Three to six months?

Left Lung clutched; Right wept. Mind bumped walls in a padded white room. Heart knocked like an engine throwing a rod. *Why, Halmoni?* She ate healthy Korean-style, with veggies, fruit, fish, beancake, and brown rice. She did aerobics by lifting, rolling, and pushing patients. She had worked hard to provide for her children. White Knights were her only vice.

She choked up a clot that looked like Dead Husband's liver.

Trying to kill me so I can join you at Evergreen Cemetery, Jae Pil? Selfish kaesaekki.

Kyong Ah folded the clotted tissue and slipped it in her pocket. She pulled a White Knight from her bag and placed it between her lips, her fingers trembling. No fire, but the ritual motion somehow calmed her. She inhaled Tobacco God's husky scent before returning the knight to the crumpled pack of warriors.

Kyong Ah emerged from the dressing closet just as Mackerel did from his bunker.

"You suck. Door not stop sound."

"What?" Mackerel's nose grew pointier.

"You heard me. You suck, you creepy." Kyong Ah coughed; two patients covered their faces against whatever incurable Asian plague she might have.

"Not contagious. Only cancer!" She shouted like a homeless prophet wandering downtown's Frank Ogawa Plaza.

She stumbled down the yellow line back to her hallway chair, now occupied by a banged-up kid with a drooping eyeball and barely hinged flap of cheek skin. Where was his mother? Big Man lay on a gurney, his breath more ragged. It was already 4:48 a.m. She needed to go to work to pay for the damn X-ray and labs. Maybe Mackerel had done her a favor by giving away the verdict. So she could avoid flushing her money down the toilet on useless treatments.

"Nurse, I got to go to work."

"Sure? I don't know who your doctor is yet and we're coming up on shift change."

"I can't be late to work. I got mean boss."

"I can leave a note for a doc to phone you with your lab and X-ray results. I'll see if they can call in scripts to help you breathe easier, too." The nurse's lustrous hair smelled of coconut oil.

"You are nice lady. Yes, please do that."

"One more thing. I want you to quit smoking. That blood is a warning."

Kyong Ah grunted noncommittally. On the way out she patted Big Man's feverish hand though he was beyond comprehension. "Hope doctor see you soon." Bad to be stuck here unconscious and alone. Like she'd be when she got worse.

In the waiting room an amputee still waiting to be seen punctuated his argument with staffers by pounding the floor with his cane. Forget waiting to ask about costs at this hour. She'd get the bill soon enough. Kyong Ah walked out into the brisk morning.

Tumor? Three to six months? What did that kaesaekki *know? Probably only seen ten thousand X-rays.*

After eating dinner out of the candy machine last night, she craved a real meal with rice and kimchi. Too early to tell her kids and deal with their reactions. Yumi would be a pain in the *eongdeongi,* accusing her of bringing this on herself. Seungsoo would freak out and disappear. Minsoo would escape through tumbling off the wagon and Evan through dope.

Kyong Ah punched in at work and stumbled through tasks in a fog until her cell rang.

Flatland County Hospital. Ssibal. *Please battery, don't die.*

"Hello, Doctor?"

"Hello, Mrs. Cho-yee? This is Doctor Tiffany Desai from ER. Nurse Ricard told me to be sure to get right back to you. From your labs and X-ray results, we'd like you to see a specialist."

Kyong Ah headed for the stairwell, cupping her shaking hand around the phone as oldsters turned their morning glory faces toward her. "What's wrong with me, Doctor?"

"We'd rather you come in and speak with someone in person."

The uncertainty in Baby Doc's voice made Kyong Ah question how many miles she'd clocked. "Don't sugar pill me, Doctor. I'm nursing aide at SNiPeh."

"Snippy?"

"SNiPeh, you know, Skilled Nursing Facility. I care for patients with every kind of sickness."

The line sputtered. Kyong Ah leapt in the gap. "What you waiting for? X-ray techie already say I have TUMOR." The words ricocheted up and down the stairwell, striking her shoulders. *Tumor. TUMOR. TUMOR!*

"X-ray tech? I don't understand. That's not our protocol."

Kyong Ah snorted. "He said I got three to six months to live. Just tell me if I have cancer or not."

"The results aren't conclusive. You need more tests."

"Kuurrh!" Kyong Ah wanted to reach through the phone and yank the girl's pigtails. Mr. Bak gave better answers through his cut throat. "And who pay for that? I got no coverage. If I going to die soon, I want money to go to my kids and grandson." Kyong Ah teared up, suspecting that Evan would snort up anything she bequeathed him. But that was beside the point. After all these years slaving, she wanted to leave her offspring something to remember her by. Yumi's new orphan girl, too. Her chest contracted painfully.

Baby Doc sniffled. "I'm connecting you to Doctor Gokul." The line crackled and popped. Before a clear voice shot through.

"Mrs. Kyong Ah Choi?"

"Yes?"

"Hello, I'm Bethany Bones, Dr. Raj Gokul's nurse here in the Oncology Department." Her voice carried a slight Texan twang, blunted from decades spent in California.

"Bones?" Good luck name for orthopedic patients; bad for someone with tumor and a dead husband in the cemetery craving her company. Kyong Ah's teeth chattered. "Oncology?"

"Yes, Ma'am." Nurse words dissolved into white noise. Terror flooded Kyong Ah's chest as Cancer Goddess unfurled a straw mat. The kind picnickers used during spring kite-flying season. The kind mourners used to wrap corpses with for burial back on Dolsan Island.

"Mrs. Choi, you there? Dr. Gokul is prescribing medications to help your breathing until your exam. Let's set the date. We're booked solid for the next two months. Truly sorry about that, but I'll be sure to call if anything opens up earlier. Go straight to ER if you run into any problem before then."

"ER? I just spent night there without even seeing doctor."

"That's right awful. I'm tagging your file. Next time tell them you're Doctor Gokul's patient. That should speed things up. Should we fax your prescriptions to Pharmacy?"

"How much visit and meds going to cost?"

"Sorry, that's not our department. I can arrange for a social worker to meet with you about financing and any other concerns."

"Don't sugar pill me. I got lung cancer, right? Three to six months left. X-ray techie said so."

"*Kuurrh!*" The phlegmy Korean growl made Kyong Ah wonder about the nurse's race. "Outrageous! Did you get the tech's name?"

"No, but he work last night. Got face like fish."

"You'd best believe I'm going to fix his wagon. Hang in there, Mrs. Choi. Dr. Gokul will get in touch with you as soon as he can. I promise."

They signed off. Kyong Ah slumped down on the stairs. Now what? Wait two months to be tested and diagnosed? If Mackerel was right, it'd devour what little time she had left.

Kyong Ah struck away tears. She fired up a White Knight to clear her mind and anesthetize the *han* and grief knifing her lungs.

II. ANGER: *Cancer Goddess*

"Makes them get frustrated
and want to hurt someone."
—Leng Fong

10. MEDIBEGGARS

Kyong Ah woke up clutching a pillow clotted with blood and snot. Mr. Bak's scar throbbed behind her third eye. She sat up.

If docs slice you down to one sound, will it be English? Or Kuurrh-ean?

She performed morning ablutions, dangling an unlit cigarette from her lips. The refrigerator was empty save overripe kimchee and a dried-up specimen jar of her sputum. She tossed both jars and opened the coffee canister; only the scent of its former occupant lingered.

"Minsoo-yah! Why you eat all my food and make me go to work hungry? That's it. You're moving out today!"

"Dang, Omma. Let me sleep. I got a job interview this afternoon." Mickey knuckled a kink in his neck.

"Think I'm running homeless kitchen? Think I got time to shop and cook for you?"

"Alright, alright. Leave me a list and I'll drop by Koreana Super after my interview. Happy?"

"No, not until you move out. You're killing me."

He burrowed beneath the comforter.

Kyong Ah pulled on her carnation print scrubs. "Stop

being slacker and get up." She scribbled a grocery list and thrust it into an envelope with cash.

Mickey groaned from beneath the comforter. "I left yesterday's mail on the counter for you."

A red-striped envelope hooked her eye. She tore it open.

"*Ssibal!* ER bill for $3,479.89 without even seeing doc!"

Mickey sat up. "Shit, Omma. What now?"

"Nothing, go to sleep." Kyong Ah's eyes watered. Halmoni's voice welled up in her ears.

"*Tell my great-grandson about that blood on your pillow!*"

Halmoni used to tuck a dried fish treat beneath a roof eave to appease Smallpox Goddess so the powerful spirit wouldn't snatch her granddaughter away. Kyong Ah chewed her lip; what bribe would please Cancer Goddess, Smallpox Goddesses' hip cousin, now lounging on Left Lung's couch? *Soju* liquor? A carton of White Knights? Bacon-wrapped jalapeño cheese poppers?

Get your eongdeongi *down to MediBeggar office today.*

Kyong Ah left a phone message for Leng that she'd be late but would make it up to her by the end of shift. Kyong Ah threw her backpack in the car, started the engine and lit up. Fire flared like vengeance over a napalmed village.

At MediCal's entrance stood a Yellow Gates of Hell guardian wearing French braids and a gun instead of a helmet and sword. She scanned Kyong Ah's eyes before moving on to the next *keoji*. Kyong Ah tried to remember the last time she'd seen a white security guard. Flatland— black. Target—black and brown. Koreana Super—Korean and black. Liquor stores—Arab and Korean. Hard people staring down hard people. Yet MediCal beggars were as sickly as Golden West patients, only many were younger. Coughers and cripples. Wheezers and twitchers. Crumpled sad sacks and big mama bellies. A stew of black, brown, yellow, and red. Sparingly salted with white cowboys and cowgirls down on their luck.

A caramel-skinned lady in a wheelchair inched forward, her arm slung around an oxygen tank like a favorite child. She sported a lemonhead jogging suit and those navy plastic slippers old Korean men wore. Her labored breathing, swollen ankles and spongy neck hissed edema and COPD, chronic obstructive pulmonary disease.

"Want me to pull number for you?" Kyong Ah asked so the lady wouldn't have to get up.

"Thanks, Sugar," said the lady, sizing up Kyong Ah.

The aide nodded.

Don't ask about her wheezing. Stick to your own side of road.

Kyong Ah checked her backpack. Green card. Driver's license. Rent and utility bills establishing residence. W-2 and income tax papers for 2004. Car registration and proof of insurance. What was the eligibility cutoff? How poor must a poor person be?

Now at the front of the line, the lady with the oxygen tank wheezed loudly. "You the ones who screwed up. Got the collection agencies harassing me day and night. I want to see that heifer's supervisor."

"You'd best lower your voice, Ma'am." The pretty young clerk's hazel eyes narrowed, Siamese cat-like.

"What if I don't?" Tank Lady yanked the plastic tubing from her face. Clutching the wheelchair armrests, she rocked forward and rose shakily on the third try.

"Then you'll have to leave." Surly Miss sneered. "Security!"

The guard strode toward them, hand on holster. "Come with me, Ma'am."

Tank Lady bulked up; her eyes spun bing-bing wild. "Make me and I'll snap that heifer like a twig in a drought."

A metallic click sounded.

"What the?"

Some petitioners crouched; others scrambled for a better look.

"Can't they see the ole gal's on a hose?"

"No freakin' fair."

"Excuse me, Miss. I think she not hear you. Look, she's wearing hearing aid." A White Knight filter Kyong Ah had pinched off sidled up into Tank Lady's ear. Kyong Ah nodded to her to play along, praying the granny wouldn't get both their *keoji eongdeongi* pitched into the street. "I'm nursing aide. Sound like her bad lung and heart condition getting stressed out. But you got doctor on site, right? Better to call them right away." Kyong Ah squeezed Tank Lady's shoulder. "Missus, how about you relax until their doctor come? May I?" Beggar put beggar's breathing tube in again.

Surly Agassi thrust out her pointy chest, armored in a metallic orange top. A vein beat violently in the guard's neck as she white-knuckled her weapon, flashing an "I-own-this-place-and-don't-you-jokers-forget-it" look before putting the safety back on.

Surly Agassi cut her eyes at Tank Lady. "Take a seat. Your number will come up when a counselor's ready. Next."

"I *still* want to see that heifer's supervisor."

"Tell that to the counselor and she'll call the supervisor. No exceptions. Next!"

Like Pockmark's Push Hands made-up rules.

Tank Lady grumbled. Went away and waited to be called.

Kyong Ah stepped forward. "Please give me application. Can you tell me eligibility cutoff so I don't waste everyone's time?"

"You have to ask the caseworker. Your number will appear on the monitor when one's available. Next."

Kyong Ah went to the waiting corral. Tank Lady patted the chair beside her. "Thanks. But my hearing's the one thing that ain't broke. If I was ten years younger, I would have taken out that dried up little hussy myself." She popped Kyong Ah's filter out of her ear and flashed two gold-plated bunny teeth. "They all on edge because someone phoned in a bomb threat yesterday."

"Really? Wait. Why they cut off your MediCal?"

A vessel in Tank Lady's eye pulsed. "They treating me like Daddy Warbucks because I got a small pension that I'm already having to tap into. Everyone warned me to hire a special MediCal lawyer to handle this nonsense. But who's got that kind of money?"

A man with a thinning Afro interjected. "Fucking Republicans raised the cutoff again. Like we don't got nothing to do but sit up in here and take their abuse. After we built this country." A lunatic fire lit his eyes. Like Mr. Legaspi's and his Battle of Bagoong.

Tank Lady hissed through a missing dogtooth. "Before Bushwhackers stole the elections, Slick Willie talked welfare deform out one side of his mouth and 'I feel your pain' out the other. Liars, all of them."

Afro Uncle snarled. "Tell me about it. Now they burning all our money on bunker busters. Drones. BBQs at Dubya's ranch and mess like that. Instead of taking care of us vets who fought their damn wars."

Kyong Ah interrupted. "Excuse me; anyone know what income cutoff is?"

"Depends," said Tank Lady. "Got a spouse, kids or grands you're supporting?"

"No, just me." Left Lung cramped.

Minsoo better be out soon.

"Used to be around $2000 for single with no dependents."

"Gross or net?"

Tank Lady snorted. "Gross of course."

"What if you only make couple dollars over that?"

Tank Lady drew a finger across her throat. "You're dead meat."

You're not poor enough! Ssibal, *you pathetic* keoji!

"Make sure your property's turned over to your kids or they'll come gunning for that, too," said Afro Ajeossi, whose right hand whorled inward like a leper's.

"Better get a lawyer to file for you. Man, I need a cigarette," said Tank Lady.

Kyong Ah's ciggies crouched. "How long it take for application to get approved?"

Afro Uncle said, "Forty-five to ninety days. But forty-five is a con for suckers. More like ninety—or longer."

Ninety days or longer? How does that calculate with Left Sponge's expiration date?

Half an eternity would pass before the docs could summon Knife, Raygun, and Poison Generals to do battle against Cancer Goddess. A California fire blazed in Kyong Ah's chest. She needed a Korean *kut* cleansing ritual to bribe and lure away Cancer Goddess. But MediBeggar made her want to hurl chairs and riot American style and reduce the place to cinders. Which must be why the windows looked bulletproof. Like at the bank. Post office. And Flatland ER with its metal detectors.

Just take your application and keoji eongdeongi *to work.*

She bid farewell to her fellow *keoji.* The guard's shiny gun hooked her eye on the way out.

What would Gun God taste like? Steel rage? How much bloody I&Os would it leave for your kids to clean and bag?

11. B-WORD

"Let's try something new. Step on top of my feet," said Kyong Ah pulling Mrs. Santos up from the wheelchair.

"Ba. Ba. Ba." Mrs. Santos' joints sang like corn kernels on a hot skillet. Her face showed no pain, but that could be because of her stroke.

"Ready to dance?" Kyong Ah slipped her arms around her partner. "Right. Left. Right. Left. Great job! What kind of music you like?" Kyong Ah should bring her Kim Chu Ja tape to work; the songstress could get anyone with a pulse up and moving.

"Bal. Bal. Bal," said the granny. Her eyes filled at memories of children following her like a train around the playground.

Kyong Ah panted as they shuffled to the wheelchair. Aide lifted and bent patient's legs. "Feel less stiff. Winny and PTs going to be happy."

A cough devil dropped out of the sky. Kyong Ah hurried to the bathroom, shut the door and hacked into a wad of toilet paper. She massaged the pain in Left Lung, pressing bronchioles to expel mucous. She studied, logged, and flushed her sputum, almost tripping over Mrs. S and her wheelchair when she emerged.

"*Sesangeh,* what in the world! How you get here?"

"Bal. Bal. Bal." Mrs. Santos' ocean eyes frothed with fear she'd never see her charges at the children's center again.

"My cough scare you? Just allergy. How about haircut? I need one, too." A smile warmed half of Mrs. Santos' face; a nerve on her opposite cheek twitched.

The aide's cell rang as she parked Mrs. Santos in the TV corral. "Hello?"

"Kyong Ah? Lincoln Whang here. Report to my office at the end of shift."

Kyong Ah's brow spiked. *Named yourself after hero who freed slaves? Give me break.*

"What's it about, Mistah Whang?"

"We'll talk when you get here." He hung up.

"*Kuurrh!*" She motioned to Leng. "Pockmark tell me to meet him at end of shift. He ask you, too?"

"No. About salt shrimps?" Leng scowled. "Wait, didn't you say Boy suspect Pockmark might sell out to Cove-haven? Maybe he call us in one by one to see how much pay cut we accept. Divide and conquer."

"He call anyone else?" Kyong Ah tore off a nail and grimaced.

"I not hear anything."

"Why me?"

Leng's brow bunched. "Maybe he want to start on bottom."

"Then why he not call Custodial or Laundry first?"

"Maybe he did and make them promise not to talk."

Kyong Ah nosefarted. "No one can keep secret in this

place." She fondled her White Knights.

"What you going to do?"

"I got no choice but to go."

Leng lowered her voice. "Don't say anything. Don't sign anything. He's *baahk gaap ngaahn* pigeon-eye bully. Got *ahead* during Great Leap *and* Cultural Revolution. Devils like him did my Grandpa in. Watch out." Leng's eyes whipped banner red.

"I will." Kyong Ah's big eye narrowed and small eye widened.

By meeting time, Kyong Ah had rehearsed responses and hoiked out as much mucous as she could. If it was about Mr. L's damned shrimps, she'd feign ignorance. If it was about Pockmark selling Golden West and letting her go, she'd negotiate to leave as late as possible. Her heart drummed against elevator walls. The hole in the back of her head that smoking used to fill ached. She swallowed an antihistamine, praying it would contain her cough. *Call him Boss, Boss, Boss.*

The first thing that caught her eye was a large picture of Pockmark seated in the middle of a bunch of Chinese old guys in suits at a banquet. *Cronies.* Over in the corner were golf clubs, some balls, and a strip of Astroturf. He probably belonged to some suburban country club.

With more crooks making money off working corpses like us. Ssibal nom.

"Have a seat." Pockmark motioned for her to sit opposite him in a chair so low she had to look up, like a peasant groveling before the landlord.

Kyong Ah made her face smooth as a freshly made bed. Pockmark's glasses magnified his pigeon eyes. He ran his fingers through his oily combover.

She shuddered. *Poor Missus Pockmark. Imagine having this worm climb on top of you every night.*

"Why you want to meet, Mistah Whang?"

"You know, don't you?"

"No."

"What did you say to Legaspi that got him so worked up?"

"Nothing."

"So writing that complaint letter was his idea, not yours?"

"Letter?" A wooly cough scratched Kyong Ah's throat. "He got million suggestions. He's super smart guy."

"Where'd he get the paper? And the pen?" Pockmark waved yellow lined paper peppered with the words "*bagoong*" and "shrimp." If only he'd stop shaking it so she could see if it bore her name. So she could stretch the truth wide enough to cover her *eongdeongi*.

"He asked me for them."

"Hah, so you admit you helped him?"

"No, but he not like our patients with broke brain or tongue. You can't fool him. He's vet."

"If he's so smart, how'd he fall down and break his arm and ankle?"

Kyong Ah started to cough.

Not in front of Pockmark.

She swallowed snot salty with blood, *bagoong* and fear. "Not contagious. Only allergies. If you don't give him his shrimp, he's going to make super big stink." Kyong Ah opened her mouth. Closed it. Like a fish trapped in a tank. "And Missus Santos say she want shrimps in her *jook* like

Mistah Rheegasepee."

"Who?"

"You don't remember Missus Santos? Real little. Had stroke."

"Stroke? So she's paralyzed? Can she talk?"

"Part paralyzed, but she can say some words."

Pockmark hissed. "So she's no threat."

Kyong Ah's third eye blackened. Like the sky over the Richmond refinery on a stay-in-your-house-with-the-windows-locked alert day. She smelled gasoline gushing down the ditches of Pockmark's face and then burning flesh.

Now, she crushed a White Knight in her pocket, releasing the smell of Tobacco God's iron red plantation soil. She gripped the sides of her peasant chair, speaking in a quiet, low voice. "Po-oss."

"What?" Pockmark's snake pit face writhed.

Blood curdled in her throat. "What about Mistah Rheegasepee and Missus Santos' request? And Mr. Sorro. Mrs. Robles. Mr. Veracruz. Domingo. Viernes. Gacatan. Dalugdug. Cabatic." She salted in as many Filipino patient names as she could remember.

"We'll decide later." His eyes bulged and shifted.

Leng was right; he did look like a pigeon. *Scavenger.*

Pockmark cleared his throat. "By the way, Morningside is closing down and sending us some of their patients." He leaned forward, his pores throbbing with menace. "Lot of changes in this industry. You're a trusted and valued employee, Kyong. Let's keep it that way."

Kyong Ah's BS-o-meter careted.

Go ahead, make me eligible for MediKeoji, you ditch face

creepy.

But she kept her yap shut. Just until she could file her app at MediCal and endure their ninety-day purgatory period.

"You're dismissed." Pockmark rustled papers on his disheveled desk.

Probably complaints and lawsuits.

Kyong Ah caught herself mid-bow and straightened her American back. A cough rumbled up her throat as his phone rang. He covered the receiver and thrust his chin at her. "Shut the door on your way out."

Leng, Luz and Remy were gone and Swing Shift was setting up for dinner by the time Kyong Ah returned down-stairs for her backpack. She headed to the garage. Later she'd call Leng to debrief. Didn't sound like Boss was sell-ing Golden West. More like expanding at the expense of a smaller fry.

She tapped her temple and took out her ADL notebook.

—*Mrs. S try to dance on my feet*

—*Don't know how she wheel self across room with one hand*

—*She say ba & bal*

Maybe Mrs. Santos was saying "ba" to support Mr. L's *bagoong* campaign. But what about "bal?" Which meant foot in Korean, an odd coincidence. Unless Mrs. Santos was trying to say "ballroom dancing."

Kyong Ah's air sacs bubbled oxygen red.

12. GAMETIME

Kyong Ah was cranking up the bed for Mrs. Loveless, a new hip replacement patient, when Flatland called. Then the line disconnected. When no one called again, she cursed beneath her breath; she'd have to call them back and pray the right person would pick up.

"I have to make a call, Missus. I be right back."

Mrs. Loveless hissed. "Do I look like I'm going anywhere? Can't you give me something for this pain?"

"Right. I tell nurse you want to see her."

"She on another break? Call her pronto." Apparently Mrs. Loveless didn't realize that the more she demanded that staff hop rabbit speed, the slower they turtled.

Kyong Ah retreated to the stairwell and called. "Hello, sorry, did someone call me from this number?"

"Kyong Ah Choi? Bethany Bones here from Doctor Gokul's office. Just had a cancellation. Can you come in today at 3:30 for an exam?"

"I'm at work. How much it cost?"

"Sorry, you'll have to talk to Billing. But bet it's about the same as the appointment you have scheduled two months from now. Sooner the doctor sees you, the better."

Some keoji *died and gave you their space. Gametime.*

"Okay, I take off work."

Kyong Ah found Leng restocking diapers in the supply cabinet. "Leng, sorry but can you cover for me this afternoon? Got to see doctor."

"What's wrong?"

Tell your friend.

"I don't know, maybe asthma or emphysema."

"I knew it. Those cigalettes. What they say at MediCal other day?"

"They give me application. But other people already on MediCal say maybe I make too much to qualify."

"On our pay? That's mess up. But better find out for sure. I cover you, *mo muntai.*"

"Thanks, you are good friend. I make it up to you. Where's Fely? Hip replacement in #313 wants more painkillers."

Leng eyebrows jumped. "Already? This going to be another fun day. Anyway, she have to wait until Fely finishes First Floor. Or Registry nurse show up."

In the late afternoon, Kyong Ah joined the condemned in Flatland's oncology waiting room. A gaunt grandpa with sunken orbs heaved into an airsickness bag. A couple sat holding hands; the husband struggled to straighten his curling spine each time his blonde overly cheerful wife whispered in his ear. A thick man wearing denim overalls furled and unfurled coughs long as an anteater's tongue. A fifty-something woman wearing a batik scarf over her bald head crocheted an afghan square with rainbow-colored yarn; though she looked like a Holocaust survivor, her deft hook looped confidence.

Kyong Ah should have told Leng the truth. Why lie now? She checked off symptoms on the form and admitted to smoking almost fifty years.

Left Lung hacked until the perky daffodils in the picture frame shrank, the magazines grew oilier and the crochet hook hovered mid-air. Anteater Uncle's cough growled in rhythm with hers. But unlike in ER, these patients leaned closer. As if to discern from which clan her Cancer Goddess hailed.

Kyong Ah made a Buddha half-smile in spite of herself. Did these beggars have gods and goddesses for every problem like Halmoni had? Birth Goddess for barren aunties. Tree God for woodcutters. Farming God for farmers. Dragon God for fishermen. Smallpox Goddess to make babies get sick so mothers would better appreciate those who survived her terrible embrace. Old time Koreans called her "Guest." Visiting Smallpox Goddesses had sailed up the Taedong River with the Americans. Or was that the French, Brits, or Russians? Or Chinese and Mongols? Whatever. Disease-bearing goddesses loved to have their praises sung. They were to be eased and appeased. Not exterminated western Terminator style. According to Halmoni, with luck and ingenuity, petitioners might even please the goddesses into erasing scars and bestowing health and long life on the family.

But what about Cancer Goddess? Did she play by Korean or American rules?

The Hanja Sino-Korean character for cancer pulsed behind Kyong Ah's third eye; a mountain of boxes—probably tumors— piled inside the radical for sickness. She shivered.

"Kyong Ah Choi?" A tall, towheaded nurse spoke, sounding like the lady on the phone. She must know something about Koreans; most people called her "Choy" or "Chwee" instead of "Choi." The nurse's daffodil scrubs matched the picture's perky flowers. Her clipboard covered her upper right chest, where they'd removed a breast so many years ago that the nurse had stopped strapping on its stand-in.

A survivor.

Kyong Ah noticed but pretended not to.

Bones noticed her pretending not to notice and smiled. "I like your scrubs. Plum blossoms, right?"

Kyong Ah nodded.

"Thanks for coming on such short notice."

"Thanks for fitting me in."

After the nurse took Kyong Ah's vitals, she sat on the exam table in a blue paper candy wrapper for the cold part of an hour. She should have snagged an oily magazine from the waiting room. She was on the verge of dressing and going out for a verboten smoke to plug the throbbing hole in her skull when a knock sounded and the door opened slowly.

"Kyong Ah Choi? I'm Doctor Raj Gokul. Sorry to keep you waiting." The doc looked at least six feet tall, his skin bark brown. A bit of silver kissed his temples and sadness darkened his eyes.

Not a bad face to look up at—if it was your last.

Kyong Ah felt embarrassed beneath the blue wrap. She should have worn lace panties instead of her workhorse blacks.

He questioned her on symptoms. "Let's do the exam–

ination, shall we? Then we'll send you to start tests."
The doc checked her throat, nose and mouth. He listened
to her chest, tapping it and making gushy sounds. He'd
been eleven when cancer's hard, crab-shaped tumor had
roosted in his mother's stomach. The disease took her
quickly and then pesticide poisoning, his father.

"Here, Doctor." Kyong Ah handed him a Rorschach
I&O tissue she'd produced earlier.

"Thanks." He pulled a penlight from his lab coat
pocket, poked the clots with a tongue depressor and put
the tissue in a specimen cup with her name and date. Then
he asked her to dress and meet him down the hall.

Stacks of files engulfed his office. A UCSF medical
school diploma hung on the wall; the shriveled fern in the
window looked like it'd suffered Raygun General therapy.
Kyong Ah sat in a plump leather chair the color of ox blood;
at least she could talk eye-to-eye with the doc.

Screw you, Pockmark.

Hemp mourning threads tickled her throat; she swallowed. "Don't sugar pill me, Doctor. I'm nursing aide at
SNiPeh and take care of many cancer patients."

The doc's eyes held cloudbursts, his large, dark pupils
brightened by honey flashes before turning darker still.
Now his left eyelid stammered slightly. He scanned her
face searching for mutant cells lurking behind her skull.

"Nursing aide? That's a lot of heavy lifting."

"Yes. I'm more out of breath. Inhalers not help much."

"Tell me again when you started spitting up blood?" A
musical lilt Kyong Ah could not identify danced beneath
his faint Indian accent. African? Caribbean?

"Few weeks ago. But not that much in beginning."

Kyong Ah pulled out her notepad and read the incidents she'd recorded.

"That's impressive tracking."

"I do same for our patients."

"I'd like you to make a biopsy appointment, go to the Lab for tests and come back for your CT in Radiology." He gave her a sheet on how to prepare for the CT.

"I already took X-ray in ER. Techie said I have tumor, not much longer to live. That cost me $3,500. Talk to you today going to cost how much? To tell me same thing?" She blinked back tears.

"I heard about that—completely unethical!" The doc's eyes stormed. "Here's your X-ray. See?" He outlined it with the tip of his pen. "The image quality isn't sharp enough for anyone to make a clear diagnosis."

Your tumor is shaped like your country—ssibal! With your bum fortune, islands off your homeland's coasts will soon spot your lungs, too, and crawl with crabby cancer cells.

"The biopsy will tell us whether it's benign or malignant. I don't see any other problem areas, so let's keep our fingers crossed."

"So where does the blood come from? Tell me truth. No matter how bad. So I can prepare while I still have time and strength."

"I can't say definitively until we see the results of your biopsy." The date on his diploma said she could be his thousandth patient. Getting a doc still uncomfortable with death was good. "Okay, tell me what happens if I *don't* have cancer."

"If the mass is benign, you should still consider surgery to get it removed."

"What if I do have?"

"If you test positive, we'll probably recommend surgery and then a course of chemotherapy and radiology. And after that, we would continue checkups to make sure it doesn't return. Of course, it all depends on whether you've contracted small cell or non-small cell carcinoma."

Kyong Ah sat on her shaking hands. Her mind stuttered on the deathbed ravings of Mr. Jefferson, a former patient whose non-small cell cancer had metastasized to his brain. He'd stopped recognizing family members, who fake smiled or wept through his curses.

Please Kwan Seum Bosal, help me not lose my mind.

Wondering if Flatland had been able to help Mr. Bak, she forced down despair. "How long it take to recover after treatments?"

"Depends on the patient. It takes at least a month after surgery and two-to-six weeks after each chemo or radiation session, longer if done concurrently or there are complications."

"How much I got to take off work?" She'd seen how oncology generals exterminated whole villages to kill cancer bandits laying siege to her patients.

"Each person responds differently. If your job involves a lot of physical labor, you'll need to talk to your employer soon."

Kyong Ah nosefarted. "Boss will fire me."

"You might be able to contest it."

"He find way. He got away with bad stuffs in China without getting catched. Then how can I pay hospital bills?"

"You should be able to work out something with Billing. We're the hospital of last resort for our patients. But if that's the kind of boss you have you might wait until after the biopsy and your prognosis is clearer before speaking with him."

Kyong Ah batted away tears. "No fair."

The doc pushed a box of tissues to her. "Yes, this is a grossly unfair disease. We're here to help you fight it. Look, Mrs. Choi, our patients find it comforting to identify people to act as their support network through this challenging process. Staff organizes support meetings." He scribbled orders and scripts and looked up. "Promise me you'll stop smoking."

Kyong Ah fingered the now shredded tobacco in her pocket. She shook the doc's large, mahogany hand, provoking her curiosity about how it wielded a scalpel. She wasn't surprised that the first available appointment was a month away. Cancer Goddess might prod some other beggar to surrender their spot to her like today. But the doc's fluttering eyelid and support network advice pretty much confirmed the X-ray tech's verdict. She needed to get that damn MediCal application in ASAP. Visit Borisa Temple to chant thanks to Buddha and Kwan Seum Bosal and leave offerings of green tea and money for the nuns to buy fresh veggies. And kick Minsoo out.

By the time Kyong Ah left Flatland, blackness embraced Oakland. She wept up at the sky. Knowing Cancer Goddess and her legions must already blanket Left Lung's valleys and hamlets.

Where are you now, Halmoni? Help me appease Cancer Goddess. She's general and smart survivor. Like you. Please lure her away like you did Smallpox Goddess.

13. HOME

On the way to the kitchen for breakfast Kyong Ah tripped over a lumpy green army sack. She peered inside. A .357 Magnum Gun God slept atop Minsoo's fatigues.

And you were wondering how gun would taste.

She yanked the comforter off her son. "Get up! Why you bringing more junk here when you about to go?"

"*Yaah,* Omma! Charleena pitched all my stuff out." Mickey sat up, rubbed eyes and scratched stubble. His hair bristled like a hedgehog's. "We got loud. Neighbors called the cops. Lucky they didn't haul me in."

Kyong Ah sucked her teeth. "Am I supposed to feel sorry? I got my own troubles. Get out!"

Tell him about your Flatland and MediKeoji visits. And Cancer Goddess' long shadow.

"Cut me some slack, Omma. Got a promising interview this afternoon at Kwon's Body Shop. My main man Marvin's there pulling for me. I'll be out before you know it."

Kyong Ah shook her head violently. "When I get home, your craps better be gone."

Mickey sat up and lit a cigarette.

"Put that out. I'm trying to quit," she said, nearly

slapping it out of his hand.

"Quitting? Alright already." Mickey pulled the comforter over his head, mumbling. "No wonder she's so damned mean."

"What?"

"Nothing."

Later, at work, she ran into Boy as he pushed a wheelchair stacked with cartons of Ensure. "You got to take the stairs. New patient's barricading the main elevator. Unless you guys pry her out, she's going to be the third 5150 pickup for Flatland Lockdown this week."

Kyong Ah's head throbbed. She drew a stealth sniff of the smoke clinging to Boy's scrubs. The hole in the back of her skull contracted nicely.

"Haven't seen you in the Lounge lately." He grinned one dimple deep.

"Too tempting. Trying to quit smoking. I take service elevator."

"You can't. Repairmen are messing with it again. You guys need to liberate the main."

Kyong Ah climbed the stairs; stopping to suck her emergency inhaler at the top of each flight. Her calves stung as if from Halmoni's green switch.

Please, Kwan Seum Bosal, one small miracle. Don't make me lift anyone today.

Kyong Ah emerged to find a snowy-haired mountain elf encamped in the elevator, her walker half in and half out. Wearing a fire-engine-red jogging suit, she clutched a pink Tinkerbelle backpack. She tugged at a surgery bandage wrapped around her head.

Leng stood to her left; Kyong Ah got on her right. Leng

covertly tilted her head twice and vee'd her fingers signaling dementia and potential for violent behavior. Kyong Ah frowned; the granny's 24-karat gold hoop earrings should have been given to her family during check-in so the aides wouldn't get blamed if they disappeared in a fit of generosity or paranoia.

"Cheung Tai Tai, you must be hungry," said Leng in Cantonese, wearing a watery *jook* smile.

"No! *Fan okey!*" Mountain Elf shook her Tinkerbelle pack; it clacked like oracle bones.

"Go home? Later. After try super tasty *jook.*"

"No! Take me home right away!" Mrs. Cheung shouted in English, expanding her audience to the multi-culti mix of oldsters lining the hall. "Or kill me!" Buck-eyed, she scissored fingers against her throat, planting a sock foot on the bridge between Golden West and Fifty-One-Fifty Nation, land of the involuntary, seventy-two-hour psychiatric hold at the county hospital.

Leng pulled the scissor hands from Mountain Elf's throat. "How about breakfast first?" Kyong Ah fetched a bowl of *jook* from the cart.

"Take me home or kill me!" The granny shrieked, morphing hearing aids into instruments of torture. Pre-fall and pre-dementia, Cheung Tai must have been a feisty, independent woman and real ballbreaker, marshalling those around her with hot-blooded determination. But after Dementia Demon moved upstairs, the mighty waves of willpower crashed blindly. Now trapped within Golden West's upset-stomach-pink walls her chi surged in service of the prime directive: *home or death.*

Leng's smile tightened. "No one goes anywhere until

they eat their food and medicine first." Leng nodded to Kyong Ah. "Go ahead and take care of others. I stay here."

Kyong Ah joined Luz and Remy in distributing meal trays.

Mr. Legaspi raised his cast to Mountain Elf. "You tell them, Lola. The food here sucks."

Mrs. Loveless thrust her fork in the air like the broom she struck against her apartment ceiling at the head-bangers upstairs. "Can't anyone shut her up? She's giving me an f-ing headache! Get me out of this place. I'm drowning in refugees. Can't you hire any Americans?"

"What refugees?" Luz's thick unibrow scrunched. Her bracero father had come legally on a train to work the fields. Luz, her mother and siblings had followed, gaining citizenship during a period of amnesty. Now, Luz fingered the Virgin de Guadalupe pendant from a pilgrimage to the Basilica in Mexico City. She lifted her eyes upward and whispered. "Blessed Lord, are you hearing this *tontería?*"

Remy thrust her chin out. "And what's wrong with being a refugee? The pilgrims were refugees. *¿Qué no?*" Remy, who used to be a midwife, had narrowly missed a death squad in Chalatenango Province, El Salvador.

"You take me home!" Electricity crackled in the tucks and folds of Cheung Tai's brain.

While Leng concentrated on Cheung Tai, Kyong Ah parked Mrs. Santos beside Mr. L. "You hungry, Missus S? Sorry we start late."

"Ho. Ho. Ho." Mrs. Santos' Santa-stutter belied the terror in her eyes.

"Home, Ate, home. The old lady wants to go home. We all do." Mr. L shook his toast in Kyong Ah's face. "Why can't you people just let her go?"

Do not discuss one patient with another. Especially one with a trumpet for a mouth like this hellraiser.

Kyong Ah glared. "You and me not her doctor. Maybe her family need to elder-proof house first so she not get hurt. Like for babies."

Yoneda San, how did you end it so tidy and dignified?

"Her family dumped her here because they're too selfish to care for her. Wish I was home watering my bitter melon and tomatoes. Probably all dead now." Mr. L's eyes grew as rheumy as Mrs. Santos.'

He needs a shave.

"You be home soon. What Dr. Chu say about your arm?

"This damn itch is driving me nuts." He squeezed a couple fingers inside his cast and scratched up ash and blood.

"*Fan okey!*" Mountain Elf's fury gave way to desperation.

"Unless there's *bagoong* for breakfast soon, it'll be me in that elevator." Mr. Legaspi shook his good fist.

"Ho. Ho. Ho." Mrs. Santos' stroke fingers twitched with electrodes of memory.

Kyong Ah massaged Mrs. Santos' fingers. "Bitter melon and tomatoes so delicious, right, Missus S? Mistah Rheegasepee, you're lucky to have garden. I live in apartment."

"So what? Grow your garden inside."

The sun did smile on a corner of her kitchen.

"Get me out of this place and I'll send you my special seeds. Took years to cultivate them in this fog."

"Deal." Kyong Ah held up her pinkie and hooked it

around Mr. L's.

If I'm above ground next planting season.

"That how they seal deals in Korea?" Mr. L grinned, not releasing her pinkie.

The aide's lungs spasmed and air sacs purpled; she sputtered. "Only allergies." Kyong Ah slipped free, hurried to the cleaning closet and sucked her inhaler. After her lungs calmed, she stepped back into the hall to the whirl of metal.

They fixed service elevator—sugo!

"*Fan okey.* Or kill me now." Fatigue wrestled hysteria inside Mountain Elf's throat.

Finger-combing her frazzled perm, Leng joined Kyong Ah in the hall. "I turn main elevator off. Let her cool down. More talk, more she get work up. When Fely come up from second floor, she can call Doc Chu and the family about giving her sedative."

Kyong Ah cast a stealth glance at the elevator, careful not to catch Mountain Elf's crazed eyes. "Wonder what's in backpack."

Leng snorted. "Toothbrush and underwear? Old lady jewelry? I don't want to know."

"Hate to 5150 her. She so little."

"Me too. Locking up old people with super-violent patients, only make them more crazy. Oldsheimers brain can't remember what went wrong. Makes them get frustrated and want to hurt someone. But we not set up for pissed-off sick, only chilled-out sick."

Kyong Ah massaged her tumor. What she wouldn't give to be in Smokers Lounge plugging the widening hole in her head. She closed her eyes.

Please Mercy Goddess, don't let cancer metastasize to brain and make me crazy like Cheung Tai.

14. GUILTY

Kyong Ah labored up the stairs of her elevator-less apartment building. The hall smelled of secondhand smoke, which stimulated and repulsed her. Inside, no Minsoo and no food in the fridge. Just his lumpy bags, which seemed to be multiplying like rabbits. He hadn't bothered to fold the mattress and comforter.

Ssibal! *If you're going to croak, you have right to croak in peace. Without cleaning up after your idiot son.*

She took his gun out of the sack and pointed it at the TV, holding her finger loosely on the trigger. Her hands shook and then quieted.

In due time. Until then don't be idiot and accidently kill your TV.

She gently returned the gun to the sack. Golden West sometimes got oldsters who'd misfired and botched their exit. She felt sad and embarrassed for those men. After holding Mickey's gun, she couldn't help but admire their attempts. Sufferers needed options. Not everyone could be as skilled as Mr. Yoneda.

Feeling morose, Kyong Ah put on Kim Chu Ja's sad girl songs, getting worked up as she replayed her *"Keojit-*

maliya," "It's a Lie," song a dozen times.

Our old dictator. And you, Jae Pil. Lying liars.

Wiping away tears, she treated herself to green tea in a celadon cup whose cranes and cracked glaze imperfections made her *maum* heart-mind smile. If only her lungs grew lovelier with each fissure. Warming her hands around the cup's belly, she sipped mountain memories of dragon-flies riding mist, netting rainbows with their wings. She wished she was on Rock Mountain Island watching the waves dance their infinite variations.

She went to the bedroom. Lifted the loose floor board under her shrine where she stashed almost five thousand dollars from her just closed savings account. Fingering a prayer bracelet of sandalwood beads, she bowed before the slight, brass figurine of Kwan Seum Bosal. The goddess's closed eyes saw deep into the heart of Kyong Ah's suffering; her mudra-posed fingers, libation vessel, flowing robe, and lotus stand offered release, soothing Kyong Ah's soul.

When Kyong Ah emerged to refresh her teacup, a red-striped envelope she'd missed in yesterday's mail caught her eye. She took another sip before opening it.

Ssibal!—$4,444.49 for the exam and tests with Dr. Gokul—on top of the $3500 you still owe for the ER visit. And all those bad luck numbers for death. Aiguh!

She raised her cup to shatter it along every predestined crack.

Be practical, Horse Woman. Don't destroy beauty that gives joy.

She stuffed the bill back in its envelope and spent the night scratching her way through forms. She drifted off, dreaming of Sally's broken heart tattoo winging around the ceiling as MediBeggar numbers spidered the walls and Mickey's Gun God glowed like a forge.

The next morning on her day off, Kyong Ah was the third in line when the MediCal guard unlocked the doors. Wearing cropped black leggings and a stretchy tunic with a cow-print yoke on top, she waited an hour to get called. Plenty of time to imagine all the reasons they'd reject her.

"Kyong Cho-ee? I'm Rashida Leonard. Follow me," said a mocha-skinned worker with marceled hair. She wore a leopard print blouse and black flip skirt.

Late forties?

A thickening waist hinted at a predisposition for diabetes and problems of the heart. Kyong Ah followed her to a back corner. Anxiety constricted the mesh capillary bags holding the aide's alveoli; the caseworker's desk looked like a tornado had landed on it.

"Let's see your application." A patron of miniaturist International Boulevard nail salon artists, Ms. Leonard's manicure featured Oakland's skyline, including longshore cranes on her ring fingers.

Kyong Ah complied. Caseworker suppressed a yawn; petitioner suppressed an urge to shake her awake. She yawned again.

"Got proof of residence? Your 2004 income tax statement? Proof of wage and income? Bank statements? Car registration? Do you own a home?"

Kyong Ah produced each document except the bank statement. "I don't have savings account or house, Miss. I work as nursing aide. Nothing left to save." Kyong Ah smiled; her face hurt.

Only answer what you're asked.

"What about checking? How do you pay your bills?"

"No accounts except for checking, I mean." Kyong Ah's cheeks screamed, *Liar!*

The caseworker leaned forward; her leopard spots constricted and shoulder blades sharpened. "Falsification of information constitutes fraud, punishable by fines and jail time."

"Eung." Air sacs panicked, fumbling the handoff of oxygen to red blood cells.

"What did you say?" The caseworker growled.

Kyong Ah chewed her lip.

You are NOT a criminal. Just poor. Stop acting guilty.

"I said, yes, I understand, Miss."

The leopard spots softened a smidge. "I need that bank statement. An eligibility specialist will make the final determination and you'll be notified by mail."

"Yes. I . . ."

"What?"

Cough ambushed. Tumor bleated. Failing to find a tissue, Kyong Ah hoiked into her utilities bill, scratching her face.

The caseworker scooted back.

"Not contagious. Only cancer." Kyong Ah struck away beggar tears. "Check my application again, Miss. I got lung tumor. Unless MediCal helps me, I'm dead. I already owe Flatland eight thousand dollars."

Ms. Leonard bit her lip. Checked her watch. Kyong Ah wanted to grab her by the spots. Then the aide's sniffer quivered; beneath the Chanel No. 5, beneath the coffee and croissant breakfast, crouched half a pack of menthol cancer sticks. The caseworker must be twitching for a fix at MediBeggar's version of Smokers Lounge.

"You smoke? Me, too. Good for get rid of stress. Bad for live long. You got to go on smoke break? No problem, go ahead. I wait."

Crimson climbed Ms. Leonard's dark cheeks. Her fingernails flashed sunset hues; longshore cranes tickled the sky's belly. "Smell it on me, don't you?" She mumbled. "You better believe I need my smokes." Her eyes smoldered. "Sick and tired of caretaking the sick and tired."

Kyong Ah muttered. "Tell me about it."

The caseworker exhaled a long, ragged breath. "My sister just got laid off and had to move in with her two teenagers on top of me and my two. And last week, another nephew gets picked up for being in the wrong place at the wrong time. And everyone's looking at me like I'm the one responsible for making sure he gets tried as a juvenile, not an adult. Like I have any say in the matter. Just cause I work here." Her eyes reddened. She stroked her manicure, the one luxury she refused to surrender.

Nodding, Kyong Ah found and handed her a fresh tissue. "You must be super good sister and mom. But being main caretaker sucks. Sometimes end up beating everyone else to grave." Kyong Ah coughed and sucked down snot.

Ms. Leonard glanced over her shoulder and walked her chair closer. "Right now you make too much to be eligible. But you're close. You didn't hear that from me. I still need to see that checking account statement." She motioned to her chaotic desk. "It'll take me two weeks to file your application—in case you need to work out anything.

Generally takes three months to be approved or denied. Sometimes longer. I can flag your application as urgent. But since we all have urgents, they cancel each other out."

"Yes, please mark urgent. Thank you very much, I appreciate." Kyong Ah prayed her papers wouldn't get lost on the lady's wrecked desk. "Oh, one more question. If I get approved, does MediCal pay for back bills from Flatland Hospital?"

"Sorry, no."

"Thank you. Have nice day."

On the way out, Kyong Ah nodded at the armed guardian, who blinked back, startled. Kyong Ah started her Hyundai, coughing and wiping blood from her lip. Praying acupuncture could protect her during the three months before MediCal could kick in—if she cut her hours or quit her job in the next two weeks as the caseworker had hinted. But work was life, measuring Kyong Ah's worthiness to walk the planet. And what would she do for money? She fired up a White Knight like her caseworker must be doing right now; it burned so good.

Kyong Ah's cell rang. *Yumi.* Ssibal. "*Yeoboseyo*, Yumi-yah? Still in Korea? You guys okay?"

"We're fine." Yumi sat in the courtyard of a teahouse in Insadong, the art district in Seoul. So elegant and calming. So different from the Yeongdeungpo factory district of her childhood. She exhaled. "We ran into some bureaucratic glitches so it's going to take longer. Since we've got extra waiting time, can you tell me where Apa's parents are buried? Might swing down there on the train. I remember his mentioning North Cholla Province, right?"

Kyong Ah drew a deep drag. "His people are from

somewhere near Namwon. I think they're buried on a hill outside the city." She remembered preparing mungbean pancakes, dried fish and *soju* for Jae Pil to offer their spirits for Chuseok Holiday.

"Do you know their names, Omma?"

"No, sorry."

"We probably won't have time to visit, but do you know where Great-Halmoni is buried? Dolsan Island, right?"

Kyong Ah smiled. "Last hill on the island walking straight south. At the top of the noon shadow of three twisted pines. Overlooking ocean. Maybe her small mound is still there. Maybe it's been swallowed up by others."

Kyong Ah wondered if Yumi would one day wax nostalgic over her grave.

Not unless they bury you next to her father, that no-good bum.

"Anything else?" Kyong Ah coughed and hoiked into a tissue.

"*Yaah,* when are you going to quit smoking? Don't smoke around our daughter. And don't expect us to come visit you in the Cancer Ward."

"You told me thousand times. Anyway, good luck with your baby. I got to go."

Kyong Ah hung up before Miss Hurry Hurry could.

15. REBELS

Mr. Legaspi paced the hallway, shouting through a rolled up newspaper. "What do we want? *Bagoong!* When do we want it? Now!" One frayed brown corduroy slipper slapped the linoleum while the other dragged behind. Cowlicks mashed his head; his eyes bulged fireball red.

Unless Kyong Ah's sniffer was mistaken, Leng and Luz were rolling carts of *jook* trouble out of the service elevator. Oldsters shuffled out of their rooms.

"Follow me. What do we want?"

"*Matyeh?*"

"*¿Como?*"

"No, first answer is '*Bagoong!*' Second answer is 'Now!' Try it again—what do we want?"

"Baboon?" said a *halaboji,* stroking a Ho Chi Minh beard.

"Zoom, zoom!" A snow-permed *halmoni* raised her fist as if honoring a misty strike memory.

"Ba. Ba. Ba." Mrs. Santos hung on her doorjamb.

Kyong Ah scooted a wheelchair under Mrs. Santos. "Mistah Rheegasepee, please sit down so everyone can have breakfast. They got low blood sugar and hungry from not eat all night."

"Where's my *bagoong*? It's D-Day."

"Eat first please."

The vet's nostrils flared. "I don't smell my *bagoong*."

"Why your eyes red? You worry about shrimps instead of sleeping last night?"

He smelled like leather and vinegar. "How could anyone sleep with that woman screaming all night? Why can't you people let her go home?"

Kyong Ah's liver fluttered.

Cheung Tai. Where is she? Sleep by day. Sundowner havoc by night. The longer she stays crazy the less likely she is ever to recover from that fall on her head.

"Eat first. Then we find out about *bagoong*."

"Why isn't Whang here to tell me to my face? I'm not wasting my time with you lackeys."

Leng muttered. "No way am I Pockmark's *jaugau.*"

"Me neither." Luz sputtered. "Why does Boss have to make it so hard on everyone?"

Remy grimaced. "Too much wax in his ears and ice in his heart."

Up went the rolled paper bullhorn. "What do we want?"

"Zoom, zoom!"

"Baboon!"

Mrs. Loveless waved a paper pill cup. "Which one of you thieves stole my painkillers?"

"I didn't take your damn pills, I got my own." Mr. L patted his pocket before resuming his role as chant leader. "When do we want it?" Mr. L's bathrobe fell open; thank Mercy Goddess he was wearing a pair of undershorts printed with barnyard animals.

"Ba. Ba. Ba."

"Mistah Rheegasepee, stop raising everyone's blood pressure. Don't make us to call your daughter Anita at work."

"Anita?" His fist fell limp to his side. He slumped into his chair.

May no one ever sic Yumi on me.

Kyong Ah distributed breakfast trays. But the *ddong* disturber was right.

Only liquefied, end-of-life grub. Why get out of bed if this was all that awaited you? Kkeojeo, *Pockmark!*

"I'm not eating this crap."

"Ba. Ba. Ba." Mrs. Santos' bloodshot eyes said she hadn't slept well.

"That's right, Ate. What do we want?"

"Ba. Ba. Ba!"

"You want to start with oatmeal first, Missus S?"

Mrs. Santos refused to open her mouth. Kyong Ah gave Mr. L the stink eye. "See what you do now? Alright, alright. Give Pock, I mean Mistah Whang until end of day."

"Then what?" Mr. L hitched up his bathrobe. "No tricks. I know my rights."

"Ba. Ba. Ba." Syllables stuck to the insides of the granny's cheeks.

Oldsters' ears cocked toward Mr. L's spit-flying mouth; their eyes shuffled across the aide's skin. Kyong Ah made her face smooth as polished jade. "I not try to trick you." She made a diversionary Buddha half-smile and swooped a spoon of *jook* into the mobile side of Mrs. S' mouth. "Mistah Rheegasepee, you got to eat or looks bad on your record. Mine, too."

"So what?"

Kyong Ah suppressed the urge to give him an oatmeal facial.

"Ba. Ba. Ba." Mrs. Santos backed her countryman.

"See! She wants *bagoong*, too, don't you Ate? Now say, 'goong.'" He rubbed his Adam's apple. "From back of your throat like this."

"Ba."

"Goong,' I said, 'goong.'" Mr. Legaspi rapped his knuckles against his cast.

"Don't bother Missus S. Let her eat."

He sniffed. "Goong, Ate. Ba. Goong. Don't let them push you around."

Kyong Ah glowered at him, tavern-owner mean. Then she put Mrs. Santos' fingers around a piece of toast and raised it to her mouth. "Good job!"

"Wait until the hunger strike." Mr. L's eyes blazed with fifty-one-fifty fury. "You people don't know who you're toying with. I survived the Battles of Midway and Guadalcanal."

"Take this crap away and get me my painkillers." Mrs. Loveless slowly rose from her wheelchair. "Holy Mother of God, this f-ing hurts! I need my pills." She plopped back down.

Luz checked her watch. "Already? You're not due for another dose until your next meal."

"Wrong. You can't add."

"Please wait for us to help so you don't fall," said Kyong Ah.

And I have to lug your heaviness around with these bad

lungs. Please have mercy, Cancer Goddess.

Mrs. Loveless rocked back and forth. "Get me the nurse. And who's Pock Whang?"

"Baboon!"

"Zoom, zoom!"

"Be right with you, Missus." Kyong Ah hissed into Mr. L's hearing aid. "Okay, okay, Mistah Rheegasepee. If you not hear from Mistah Whang by five this afternoon, I wheel you to see him tomorrow. After finish meals and meds service and exercise. Everybody more relaxed. Mistah Whang maybe in better mood, too."

"Ba. Ba. Ba."

Mr. L pumped his fist. "Tomorrow we're eating Pilipino food, Ate. Or we bring this dump down. What do we want?"

"Goong. Goong!" Mrs. Santos eyes shined like burnished gongs. As a walker sped past the corner of Kyong Ah's eye.

"Cheung Tai! Stop before she gets to elevator!" Leng held four trays.

"I go home myself!" Cheung Tai wore a thug cap pulled down low and a padded Chinese jacket over her running suit. Her Tinkerbelle pack swung from her walker handlebars. Her eyes gleamed firecracker fierce.

"Not until doctor say so," said Leng, grabbing one of the walker handles.

"You kill me!" Cheung Tai swiped at Leng with one hand, pushing the walker forward with the other. They swung in circles until Leng grabbed the brake.

"Eat first." Leng cupped her ear, signaling for Kyong Ah to call a nurse. The sedatives they'd given the granny were too wimpy to douse her fighting spirit.

"Kyong, bring Cheung Tai's breakfast to her *special room.*"

Not Rec Room again. Ssibal.

Oldsters would have to do their rehab in the hallway, throwing everyone off. Doc Chu, Pockmark, somebody had to fifty-one-fifty Mountain Elf.

Left Lung convulsed. Buying breakfast peace she'd stupidly agreed to take Mr. Big Mouth upstairs. Blowing her chance of talking Pockmark into reducing her hours to qualify for MediBeggar.

"What about me and my pain? You only wait on your own kind? Get your supervisor down here right now. What's his name, Pock Something?" Mrs. Loveless walked her wheelchair forward.

"Own kind? I'm not Chinese."

"Whatever."

Left Lung tugged. Kyong Ah scowled, trying not to get a bad attitude. The woman must be in withdrawal from whatever amount of drugs she downed at home. Probably had multiple docs writing scripts for her. Kyong Ah wondered if she sweet-talked or bullied her docs. How she'd first gotten hooked. What Evan was on.

"You must be hungry. Please sit down and eat first before we have to return trays to Kitchen. Want an extra strawberry jam for your toast?"

"Now you're talking. Make it three. And get that nurse to refill my pain pills. Be quick about it." Mrs. Loveless eased herself back down into the wheelchair, calculating how to get all her pharmacies to deliver directly here. These refugees didn't know who they were dealing with.

"What do we want?"
"Baboon!"
"Zoom, zoom!"
"Pain pills!"
"Goong, goong!"

16. S&M

Sally looked up from the magazine rack as two Asiatics walked into Good Ride, one wearing butt-cutting ebony hair and a grape miniskirt and the other, riot curls and a snug "come-get-me" tangerine halter. Sally wiggled her brows at her coworker Manny; he winked back, pumping up the volume on Salt-n-Pepa's "Push It." The store promoted a positive work environment, including dividing customers equitably. Whether hotties, like these two, or jerks like the ass who'd jizzed up the john last night.

"May I help you?" said Sally, yoking her head to the beat.

"We're looking for bridal shower gifts." Long Hair fingered a bottle of Inner Tube Lube.

"The naughtier, the better." Tangerine's perfume perked up the sleepy afternoon.

Sally steered them to the lite end of the bondage section. Long Hair whistled. Tangerine lingered at a leather harness with brass rings; she raised her languid eyes and gifted Sally with a smile that made her broke heart tattoo sizzle. Sally pressed the tongue stud into the roof of her mouth and winced.

Stop drooling, pathetic foo. Get to work.

Sally motioned to the packages of cuffs, tethers, pasties and feathers. His and Her thongs. Edible undies. "These are the most popular items for showers and anniversaries."

"How about this?" Long Hair held aloft a handcuff, mask and tickler set.

"Your call, Jadine," said Tangerine, examining a black leather corset. "Can I try this on?"

Sally almost sucked the stud off her tongue. What she wouldn't give to see Hottie model the product. That cinnamon skin and almond eyes were a mixed plate. Rice and collard greens? Mango and *pozole*?

"Sorry. We had to eliminate the dressing room."

"Why?" Tangerine's smile corseted Sally's chest.

"A few bad apples. But we're good at guessing sizes. Her eyes wandered over Tangerine's curves. "Medium bottom and large top? Medium could also work if you lace the top loosely. Like that whip?"

Jadine's mane swished as she joined them. "Let me guess. Bernard?"

Tangerine held the whip under her friend's chin. "Hey, why's your basket empty?"

The studs on Sally's face tingled. Her hips whispered, *Go for it.* "This is National S&M Month." She ignored Manny's snickering. "Whips are fifteen percent off. Want to try it out?"

"Absolutely."

"Stand like you're shooting an arrow. Unravel the line. Hold it like so. Right." Sally inhaled Tangerine's orange blossoms and musk. "Visualize the force running from your back heel. Up through your leg and torso and then down the whip to your target."

Tangerine grasped the handle. "Like this?"

"A little looser at the top of your grip. Right." Sally moved behind Tangerine, coach hand over rookie's. Like Mickey when he'd taught her how to knock baseballs in an abandoned lot back in the day. Only this time she was coach. She pointed to the potted plant in the corner. "Top leaf, front."

Manny paced. "*Watchaté,* don't hurt Rubber Boy!"

"Ready?" Sally's limbs tingled with adrenaline and desire. "One, two, three."

Whutush! The whip lassoed a single waxy leaf that Sally gave to Tangerine, who nestled in her arms three heartbeats past sporting.

"Work it, Chantel!" said Jadine.

Manny ran over and checked his plant's wounds. "You're buying me a new one, Min."

"I'll take it," said Tangerine, touching the back of Sally's hand.

"Made by tanners in Mongolia." Indeed, Good Ride strove to work with suppliers who promoted indigenous craftspeople.

"Get one, Jadine. Aren't some of your peeps from there?" Tangerine fondled the handle.

Jadine looked up from reading the back of a *Devil Wears Pussy* DVD. "Bet yours are, too. Khan Boyz pretty much fucked and pillaged their way across the globe. Talk about bondage." Jadine held up a *Brown Babe Booty* DVD, featuring the backside of a cappuccino-skinned woman twisting around to flash a cherry-lipped smile. "What do you think?"

"Get it, girl," said Chantel, adding a plain wrapper picture book to her basket.

"Anything else?" Sally wondered if they'd like to pilot her *yut* game.

"How about four bottles of Lollypop Lube? For the bride and her maids," said Jadine.

Sally rang up the lube as they performed the Asian ritual of fighting for the bill. They finally agreed that Chantel would pay for the bride's cuff and thong set and her own toys while Jadine would pay for the lube, feathers and DVDs.

"Nice." Chantel ran her fingers up the phoenix tat on Sally's right arm. "Where'd you get it done?" Again with the teasing smile and suckable lips.

After a long dry spell Sally thirsted for Tangerine's delights. Just looking at her made the studs and rings on Sally's face hurt so good.

"Dragon Den over in the Tenderloin. Need their digits?" Sally pulled up the card with the rippling dragon. Handed her business card to each girl. "Come back; our National S&M Month sale goes until the end of the month." Tangerine smiled as they left.

Babo-yah—*should have found an excuse to give her your personal digits. Three years here and still ignorant of the art of control and abandon. Leather and feather.*

"Foxes. If I was into chicks." Manny pulled out a mirror and alcohol. Began cleaning his face jewelry. "The one with the ripe chi-chis was hella flirting with you."

"Was I panting like a dog?"

"Begging to be collared. At Rubber Boy's expense,

bitch. Why didn't you get her number? About fucking time. How long since you and Nesy broke up?"

Sally dug a finger into her broke heart tat. "Almost two years. I suck."

"You wish." Manny drew his fingers across his palm. "How about a friendly wager? This being 'National S&M Month' and all, you scammer."

Sally grinned. "Good, wasn't I? What kind of a bet?"

"We pledge to get laid during your National S&M Month."

"First one laid win a prize?"

"Yeah, they get their meat beat. How about we each put $50 in the kitty? First to get laid gets the kitty. If we both lose, we give the money to some worthy cause. Like a night nursing our funk in a sleaze bar. Buy Oakland."

"Not getting fucked *and* having to fork out $50 to Mrs. Kim's Backyard Bar? Shit. Better make it $20 each." Sally knew she'd probably lose, but her studs tingled at the challenge.

They hooked pinkies. Shook hands. Bumped fists. Wagged fannies.

17. EMO

With Cheung Tai commandeering the Rec Room, Third Floor was chaotic as a village on market day. Tables and wheelchairs choked the hallways. Oldsters clacked mahjong and domino tiles as the PTs snaked wobbly patients on walkers and canes through the chaos.

Kyong Ah knocked on the Rec Room door. "Leng, it's me to relieve you. I got snack for Cheung Tai."

Leng stumbled out. "*Aiyah!* Thanks. She's killing my brains, too."

"Remy and Luz are getting everyone ready for lunch. Take break first." The aides quickly exchanged places and Kyong Ah closed the door behind her.

"*Fan okey.* Or kill me!" Cheung Tai shook her head violently at the dish of applesauce the aide offered.

Kyong Ah sniffed the air and eased Cheung Tai into lying down to get her diaper changed. They spent the next hour chanting sutra repetitions. The patient's centered on home and death; the aide's, on the tasty applesauce of now. They repeated themselves so much that their lips cracked and minds split open and thunder clouds darkened the sky over Golden West.

Kyong Ah tried distracting Mountain Elf from "kill me!" chants by asking about family visitors she'd seen. Cheung Tai's sons and daughters, granddaughters and grandsons. That got them nowhere but wet eyes and "I don't remember." Since comfort food was often wired into long-term memory, the Korean aide named every Chinese food dish she'd ever eaten or heard of. That only triggered panic and "Why am I stupid?" at the mention of *ngow nguk chow fun.* Then, when the noise outside grew loud signaling the end of lunch and naps, the aide switched to more neutral topics, asking about every object in the Rec Room. Which drew head shaking and yawns.

Finally, Mountain Elf nodded off to Tinkerbelle land. Kyong Ah sighed and covered her with a sweater. That's when she realized the granny must be shuttling between two *okey*s, one small and one vast. Small House was where she had reigned over porcelain gods, knitted afghans, photo albums and family dinners until she fell down and memory bled from her brain. Big House sat on the other side of Sorrow River where fierce, proud women who'd forgotten everything but the fire that animated their souls went for their final rest.

Please protect Cheung Tai, Kwan Seum Bosal. And give me more time before I must cross Sorrow River.

Kyong Ah pressed her exhausted lungs and quietly dialed her youngest.

"*Yeh,* Omma? What's up?"

"Need your help."

"Wait, Omma." Sally put her hand over the phone and nodded to a redneck sporting a Hell's Angel leather jacket and waiting for her to ring up his XL peek-a-boo lace bra and panty set. "Be right with you."

"Seungsoo-ah, you got name of good tattoo artist? Must be someone who use clean needles." Kyong Ah pressed the web between thumb and forefinger, where Sally wore one of hers.

"What? For you?"

"Not me, silly," Kyong Ah said quickly. "I mean, Leng's daughter wants tattoo. But Leng not want her to get AIDS."

"Got the perfect place. Dragon Den over in the Tenderloin." Sally ran her fingers up her phoenix tat. "Tell your friend's daughter to ask for Van Le." Sally's tat stung as she recited the number. "Let me know how things turn out. I got to go and help a customer now, Omma."

"Thanks, Seungsoo-ah. I appreciate. I love you."

The studs on Sally's lip scrunched up. "What's up, Omma? You're getting so emo."

"What?"

"You know emotional. Sentimental."

Kyong Ah grunted. "Okay. Bye."

"How weird." Sally rubbed her scalp. "That's twice I've given out Van's digits recently."

Manny looked up from restocking *Original Plumbing* magazines and frowned. "Why aren't you giving out your own, foo?"

"No, that was my mom."

"Wow, she getting a tat?"

"You kidding? No, she needed a referral for a co-worker's daughter. Didn't want her to get HIV from dirty needles. No, I mean." Sally grimaced. "Let me shut up now."

Manny exhaled loudly, his eyes wet. "I know what you

mean. Hey, lucky for you I'm still here. Helping you get your game on. And not pushing up Astroturf under the Coliseum."

"I know. Thanks." Sally flung her arm across her friend's shoulders, feeling pretty emo herself.

Kyong Ah peeked inside Cheung Tai's Tinkerbelle bag. Three pink sponge curlers. A tired toothbrush with parted bristles. A red leather wallet bulging with Hell Notes. The kind her people burned at the cemetery so the departed would have plenty of spending money on the other side. It didn't hurt to take out travelers insurance. The granny was ready. For Big House.

18. DRILL

"I like this style best." Kyong Ah folded open the binder, pointing to a winged heart pierced by an arrow. Similar to Seungsoo's, yet different.

Who broke your heart, Daughter?

She spoke to Van Le, an edgy tattoo artist with a cerulean dragon sizzling up his arm. He wore black jeans, black high-tops and a black dress shirt with rolled sleeves, accessorized with a skinny black tie flecked with silver threads. Sally's generation never seemed to get enough black.

Around the walls hung astonishing color photos of Japanese Yakuza and Hawaiian warriors wearing talismans of protection.

Approving of Kyong Ah's choice, the artist said, "Nice. A customer favorite. Want to add any other details?"

Kyong Ah chuckled. Beneath a soft black sweater, she wore a lightly sequined and laced purple top over black pants. "No arrow. And instead of heart, can you make two lungs? With strong wings?"

"Sure. That's fresh. Where and how big?" His tongue pressed against a chip in a front tooth as he flipped through the binder. "Let's sketch it first." He looked familiar. Like a shadow flying across tile roofs in a kung fu movie.

Kyong Ah shed her sweater and rubbed the inside of her upper left arm, close to Left Lung and high enough to be hidden by her scrub sleeve. "Right here."

"Really? Going to hurt more than if we put it on the outside. It's your call. But this is your first tat, right?" He wondered why she looked vaguely familiar.

Kyong Ah nodded, glancing at Dragon Den's violet and blue neon sign. Some singer named Tupac sang a sad song about his mom from a screen in the corner like the TV at Golden West playing soaps twenty-four-seven. Another tattoo artist worked on a girl in pigtails and yet another guy on a customer with a mountain switchback carved up the back of his skull. Kyong Ah tried to guess the ethnicity of artists and customers. Vietnamese? Chinese Vietnamese?

"No, even if it hurts more that's where I want it."

"You're the queen. I'm your slave. How about this?" Energized, he quickly drew a pair of salmon pink lungs. With wings that looked more Asian phoenix than American eagle. Like the ones running up Seungsoo's arm. Kyong Ah's eyes narrowed.

"Not bad. But Left Lung got two lobes. You know, sections. And right got three. *Yeh*, that's it. How about more red, less yellow? And tail feathers longer? Less like *bong-hwang* phoenix but more like magic red *jujak* bird from ancient Korea."

"*Jujak*? What do you think of this shade of red? How about cinnabar? Or vermilion?"

"Yes, whatchucallit? Vermilion? That's it! But how

long this going to take? Nobody break into my car, right?"

"Where'd you park?"

"Over on Turk."

"We'll take a break soon so you can move your car out front."

Van Le lined up dyes and needles. Salmon pink for lungs. Vermilion reds and oranges for wings. He swabbed her arm with rubbing alcohol.

Kyong Ah studied the torture chamber drill and needles.

Not too late to back out.

She coughed into a tissue and quickly stuffed it in her pocket.

"Not contagious. Only allergies."

"If you say so." He offered her a portable CD player and headset. "Want to listen to music while I work? Some customers do. Like at the dentist."

Union brothers of the drill.

Thinking he might mean Sally's skull thumping hip-hop, Kyong Ah said, "No thanks. Wait." She rummaged in her pack for the bottle of cough syrup she'd bought at Leng's suggestion for her "emphysema." Took a swig and grimaced. A shot of Korean *soju* would have served as a better chaser for this American-style bow to Cancer Goddess. Kyong Ah sat at the edge of her seat.

"Ready?"

"*Yeh,* let's get it over with."

He positioned her forearm on the table atop a stiff pillow and rotated her upper arm to work on the inside. He sat so close she felt like he was in her lap. He smelled like cigarettes. Lime. With the faintest whiff of fish sauce, tensing the hole in her head nicely.

Who are you, young man, and what is your relation to my Seungsoo?

The artist's needle gently entered her skin; it hurt like holy hell. One of the girls yelped, confusing Kyong Ah about who was crying whose pain. She unclenched her teeth and tried to loosen her body.

This isn't so bad. Less pain than having babies. First son, shivering blue. Yumi taking her sweet time coming out. Minsoo with the cord twisting his neck. Sally, big feet first.

Van Le pulled the drill back. "You okay?"

Kyong Ah motioned for him to continue. "More you stop, longer it take." She watched the dragon on Van Le's arm ripple and throb as if it enjoyed swimming alongside her pain.

Don't look or you'll drag it out.

She counted backwards before sneaking a peek as Right Lung emerged. Plump with promise.

"Am I only grandma you see?"

The young man snorted, continuing to ride steady on his needle. "We got grandpas and grandmas who come until they run out of space for new tats. Some keep coming anyway just to check out the new designs and smell the ink."

"Your name sound Vietnamese. Can you speak?"

"Barely." When he smiled, she wondered how he'd chipped his tooth.

"Are you Korean?" He kept his eye on the drill.

"Yes. How you know?"

He smiled. "Just a guess. Head shape. Cheekbones. But you could be Chinese with your name, Mrs. Chang."

Kyong Ah's face quivered with the needle. Nothing wrong with re-inking her name and fortune. No need to worry her kids. Was it strictly business between Dragon Den and Good Ride or Good Slide or whatever Sally's sex store was called? Or more intimate?

As Left Lung plumped, a tender bud of hope sprouted in her heart. He might be a couple inches shorter than her Sasquatch footed daughter, but he seemed nice.

And he had a job!

Kyong Ah got dizzy, inhaling his inks and smoky fish scent—and her smashed-bug blood. His sure touch made him a worthy candidate in bed. But how susceptible was he to HIV/AIDS in this line of work? He wore plastic gloves, but he worked with the blood of whoever walked in the door. Like a public toilet in the Tenderloin. Even veteran nurses got infected from accidental needle sticks. And who knew, maybe Kyong Ah had caught cancer from a patient via an invisible transmission belt that scientists wouldn't discover for another century.

Right, Choi Kyong Ah. And your White Knights are blameless.

A vision of Cancer Goddess hummed behind Kyong Ah's third eye. More gaunt and modern than Smallpox Goddess with her ample hips, skirts and hair bun, Cancer Goddess sported a stylish haircut, a purple tunic with lacy trim over pencil black pants and silver mules that matched her temples. She sucked on an ox horn cigarette holder; she and White Knight were obviously lovers.

Visualizing Cancer Goddess both frightened and calmed Kyong Ah, confirming she'd made the right decision to come here. She gritted her teeth against the drill.

"You can tell I'm Korean by how I talk, right? But you have no accent."

"That's because my mom and I came here when I was three. All I remember is a bunch of people's knees."

A cough grapple-hooked Kyong Ah's throat. "Wait."

He lifted the drill. "Go ahead."

She hoiked into a tissue. Sucked her inhaler and took another swig of cough medicine to quiet her air sacs.

"You okay? That sounds awful, Mrs. Chang."

Kyong Ah knew he wanted to ask why she coughed like a TB ward and needed a lung tattoo. Just like she wanted to ask him about Sally.

But they kept it light. Vietnamese versus Korean food. Korean versus Vietnamese liquor. The wings and lungs feathered as she walked Pain's epidermal floor.

After the two girls left, Kyong Ah moved her car. More customers arrived. Driller and drillee moved on to Korean versus Vietnamese wars. Kyong Ah's heart stopped each time the door opened, half expecting Sally to walk in. Catch her in the act of cancer treatment before she was ready to come clean.

"You know someone named Sally Min? Works at Good Slide something in Oakland?" Kyong Ah kept her voice even to catch if his drill wobbled like the needle on the TV cop show lie detectors.

And it did the tiniest bit. His tooth chip smile turned bitter. "Sure. She a friend of yours?"

"She's friend of my friend's daughter. Ever been to her store?"

"There's no right answer to that question is there? Except to say, 'have you?'"

"No way, Joe-say!" Kyong Ah's cheeks flashed the color of her new tattoo lungs. They both laughed.

The eyes, that's what this customer and his ex shared. And the sadness lining the cut of their jaws.

Hope's Left Wing unfurled in the drill's wake as the conversation drifted back to safer topics. Whose soldiers were scarier, the Republic of Korea's or the Republic of Vietnam's. And whose fish paste could grow more hair on your chest—his *mắm ruốc* or her *jeot*.

Finally, he gave her a teak hand mirror. "What do you think?"

Kyong Ah turned the mirror to inspect her tattoo from different angles. Red and pink. Purple and tender.

Dragon Den let you redraw pain's past. To gird your loins for pain's future. And whatever surprises Cancer Goddess has lining her billowing sleeves.

"This exactly what I want. Thank you very much."

"Going to be sore and puffy for a few days. But should be fine after that." He told her to baby it with plain water and not soap out the colors.

When they were done, Kyong Ah pulled cash from her bag, including a tip.

What a nice young man.

Whatever his relationship with Seungsoo might be.

"Thanks. Hope that cough gets better." His chip toothed smile showed a fleeting, almost feminine concern.

Kyong Ah's air sacs plumped with oxygen, blood and magic. "You remind me of someone."

"Really, who?" He rubbed his head. Tugged an ear with a single diamond stud like a pair she had given Sally a few

Christmas' ago.

"Older get, more forget."

Van Le walked her out to the car. "Let me know if you have any problems. And take care of that cough, Mrs. Chang."

Kyong Ah rolled down the window. "Not contagious. Only allergies."

"Right. And you just sat through two hours in the Tenderloin getting lungs drilled inside your arm." A shadow crouched behind his eyes, tweaking Kyong Ah's heart.

"Let this be our secret." Kyong Ah held up her pinkie for him to hook with his.

He nodded and complied. "Your privacy is our bond. What goes down inside Dragon Den stays inside Dragon Den. Take care, Mrs. Chang." He grinned his chip.

That's when she realized that he wouldn't tell her about his relationship with Seungsoo without her permission.

How do you like it, Cancer Goddess?

Kyong Ah's lungs smiled. She twisted her arm upwards, lightly kissing their fresh portrait. Which she couldn't have done as easily had it been drilled on the outside. Tomorrow she'd have to add fresh tobacco to her shrine. And chant the Lotus Sutra. Make an acupuncture appointment. And with the help of this new lucky scar, wing her way to recovery.

Kyong Ah watched Van Le from the rear view mirror as she pulled away and waved. He waved back.

Please Kwan Seum Bosal. Let Sally find good man to love her. Like Van Le.

III. BARGAINING: *Dope*

"More kids you have, bigger the odds
you'll produce some duds."
–Minsoo Mickey Min

19. BRINKSMEN

"Ready, Korea?" Mr. Legaspi looked up from his solitaire game. His hair swirled like a burning cane field.

Kyong Ah grimaced, glancing at her watch. "Better wash hair and shave first."

"Why?"

So you don't look like crazy bum.

"Because catch more bugs with honey."

"Or shit." The vet's eyes flared. "I'll teach Whang not to toy with me."

"Please don't swear." She touched her still tender tattoo. Her breath eased.

He shrugged and shuffled off to his room. After fetching shampoo and shaver, she met him in his bathroom. Pulled a tattered *Brown-n-Proud* T-shirt over his head and tested water temperature. Worked up a lather of baby shampoo and scratched rooster flakes from his scalp.

"Ah, that feels good. Back more. To the side."

She pushed his head beneath the faucet before toweling him dry. "Now shave."

"My good arm's broke." He rapped on his cast.

"Didn't Winny and PTs say more you take care of self,

sooner you go home? Big baby."

He made cow eyes. "That's what my Lorena used to call me." His heart tightened upon uttering the name of the only one who could rein him in. On her deathbed, she'd passed the baton to their daughter.

"Hold still." Kyong Ah worked quickly, the shaver rasping against his leathery chin. She stood back and inspected her work. "Not bad. Now you ready for Mistah Whang." Red light *nunchi* flashed inside her third eye.

He's going to hug me. In this close, wet place.

She leapt out of reach. Despite a compromised lung, she could still deflect the grabby hands of yet another Golden West hornster. Though weak of limb or mind, many of the old fools had not yet lost desire.

"Ooh, you're a fast one aren't you? I like that." Mr. L grinned and slapped his cheeks. "Soft as a baby's butt."

"*Yaah!* How about magic word?"

"What? Oh, thanks—Korea."

Kyong Ah got a wheelchair, her shoulders stooping for the caning to come.

"I don't need that thing anymore."

"No, but I need excuse to go with you. But if you want to go alone, better for me."

"No, push me." He parked his bony behind in the chair.

The elevator wheezed them up to Fourth Floor.

Fool—wheeling fool.

"Remember, catch bee with honey. Or you give him no choice but to reject you just to prove his power. And don't tell him you say anything to me or you get me fired."

Mr. L slapped his cast. "I'm no snitch."

"And no swearing. Remember—honey."

Upstairs, Mr. L struck Pockmark's door with his cast. "Open up. It's me, Wahat Legaspi. Time to talk."

The aide shook her head.

Let patient be hero. You are only his mule legs.

Pockmark cracked the door open, his hair freshly dyed super black. He spoke *ppalli ppalli* VIP like Yumi, his pigeon eyes snapping. "I know who you are. Something urgent came up. Friday next week at 3:30 is my first free opening. Come back then."

"You promised to decide about my pood *yesterday.* This is bullsheet. You'd do it if I was Chinese. That's discrimination, goddammit."

Kyong Ah's lips parted but her tongue stuck to the roof of her mouth. She squeezed Mr. L's shoulder telepathically.

Remember? Honey.

Pockmark's eyeballs pinged between patient and aide. As if she had any control over Mr. L's big yapper. "Swear again and we're not talking, period."

Mr. L's eyes bulged like lotto-ball curses were tumbling inside his skull. "I'm busy next Priday. You answer me now. Or else."

"You threatening me?" Pockmark bulked up, standing on tiptoe in his elevator shoes. His crater face throbbed, menacing.

"I'm not leaving until I get my *bagoong.*" Mr. L put his hand over Kyong Ah's, still frozen on his shoulder. "Right, Korea—I mean Kyong?"

Kyong Ah's tongue flopped like a fish on a cutting board. Gutted, scraped, and ready to be salted down in a vat with Mr. L's shrimps.

Pockmark's eyes narrowed dangerously. "Don't make me call security." Miscreants back home got their hard heads tenderized by thick-knuckled guards. Here he had to work his ass off and suffer insults from idiot nobodies like this one.

Security? Left Lung grunted. BS-o-meter careted. Golden West didn't need muscle to handle its calcium-depleted, flimsy-limbed oldsters. But if a dementia patient got really militant, the aides could call Boy or Romy from First Floor to bear-hug and sweet-talk them until Fely or Inday administered sedatives. Would GW's Filipino staffers manhandle a countryman for Pockmark over a couple shrimps?

Could be you soon, fighting for kimchi rights at some SNF— if you're lucky enough for MediKeoji to cover you.

"Mistah Whang, no need to call um, security. How about ask Kitchen to try shrimps one week? If vital signs good, keep going. If not, at least everyone tried their best."

Mr. L turned up his hearing aid until it screeched. "Right, what she said."

"Oh, and how about for Missus Santos, too? They eat together."

The one you said was no worry because of her stroke, you ditch face creepy.

The boss' cheeks mottled like a big-pored orange skin hiding piddly fruit. "No exceptions. It's not fair to the other patients."

"Don't make me go on a hunger strike. My nephew Toñio is an editor at the *Oakland Trib.* Want to lose all your Pilipino customers?"

Pockmark sputtered; his face flushed China red. "Alright. One week trial, just for you. If you say a word to anyone else, the deal's off. Now go. I'm busy." He cleared his throat. "Kyong Ah, you stay."

"Why? You said you were super busy. I got to take care of patients."

"It'll only take a minute." He pigeon-eyed and pulled her in, closing the door on Mr. Legaspi. Kyong Ah reluctantly sat in the peasant chair as the boss mounted his throne. "What's your relationship to that big mouth?"

"He's my patient. That's all."

Stand beside hornet's nest and you're bound to get stung.

"Where'd he get this crazy shrimp idea from?"

"From hisself." Leng was right; back in China, Pockmark must have been a party bureaucrat squeezing shrimps and eating bribes.

"This shrimp stupidity sets a bad precedent, don't you agree?" Pockmark nodded so she would, too.

"Why? Americans say 'customer is always right.'"

"Except when they're mentally impaired. Then it's harmful, even dangerous."

Tumor sweated.

Please don't fire me, Pockmark.

She made her voice honeybee sweet. "Boss, you made super good decision today. Taking away everything from old people makes them depressed. Harder to heal."

"Don't lecture me." Pockmark's eyes lingered on her chest longer than was decent before climbing to her now hot face. "Who takes blood pressure readings on your floor?"

"Fely and Inday, of course."

"You aides never do it?"

Kyong Ah bit her lip. They did sometimes when short staffed. But they weren't supposed to. SNF Standard Operating Procedure. Feed hierarchy. Starve underlings.

"No, Po-oss. You know that's nurses' job."

Pockmark's eyes bucked. "I want you to take Legaspi's blood pressure for the next two weeks. Keep me appraised of the results." His crater-face palsied. "This shrimp test better fail."

Her eyes narrowed sniper tight. "Boss, you selling Golden West to Covehaven?"

Taichi Push Hands that!

Sweat beads popped through the pores on Pockmark's nose. "Why, what have you heard?"

"Nothing. I got to go." Kyong Ah fake smiled, opening the door and backing out so quickly she almost tripped over Mr. Legaspi's wheelchair.

"What happened? Didn't cut a side deal on my *bagoong*, did you?"

"Shh!" She shot him a frosty look.

They waited until she had pushed him around the corner. "Mistah Whang said you can try for one week and see how you do."

He pumped his fist. "We won, Korea! Pirst battle anyways. After this, *pancit!*"

The elevator opened. Kyong Ah winced.

Pockmark blames me for Mr. L's demands. Trick oldsters into eating another bite of jook, *or laying down for a nap, okay. But faking Mr. L's blood pressure readings for Pockmark's power trip? No way, Joe-say.*

Boss had made her sweat; her armpits smelled like

kimchi stuffed with *jeot* and oysters. Standing behind patient, aide massaged her tumor as the doors closed and the elevator rattled down to Third Floor.

20. HUBBLE

Kyong Ah's cell rang as she started her car after work. *Flatland.* Ssibal!

"Hello, Mrs. Choi? It's Bethany Bones from Dr. Gokul's office. Know we had you scheduled for your biopsy next month. But a slot just opened at 11:45 tomorrow morning. Any way we can get you down here?"

Cancer Goddess took someone out to free space for you. As she may take you out one day to help another keoji.

"Mrs. Choi? Can you come in?"

"What choice do I have?"

"I'll take that as a yes." The nurse gave her food and drink instructions for the next twenty-four hours. "Please arrange for someone to pick you up afterwards. Any questions?"

"How much this going to cost?"

"You still haven't talked to a social worker?"

"They left cancellation message on my phone but didn't return my calls for new appointment."

"Sorry. Let me see what I can do." She asked Kyong Ah to come in early to fill out forms and they signed off.

Kyong Ah touched her chest.

Bet Doc G will cut right here.

She pulled out the crumpled pack of White Knights she'd been toting like a talisman and lit up, inhaling Tobacco God and stroking her tattoo in the cool darkness of the garage.

Cancer Goddess, please accept this incense-leaf offering.

"Wa!" Leng rapped sharply on the window. "Give me cigalette. What about you cough?"

Kyong Ah rolled down the window. "I need this, Leng. I go under knife tomorrow."

"What? For you empeeseema?" Leng leaned through the smoke cloud and listened to her friend's jagged breath.

White Knight trembled on Kyong Ah's lip. "They think its lung cancer, Leng." The C word curdled against the low-roofed garage like car exhaust.

"*Aiyah!* You sure? What stage?" Leng grabbed Kyong Ah's shoulder; the teddy bears on her scrubs looked on in sympathy.

"Biopsy tomorrow will tell. But I already know from way doc look at me." Kyong Ah shut her eyes against tears.

Leng opened the passenger side and slipped in, her flat nose scrunching like a silkworm. "Give me cigalettes."

Kyong Ah surrendered the White Knight to Leng; his brothers-in-arms crouched lower in her pocket. "I owe big time. After biopsy, super big time. If Doc got bad news, I can't afford treatment."

Wrinkling her nose, Leng crushed the cigarette in the ashtray. "What MediCal say? What you kids say?"

"MediCal won't decide for three months. Haven't told kids yet. Why worry them for nothing?"

"Choi Kyong Ah, that's clazy! Something like this, you

got to tell them. Or else they going to be super piss off. Maybe they can help pay bills and take you to appointments. I going to burn incense before Longevity God and Guanyin for you." The two women shared belief in Mercy Goddess.

"Don't tell anyone, Leng. I can't stand people looking at me like I'm going to gas chamber."

"Hey, I can keep secret. You don't know how many I got locked here." Leng thumped her chest and struck tears from her cheeks. "Promise me you tell you kids."

"Maybe."

Leng thrust out her pinkie. Kyong Ah reluctantly hooked it.

"Now gimme cigalettes you hiding in pocket." Leng held her palm out until Kyong Ah surrendered Whitey's brothers.

By the morrow, Kyong Ah's bare chest was dressed as if with holiday table dinner linens while Doctor Gokul and a pale hulk of a radiologist, ironically named Doc Brown, checked the CT scan to guide insertion of the biopsy needle into her tumor.

Doctor Gokul rested his big blue plastic hand on her arm. "Are you all right?"

"*Yeh,*" she lied.

"The mass in the scan looks about the same size as your previous X-ray. Right now I don't see any others. Good signs. We're going to give you a local anesthetic to numb the area."

He stuck a needle in her chest that kicked like a devil's hoof. She balled her fists to keep from screaming.

If little needle hurts this much, what about big needle?

Kyong Ah's eyes widened when she saw the North-Korean-Taepodong-Missile-sized needle Doc Gokul readied to launch into her chest.

Poor Mr. Bak. They thrust this missile in his neck. Then their jackhammers and shovels.

"Can you still feel this?" The doc pressed near where he'd given her the shot.

"Yeh."

He gave her another shot. Her teeth hummed.

"Better? Now I need you to lie perfectly still. Don't cough."

"Wait!" Kyong Ah turned and hoiked up as much phlegm as she could into the container Nurse Bones held to her lips. Patients gurgled and moaned in adjoining theaters—Flatland needed better soundproofing. Her brain bubbled.

"Remember, try not to move or cough." Doc Gokul's sky blue shower cap and gown prepped patients for flights to heaven. "Ready? Can you hold your breath a moment?"

Before she could respond, the doc pushed in the biopsy needle.

Pain! Pain! Pain!

The missile nosed down, down, down. Past her muscle defense shield. Coal mine bronchial shafts. Mucous fortunetellers. Red cell alchemists.

Can you hold your breath?

Half Taepodong, half Mars Hubble mission the needle ferreted about for mutant cells with abnormally dark, raccoon-eyed nuclei.

Please show doc creatures hiding in your sleeves, Cancer

Goddess.

Left Lung shuddered. Tattoo glistened. Hubble vacuumed up payload. Her flesh tugged around the needle.

Spare me, Cancer Goddess. Help me Kwan Seum Bosal.

How weirdly intimate. To have strangers dig inside your chest. Trawl sponge crevices where only smoke and sorrow had tread before.

Can you hold your breath?

Time photosynthesized inside bronchioles and purpled alveoli.

"That's it." Doc Gokul slowly extracted the bloody needle, bruising cells and re-charting blood trails. He taped dressing over the puncture wound and touched Kyong Ah's arm. A vision of cancer cells proliferating flashed behind the doc's third eye. His mother's? This patient's?

"Please lie here on your side while the wound seals up. We'll get back to you with the results within the next week."

"Can't you tell me now?"

"Please be patient a bit longer." Doc G squeezed her hand, blue glove off now, before leaving with the radiologist.

Nurse Bones inserted pillows beneath her. Kyong Ah lay there until her toes and fingers tingled with feeling again. The nurse returned and transferred her to a recovery room away from the troubling sounds of the missile launch pad. Kyong Ah worried over unfinished tasks should the results be unlucky. Cleaning her apartment. Dividing up possessions between her kids. Making sure they didn't get stuck with any bills. Or fight over meager spoils like her patients' families often did.

Endure. Wait for biopsy results.

The nurse asked questions to check her coherency before letting her leave. "Call if you get a fever, severe chest pain, have difficulty breathing, or cough up blood." Grey streaked Bones' wheat curls; her comforting farm girl smile made Kyong Ah wonder what kinds of crops and stock her people tended.

"I already cough blood."

"Sorry, I mean more than usual. Stay away from heavy lifting for a while." The flat half of the nurse's chest summoned a fresh wave of respect from Kyong Ah. She must have paid a fleshy toll to Cancer Goddess to survive and help new victims.

"I'm nursing aide."

"Right. So you know this is the time to use sick leave and ask your co-workers and family for help. Is someone picking you up?"

"No. Can you call Veterans Cab?"

"Sure, got them on speed dial. Transport's coming soon to take you downstairs."

"Thanks. I appreciate."

Kyong Ah touched the rim of her wound gingerly, hoping the pain would be tolerable so she wouldn't have to use sick leave when the meds wore off. "I have one question, if you don't mind."

"About this?" The nurse thumped the flat side of her chest, as she did with patients ready to wade in deeper. "Lost it to cancer twenty-three years ago. When methods were rougher. Largely been in remission since then. Though there were a couple scares." When she smiled her eyes turned a green shade of blue. "Doctor Gokul is the best. You're in good hands."

"Thanks for telling me."

"You'll find that the more you talk about it with family and friends, the lighter the load."

"Maybe," said Kyong Ah. Doctor, radiologist, assistant and nurse. Plus CT scan, drugs and needle. White Man's Medicine was good at running up tests and bills. But it remained to be seen if WMM was strong enough to search and destroy Cancer Goddess, Terminator style.

21. PAINKILLERS

Kyong Ah's biopsy puncture burned. She winced and let go of the breakfast cart. "Be right back, Leng." She ducked in the bathroom and spit bloody glop into the toilet. The tarred tumor on the stop smoking poster shuddered. She sucked on her inhaler and reemerged.

Crash!

"Sweet Jesus! I'm hurt! Help me!"

The aides rushed to the noise; Mrs. Loveless lay twisted on the floor beside the bed, her hands shaking, her blue eyes streaked red with pain.

Kyong Ah crouched beside her. "Where it hurt, Missus?"

"Everywhere!" The patient pointed to her newly pinned hip. She tried to sit up. "Jesus, Mary, Joseph!"

"*Híjole*, don't move!" said Luz. "I'll get Fely. Be right back."

"Next time press button and we come help you, Missus."

"Get me water. I'm dying of thirst." She swabbed her brow with the sleeve of her pale blue gingham dress.

Kyong Ah returned from the bathroom with a paper

cup. She lifted the water to Mrs. Loveless' lips and spotted two fatso pills squatting on her tongue. Like when Sally was little and used to snack on pebbles.

Weird. Not meds time yet. Kyong Ah hooked them out with a finger. They splashed into the cup as Mrs. Loveless bit down on Kyong Ah's pinkie.

"*Ssibal,* no biting!"

Fely rushed in. "Good grief, stop that right this minute!"

Aide tickled patient to free herself. "I caught her eating these."

"Mine!" Mrs. Loveless lurched forward. "Ow!" Her face twisted as if she'd unpinned the surgeon's work.

Fely pocketed the wet pills.

"Those are mine! She stole my Tylenol!" Mrs. Loveless shook her fist at Kyong Ah.

Fely's voice tightened as she squatted on the floor beside the patient. "Tylenol? We agreed that you'd let us take care of your medications. Let's check and make sure you're all right."

Remy shook her head at Luz. "Don't strain your back again. Let me do it."

"Thanks, Remy. I'll wrap up food service." Luz left as Remy helped Kyong Ah push the bed aside to make more space to maneuver. Fely counted to three and they hoisted the patient.

"Lord! Lord! Lord!" Mrs. Loveless grabbed her hip; a baggie hit the floor. "Mine!" She lunged and screeched in pain.

Fely scooped up the baggie; her lips flat-lined. "Kyong Ah will stay with you while I call a doctor to come check your hip."

"Not her! I need those!" Mrs. Loveless lunged at them. What her stupid jailers failed to understand was that the scripts and meds she'd earned through falls and fractures were the only doses of relief she got from the bottomless grief that engulfed her after her son Tommy's suicide.

Kyong Ah held up her hands and backed away. Outside, Fely held the pills against the light. "Looks like oxy to me. Too soon after her hip surgery to be that hyped. Wonder how long she's been hooked. Is it my imagination, or are we getting more addicts?"

"We getting more." Kyong Ah rubbed her finger. "She got teeth like horse."

"Biting, a regression to toddlerhood. Only going to get worse." Fely sucked her teeth. "Upstream, docs shower patients with scripts. Downstream, we catch the flak. Bet she's re-injured that hip. Watch her docs reward her with more painkillers."

"Somebody else got to watch her. She hate me."

"Doubt if she likes anybody. Unless they give her what she wants."

"*Yeh.*" Painkiller God saved and soothed, conquered and condemned worshippers. Like his cousin Alcohol King. Kyong Ah patted the White Knights riding her hip.

That was the trick wasn't it? To die with dignity before anyone stepped between you and your addictions.

Mrs. Loveless cursed "you refugees" for the good part of three hours before Fely reached her son Johnny at work to approve sending her back to the hospital. Kyong Ah wondered if she'd had that mouth on her before Painkiller God came to roost. From family members' stories, patients often retained personality quirks they'd had before the onset of their illness—only more so. Like a crabby man falling out of his wheelchair while trying to hit someone. Or a tender-hearted man spending his entire stay weeping.

But Kyong Ah had to give Mrs. Loveless credit; where her hips failed, her mouth—and teeth—took up the fight. More than Mr. Bak or Mrs. Santos could. She commanded attention, if not respect.

Kyong stayed out of sight, busying herself with bathing patients. Surrendering this ADL provoked different responses, depending on the patient. Some, like Mrs. Jeters, curled inward like fetuses. Others, like Gramps Kennedy, shouted, "Get out! I can do it myself!"—although they couldn't. Others relished a good scrub and vanquishing the SNF smell, if only for a moment. For those who welcomed the wash, Kyong Ah liked to soap up two cloths, rubbing in opposite direction circles, Korean bathhouse *ajumah* style. To bring poisons up to the surface and send them swirling down the floor drain. But today's compromised lung forced her to economize.

She still worked up a sweat on Mrs. Aasha Singh, paying special attention to bottom folds and holes as the granny alternated butt bones atop the plastic washing bench. Mrs. Singh had been suffering from a stubborn urinary tract infection. The antibiotics she ate to kill the infection gave her diarrhea, a likely culprit in prolonging the problem. While some patients refused to be washed "down there," Granny Aasha sighed with pleasure throughout the cleaning of funk's favorite hiding places.

Kyong washed carefully around her wrist casts.

"Shampoo, too?"

"Please, would you?" Mrs. Singh let Kyong Ah undo her bun and wash her long grey hair.

"Thank you. I'm so useless." The granny wiped her eyes.

Kyong patted her back. "That's okay. You'll get better."

"Think so? They say when old women fall down, it's the beginning of the end."

"Not always. How you hurt your wrists?"

"Fell down in the tub. Like an idiot."

"Not idiot. Easy to slip when wet, even for young people. Get your family to get you bench like this, and handrails." After drying, patient gnashed teeth as aide pulled a mustard *salwar kameeze* over her head and arms. Kyong Ah had seen a couple of daughters come refresh Mrs. Singh's supply of scarves. She placed a gold one with panels parading elephants, tigers, and peacocks around the granny's neck.

"Like it? Yours." Mrs. Singh placed the scarf around her aide's neck.

Kyong Ah smiled and returned it. "No, that's okay. I can't."

"You must."

"Maybe another day. I got to take care of others now. Thank you. I appreciate."

Kyong left, making prayer hands in gratitude to the granny and to Kwan Seum Bosal for giving her a Singh after a Loveless.

Finally, the elevator doors rattled shut on Remy, Gabe from Lifeguard Transport, and Mrs. Loveless and her curses. Kyong Ah waited a bit before heading to her car to make sure she missed them. The old woman had sorely tested the aides' Golden Rule: to provide quality care unto others as one would want for oneself—no matter how evil and prejudiced said care recipient might be.

At Oakland Public Library Main that evening, Kyong Ah's web search on lung cancer crawled like a turtle up a steep grade. Around her, disabled oldsters pecked on Medicare forms. Kids cut and pasted book reports between videogames. Hopefuls spruced up résumés before the rising voice of a pissed-off vet in camo informed patrons that the "fucking printers are busted again."

The PA crackled. "The library will be closing in ten minutes." Kyong Ah skimmed an article about lung surgery, scribbling its lengthy link before following other computerless beggars past the turnstile. Since the Main was only open a couple nights a week after work, she'd have to learn to ride through the idiosyncrasies of the turtles at the small branches, too.

Time's wheezing away. Speed up before you run out of options.

Kyong Ah sat in her Hyundai. Exhaled. Called Yumi, ready to prostrate herself for MediBeggar advice. Yumi's message clicked on, giving a Flatland psychiatric emergency number and dates she'd be out of the office.

Yaah! Cancer Goddess already sitting on your brain? Yumi is in Korea with Agi, picking up their baby.

Kyong Ah hung up and dialed again. "Seungsoo-ah. It's Omma. You at work?"

Sally turned down the volume on Marvin Gaye's "Sexual Healing." "*Eung.* Wait a minute, Omma."

Sally covered the phone and nodded to Queenita, a Good Ride regular. "Right with you, Queenita. Sit down and take a load off."

"Jealous? More of me to lick." Queenita put down her basket of goodies, removed a black patent leather stiletto and rubbed her arches. Her Rio Red toenails glimmered.

"Whatever you say, Queenita," said Sally, smirking as she returned to her mother. "Got a customer. Let me call you back, Omma."

"Wait. I need you to buy to me computer. How much money you need?"

"What?" Sally's eyes narrowed when the Beavis and Butthead look-alikes who stuffed porn down their pants walked in.

"I need Internet."

"What for? Laptop or PC?" Sally caught Manny's eye and poked her chin towards the perps.

"Small is nice. So is fast."

"What's your price range?" Sally fingered the mace beneath the counter. Then the handcuffs. Then the Mongolian whip.

"I don't have much money. But not so cheap it's too slow."

"Okay, I'll get back to you."

"Thanks, Sally. I really appreciate."

Manny shouted. "If you're too cheap to pay for products, stay your ass home and download your shit like normal pervs. Hey, what's that in your pants?"

"Want some of this, faggot?" Beavis clutched his crotch. The store reeked of testosterone, pimples and semen.

"What's wrong, Seungsoo-ah?"

"Nothing, Omma." Sally covered the phone. "Drop the goods and get out before we call the cops."

"Ma-ma-make us, fa-fa-fairy," said Butthead.

Queenita yoked her head. "Hey, fu-fu-fuck you, pencil dick!"

"*Aiguh!* Want me to call police, Seungsoo?"

"No, Omma. Let me get back to you. Bye." Sally jumped in front of the counter with a Temüjin whip. "Put that back."

Butthead blanched. "Fuck you, faggot," said Beavis, pulling down racks and stuffing more DVDs in his pants.

"Faggot? Those flicks you're ripping are men-on-men, asshole." Manny hurled a Jell-O-blue glitter dildo like a spear; it brained Butthead who dropped the movies, rubbing his hand against his jeans like he'd been slimed.

"Fu-fu-fudge packers!"

"Pussyeater!" yelled Beavis, his voice cracking as Sally's whip drew blood from his earlobe, and Queenita's carefully aimed stiletto, from his brow. Beavis tripped over a supersized vibrator, knocking over Rubber Boy as he and Butthead fled.

"And don't come back, fuckers!" Manny righted his wounded plant, scooping in spilled dirt.

"*Aiguh,* Seungsoo-ah, you okay?" Kyong Ah shouted.

Sally fake laughed. "Oops. Thought you hung up. Don't worry, Omma. Just some guys horsing around. I'll check out that computer stuff soon as I can."

Pussyeaters? Faggots?

Kyong Ah hesitated. "Thanks for getting computer. I love you."

Sally grimaced. "Right. Got to go."

Kyong Ah hung up.

What did I do wrong with my kids? If first baby hadn't died, maybe they all would have turned out different. Or if their apa was not no-good bum. Or their omma was not single mom loser.

Kyong Ah sighed, vowing to get Minsoo out ASAP. If Dr. Gokul was going to give her bad news, she needed to fall apart in the privacy of her own grief. Not while cooking and cleaning for her rockhead son.

22. ODDS

The service elevator creaked open, releasing the scent of ocean salt beds. Oldsters leaned forward like fisher-wives waiting for husbands to dock boats laden with the day's catch.

"His *haam ha* here on top." Dong pointed his chin at a dollop of purple treasure.

"Smells like ours but stronger." Leng's flat nose twitched; her Nemo scrubs shimmered.

"How you get Pockmark to give in? He super piss off."

"Mistah Rheegasepee is vet and know how to fight."

"That my *bagoong* I smell? Hurry-up."

Kyong Ah and Leng distributed the trays. All eyes turned to the hellraiser-in-chief. Mr. Legaspi sniffed his tray as if imbibing the supple bouquet of a Francis Ford Copula Pinot Noir. "Aged to perpection!" He shouted so the semi-deaf could hear, folding the paste into his *jook* like whipped egg whites into a lemon meringue. He closed his eyes, ingesting a spoonful and moaning as his neighbors savored their gruel while smelling his.

"What do we want, Ate?"

"Ba. Ba. Ba." The bumps on the strong side of Mrs. S'

tongue flooded. Setting off quivers of excitement up and down both sides of her throat.

"When do we want it?"

"Goong. Goong. Goong."

Mr. L spirited a smidge of *bagoong* into Missus Santos' *jook* and winked.

"You understand everything, don't you Missus S?" Kyong Ah stirred in the tiny sea creatures, placing a spoonful on Mrs. S' eager tongue.

"Ba. Ba. Ba."

Mr. Legaspi extracted a blue plastic hospital glove from his plaid bathrobe pocket.

"Where you get that?"

He grinned and blew into the pinkie. Spooning in the remaining shrimp, he tied it off like a spent condom. "For later. How you think I survived the Battles of Midway and Guadalcanal? Talking to Whang soon? Tell him the *bagoong*'s fine but I want it for lunch and dinner, too. And what's happening with my *pancit, adobo* and *pinakbet*?"

Perhaps Pockmark was right; give an inch, give an ocean.

During break, Kyong Ah sat on an overturned bucket in the broom closet, massaging the hole in the back of her head. Her cell rang.

Flatland.

The roses on her scrubs top withered.

"Hello, Mrs. Choi? Bethany Bones again. Can you come in tomorrow at eight a.m. to review the results of your biopsy?"

"Is it cancer? Tell me now. I'm nursing aide."

"I know, don't sugar pill you. Dr. Gokul wants to talk to you in person."

Translation: you're a goner.

"Please consider bringing someone with you for support."

So they can bear-hug and restrain you when you lose it.

Kyong Ah signed off and splashed water on her face, remembering the microwave grey cast of radiation patients' skin. Soon she'd need a wig from one of the Korean shops on Telegraph Ave that black women patronized. Crazy curls. Bullet-straight bangs. Mini-braid waterfalls. What would look best on a cooked crone's dome? Combover's Revenge. After all the jokes she'd enjoyed at Pockmark's expense. She hoiked and washed bloody mucous down the mop sink and stumbled out into the hall. Her big eye flooded; its small mate blistered.

"You look terrible." Leng stuffed a bag down a hazmat chute.

"Flatland called to come in tomorrow morning at 8."

"About you biopsy? What they say?"

"They not want to tell me over phone."

"You talk to you family yet?"

"Why worry kids before I find out for sure?"

"*Aiyah!* Don't be so pighead. It's kids' duty to worry about parents who raise them. You know patients with family visitors get best care. More eyes, more hands, more better. Want me to go with you?"

Kyong Ah shook her head violently. "Who work floor if we both gone? I appreciate."

Leng seized her hand with scorpion intensity. "Guess what? I going with you."

"No, too much trouble."

"Listen to me, Kyong. Hard for people like you and me

to stick up for self when sick. Easier to fight for someone else. I do for you this time. You cover for me plenty when I take my old guy Jimmy to hospital." Leng massaged her husband's legs each night, not sure whom his Parkinson's or her arthritis would strike down first. "I ask Remy and Luz to cover for us."

Kyong Ah pushed away tears. "Please don't tell them about biopsy."

"*Mo muntai.* No problem. I pick you up early."

"Thanks." Kyong Ah wiped her eyes and hugged her friend, relieved that Leng would drive, her perm barely visible above the steering wheel.

The next morning the two aides sat in Doctor Gokul's red leather chairs. The doc extended his hand to Leng. "So good of you to accompany your friend, Ms. Fong."

Leng fluffed her perm. "Thanks, Doctor. Kyong and I take care of many, many cancer patients."

"Valuable work, indeed. Mrs. Choi, let's review what we've found from your biopsy and blood work." He posted her X-rays and CT scans. "The good news is that the mass hasn't grown or metastasized to other sites since your first visit." Doctor Gokul lowered his pen pointer and looked Kyong Ah directly in the eye. Unblinking, she returned his gaze. His left lid fluttered.

Here it comes.

He cleared his throat. "The bad news is that the mass is cancerous. I'm so sorry."

Assassin cells climbed Grief's veins. Wolf fear mounted her lungs.

The doc's words faded in and out—"non-small cell," "less," "more," and "invasive."

"C-A-N-C-E-R?" she said slowly in case he wanted to interrupt and correct her. Blood and terror pummeled her chest. "The X-ray techie was right."

The doc pressed his fingers into the desk, his eyes exploding in anger.

Good; he is no Mackerel. Death still bothers him.

"Pay him no mind." His dark eyes softened as he exhaled. "Your illness is in Stage One. As far as we can tell, the cancer has not spread to the lymph nodes or other parts of the lung, chest or beyond. There's a good chance that if we take strong measures now, we can defeat it."

A bullet clicked into a chamber. "What measures?"

"We'd recommend performing surgery to remove the malignancy as soon as possible. We may do a thoracotomy to extract the tumor. We'd prefer a thoracoscopy with a small video cam that's less invasive—if the cancer does not spread between now and then."

Leng squeezed Kyong Ah's arm. "How long take for surgery and rehabs?"

"Depending on which procedure, if all goes well, several hours for the surgery, followed by a hospital stay of anywhere from three days to a week to recover while we monitor your progress. We send the tumor to Pathology to be analyzed and they'll get the report card to us about two weeks after surgery."

Kyong Ah watched the doc's lips move as memories of past skeletal, bald, listless and delirious patients bubbled through the hole in her head. Santiago. Chang. Acuña. Jefferson. Seto. Yoon. Wong. Bak. Kyong Ah's lips clacked. "How much all this going to cost?"

"You need to talk to a social worker about that."

"They cancel my appointment."

"If you got MediCal, they pay, right Doctor?" said Leng.

"Yes, for some procedures."

Kyong Ah swallowed a clot. "I low income, but maybe not enough for MediCal. If you had no money and had to choose one treatment, which would it be?"

"That's not how we do it." Dr. Gokul frowned and loosened a tie decorated with small blue elephants. He eyed a warning notice that he'd gone over budget with his patients again, shook his head and turned it over. "Treatment decisions are based on the nature of the cancer."

Kyong Ah's eyes burned. "No, choose one treatment for me, please, Doctor."

"I can't do that." He studied his hands as if assessing how many cancer jungle hectares they'd chopped through. "If you're truly in Stage One, we may be able to hold off on radiation and monitor your progress. But not so long that we risk undermining your progress with surgery and chemo."

"Can I still work while getting chemo?"

"Depends on your job. If you're a nursing aide, you won't be unable to do heavy work. And it's not good to expose yourself to contagious illnesses from your patients when your white blood cell count is down during chemo."

"So you're saying she can't work?" asked Leng.

Kyong Ah's tattoo burned. "What's my odds for surviving?"

"You have a good chance of recovery. We caught this relatively early. The wild card is that you smoked for a long time. You've quit since we last talked, haven't you?"

"Yes." Kyong Ah scratched the hole in her head and

squeezed the White Knight talisman hiding in her pocket.

"There are a number of variables, like age, gender, health and smoking history. You're sixty-three, right? In the case of someone with your profile, I'd say the chances are fifty to sixty percent over five years. Any other questions?"

A one in two chance you'll be pushing up grass next to Jae Pil that bum by the time Yumi's kid begins kindergarten.

"Any chance I won't make it out of surgery?"

"Of course there's always a possibility. But your probability of success is good." The handsome doc's lips smiled; his eyes didn't.

As they headed up International to work, Kyong Ah watched the clusters of uniformed school kids cross the street with their Dora the Explorer and Ninja Turtle backpacks. Who among them would one day battle Cancer Goddess? She grunted. "I'm worth more dead than alive."

"*Aiyah,* don't talk like that! You got to think positive to beat this. But why they not schedule you surgery faster than nine weeks?"

"That's Flatland. If somebody die or run out of money, they see me sooner. Anyway, I already owe $7,000—not counting biopsy and today's visit. Surgery must cost hundred thousand. Doubt if they do it if look like I can't pay. I got to quit work to qualify for MediCal. Maybe good they not schedule me right away so I can get MediCal first. You think Pockmark hire me back if I survive?"

"Hard for Pockmark to get good help like us. But depend on how long you out."

"Thanks for taking me to hospital. I treat you and your Jimmy to dinner soon."

"Don't worry about it. Promise me you tell at least one of you kids—tonight."

Kyong Ah reluctantly hooked pinkies. When they reached work, Kyong Ah hugged Leng, sure her friend would live until she was ninety-seven with a perm fluffy as the clouds smiling over her beloved Mount Tai.

23. CARDED

The headline, "Marijuana May Cut Lung Cancer Tumor Growth in Half," caught Kyong Ah's eye. Tattoo Wings fluttered. Though normally she would have nosefarted at the green magazine atop the mailers beneath her box, today she decided to borrow it, marveling at how a stoner neighbor could subscribe to *Medical Marijuana* without fear of prison. Only in a laid-back nation with inhalers-in-chief Clinton and Bush was such leniency possible. She tucked the magazine in her grocery bag and climbed the stairs.

Mickey was out. The fridge was empty and his junk still cluttered the living room. But at least she could read in peace.

Thank you, Mercy Goddess.

Kyong Ah flipped past cannabis growing tips, dessert recipes and club ads to the feature about a study that had found the active ingredient, delta-tetrahydrocannabinol aka THC, had cut cancer tumor growth in half. The co-authors were two white knights, one bald, the other, pony-tailed. On the upside, Harvard brains had pioneered the study; on the downside, the results were from lab mice, not human beings. Kyong Ah pictured test subjects smoking mouse-sized cancer sticks; the hole in her head contracted pleasantly. Oakland must be a hub for clinical trials. A bud of hope sprouted inside her *maum.*

Kyong Ah added a half bundle of *ssuk* to the pot, remembering Mr. Yoneda's mugwort *mochi.* Sitting down to her beanpaste stew, she continued reading. THC must be a powerful elixir; sellers brewed it in salad dressings, spirits and jam. Was it tasteless? Or sweet like the decadent smoke wafting from beneath her grandson Evan's door?

Kyong Ah opened a red-striped Flatland bill. They hadn't charged for the biopsy visit yet, but at least they'd subtracted the $250 she'd paid to stave off getting forked over to a collection agency. Like protection to keep gangsters from chopping off your fingers.

She brewed *nokcha* green tea in her celadon cup, soothing her soul. Cupping its belly, she inhaled its fragrance and remembered the kindly nun Seong Hyo at Hyangil Temple back home. Wisdom's Big Sister. She'd poured tea to dilute tears Kyong Ah spilled over Jae Pil's cheating. The nun had counseled her to remember his good points, endure and forgive him. But over time the nun's "endure" and "do your best" words had dried up to no more than a sigh.

Left Lung tingled; in Korea they must have already figured out *nokcha*'s impact on cancer. Oakland Public Library Computer Room turtles groaned, retracting their heads. At work only the nurses typed; a two-fingered aide researching cancer would arouse suspicion. She needed her own computer to check.

Drink your nokcha. *Play your Kim Chu Ja ballads. Don't chase whatever monkey idea swings through your mind. You promised Leng to tell your kids.*

Her brow spiked. Big eye itched. Small eye watered. Considering Yumi made her stomach burn; Minsoo, her liver; Sally, her heart.

Sleep on it.

She hid the dope magazine under her bed. That night happy marijuana leaf T-shirt ads danced through the hole in her head.

In the morning as Kyong Ah was leaving for work, Mickey sat up and cracked his knuckles. Got up and thrust his legs through overalls. "Congratulate me, Omma. New job starts today."

"Great! So you'll be moving out tonight."

Mickey's forehead tensed, pulling his spiked hair straighter. "*Yaah,* Omma, cut me some slack. I got to find a place first. At least let me stay until I save enough for first and last month's rent." He instinctively reached for a skull and crossbones ear stud Sally had given him a couple Christmases ago. He smiled. Still there. But he was missing it's mate. Charleena and his exes had turned him into an urban refugee who lost valuables with each uprooting.

Kyong Ah threw up her hands. "No. That's too long. I already cut you slacks. I got my own problems, Minsoo."

Like homeland-shaped tumor growing in your lung. Tell him.

"You got to go. And don't eat food I bought yesterday."

"Dang, Omma. Why you got to be so hard? At least I'm working. Isn't that what you wanted? Never satisfied."

"And look for place to sleep in newspaper. Not bars."

"Umm." Mickey rubbed his scratchy chin; where the hell was his shaver? He checked the stuffed pillowcases, hoping for a lucky feel. He pulled out a cigarette, remembered the no smoking prohibition and stuck it in a back pocket. He'd wait until she left to sneak a puff.

All day at work marijuana leaves tickled the hole in Kyong Ah's head. After shift, she hurried down to Medi-CannBee Cannabis Club and stood in the information line. A redhead named Carrot Juice seeking "Mary Jane" for bad PMS swore it was a fairy herb for whatever ailed you. By the time Kyong Ah made it to the front, three oldsters and two youngsters had told her marijuana could shrink lung tumors. She was dying to believe them, but since they'd all read the same article she had, their advice didn't really count. Plus they were potheads.

"Morning. May I help you?" asked a young lady with mahogany skin and fat dreads that kissed her shoulders.

"Is it okay to smoke marijuana if you got lung cancer? My doctor said to quit smoking cigarettes, but he didn't say anything about marijuana."

"Ooh. That's a question for Dr. Corinne Watanabe–Chin. Have a seat over there and the doc will be right with you." The receptionist's sunny disposition and insider knowledge would make her a great marketer for a fragrant farm in Mendocino.

"Can I get a referral for ID card? My doctor is at Flatland, but I don't know what he going to say about this."

"Doctor Rinne can help you get your MJ ID card, too."

MJ. Like GW oldsters' mahjong, another happy game

of chance. Kyong Ah smiled. Everyone was so friendly.

"How can I be of service, Ms. Choi?" said the doctor whose ropy hair reminded Kyong Ah of that woman—one of Mr. Yoneda's people—who'd married that Beatles guy killed by a crazy.

"I have lung cancer."

"I'm really sorry to hear that. Do you mind telling me your diagnosis?"

Kyong Ah made an oval with her fingers over where Cancer Goddess sat enthroned. "Stage One. Non-small cell. I saw article that marijuana can shrink lung tumors. What you think, Doctor?"

"In the latest *MMM?* Everybody's asking about it. Have you already started your cancer treatments?"

"No, I got surgery in six weeks, but no health coverage. Please don't sugar pill me. I am nurse's aide in SNiPeh."

"You might consider joining a clinical trial on marijuana's impact on lung and throat tumors. But the studies won't be completed for three years. If you qualify to participate, you could get your medical marijuana for free. On the other hand, the trial will also dispense placebos. If you don't have time to waste, that may not work for you."

"Placebo? You mean sugar pills?" Kyong Ah nose-farted.

"Well, I suppose you could say that, but in this case, substituting a different herb. And you CANNOT supplement it with cannabis on your own or it will throw the results off for future patients." The doc had participated in such a clinical trial during her bout with cervical cancer. Fortunately, she hadn't pulled the sugar pill straw. She took in the no nonsense set of this woman's jaw. She'd be an excellent trial subject.

"I need help now. What you think about me using this Korean plant, too?" Kyong Ah pulled a sprig of *ssuk* from her pack.

The doctor fingered and sniffed it. "Artemisia?"

"I don't know. In Korean we call it *ssuk.*"

"*Ssuk?* It's mugwort in English, *yomogi* in Japanese and *ngaai hou* in Cantonese, if I'm not mistaken. A great blood cleanser, all around tonic and anti-depressant, too. Let's go online and check its use on cancers and lung diseases." The doc clacked keys until *ssuk* pictures scrolled up.

Kyong Ah pointed. "That's *ssuk!* Please write down English name for me."

"Also fights fatigue and strengthens dream and prophesy powers. If you believe that sort of thing. But illness can open a mind up to different possibilities. I'll print this out for you. Have you smoked marijuana before?"

"No. But I'm sure my kids and grandson do. What if I smoke *ssuk,* or whatchucallit? Mudwort with marijuana?"

"That's mugwort. Given your illness, the safest method would be to stay away from smoking and ingest it through marijuana brownies or cookies, keeping track of what amount works best for you. Here are some recipes. It's best to keep a daily record of intake and effects. Then you can determine the best dosage of each."

The doc gave her the printouts in a sage green folder decorated with a tiny, hopeful marijuana leaf. "The jury's still out about marijuana's impact on tumor reduction. But many studies attest to its effectiveness in helping with appetite and pain issues, especially as one recovers from surgery, radiation and chemotherapy treatments."

"Thanks, Doctor. You people are real nice." Tattoo hummed.

So different from MediCan't.

"Want me to issue a doctor's referral so you want apply for a cannabis club card?"

"Thank you! I really appreciate."

The doc signed a note recommending medical marijuana to alleviate the painful effects of cancer—and its treatments. Kyong Ah hurried down to the county health center as directed and stood in line. She lucked out and saw a caseworker before they closed, plunking down her application and $100 fee. So as not to look like a goofball stoner, she did not smile for her ID picture.

Kyong Ah returned to MediCannBee the next afternoon, using her temp ID and cash to buy brownies and a small bag of herb. Although California voters had given the thumbs up to medical MJ, she tucked her stash in the bottom of her pack. She wondered if Yoneda San and Dr. Watanabe-Chin, now helping her manage Cancer Goddess were descendants of the invaders whom great Admiral Yi Sun Shin had deployed his turtle ships against to defend the motherland in the 1590s.

"Halmoni, only in this crazy country."

"You're getting help from our colonizers? Don't turn your back for a moment or you'll end up their sex slave in some wintry barracks. And you promised your friend to tell my great-grand-children that you're sick. What are you waiting for?"

"Sorry, Halmoni. So different here from back home."

Kyong Ah sighed. Halmoni had taught her how to harvest low tide treasures and how to salt fish away for a rainy day. Which leaves, berries and roots were safe to eat. And during the war, how to hide from soldiers and bombs. Kyong Ah had taught her kids how to keep a roof over their heads and food on the table. Well, the girls anyway. Maybe she had earned the right to ask for a little help.

"*Kuurrh!*" Kyong Ah grimaced. MJ eliminated Mickey as a support network candidate; indulging in herb while condemning his drinking and doping would be hypocritical. That left the girls.

Meany or Porkypine.

24. EDIBLES

Kyong Ah expected Mickey's stuff to be strewn across the living room. Instead, she found everything neatly folded and stacked with only a faint smoke residue. She looked at her watch, half worried, half relieved that he'd been returning late each night. Probably out tomcatting around the bars and pool halls for a new playmate and place to park his gear.

She opened the fridge. *Maum* smiled; inside sat a stew-pot with a note from Mickey taped to its lid.

Here's gumbo from Charleena's recipe with Andouille sausage. Like Louisiana style maeuntang. *Thanks from your favorite son. Enjoy!*

Kyong Ah warmed a bowlful. Chunks of peppery smoked sausage danced with okra and shrimp.

What a good son.

He'd been the only kid to watch her cook, testing her recipes with handfuls of chili powder and garlic. Of course, there was the time that he'd set the kitchen curtains on fire frying cheeseburgers for him and Sally when she was at work. She and he had repaired the damage without the landlord any wiser. Maybe she shouldn't be evil to him;

losing his girl, home and job must be hard.

After washing the dishes, she peeled back the Maui Wowie brownie's hula-girl wrap and sniffed. Chocolate, sugar, and butter with bark seed undertones. She took a bite; her nose caterpillared. Blue Kool-Aid sweet. Why couldn't they dust it with dried seaweed for salt lovers?

She took more bites, sloshing it down with green tea and releasing its damp jungle flavors. Things go better with *nokcha.* A blood cleansing leaf uncurled behind her third eye. Although *ssuk* was best dried on a thatched roof, she spread it across cut open grocery bags on the kitchen floor beneath the windows.

Brownie and green tea accompanied her to the living room to watch TV and massage tumor. By the time the weather lady waved in pressure systems, Kyong Ah wore a beatific Mercy Goddess smile. A fungal idea sprouted through the hole in her head.

Kyong Ah winged her arms for balance as she rose and concentrated on each step to the kitchen. She pushed a chair to the counter. Climbed. Swooned. Pulled down a kimchi bottle filled with sweet rice. She stepped down, her brain taking three beats to catch up with her feet.

Swish, swish, swish.

She washed sweet and regular rice in a pot to a farmer's *samchae* work beat. The sound made her suck her tongue with longing. She left the grain to soak overnight. She couldn't remember when she'd last made ricecakes flavored with *ssuk* and pinenuts. Probably since she'd kicked out Jae Pil. Hard to honor labor intensive holidays when Dead Husband wasn't there to pressure her into feeding his nostalgia.

If those MMM hippies who look like they spent night in barn can bake sweet hay brownies, you can create something suitable to your salt-loving taste. Like Mr. Legaspi's bagoong. Or Yoneda San's ssuk mochi.

Kyong Ah enjoyed her buzz, sipping *nokcha* to dilute the spacies. She picked up a marker, wondering if it enjoyed its own bracing smell.

What was I doing other night?

She grinned and pulled out a stack of grocery bags. Their ebony marker calligraphy urged her on.

Yumi. Agi. Baby Girl. Minsoo. Evan. Seungsoo. Leng & Luz & Remy.

She had little of monetary value to leave. But from work, she knew that didn't stop people from getting ugly. Whenever families started wrangling over her oldsters' belongings, she'd announce an urgent need for a sponge bath, to empty bedpans, or whatever it took to shoo away vultures and vampires.

She hoped her kids wouldn't fight over her measly possessions. Or about her care if she hung around past when she should have already croaked. She grinned with stoner wisdom.

No way Joe-say. Better make hard decisions for kids while your brain's still working. Get to work.

Yet she took forever arranging the gift bags in the hallway.

Next time work first, brownies second.

She filled the tub and soaked to advanced prunehood. Soaping her *ddae* scrubber cloth, she scratched every inch, lifting off layers of willing and unwilling skin. Satisfying as a night in a Yeosu *jjimjilbang* sauna.

Too bad you can't scrub away your tumor like ddae *outer skin layers. Bet Cancer Goddess loves good, hard scrub, and rest on heated stone floor, too.*

Kyong Ah got into bed, cuddling Pillow Monster as she fell asleep, hoping to catch a glimpse of Mr. Yoneda.

Mickey came home in the middle of the night, knocking over a chair, slamming the cupboards and crashing his mother's Maui Wowie dream.

"*Ssibal,* Minsoo!" she yelled from her bedroom. "If you want to make rackets, get your own place!" Growling, she put on a bathrobe.

"Did you try my gumbo, Omma? What's up with the bags in the hallway? Could have broke my neck. Any Tylenol?" He smelled like a beer keg. He wore an Oakland Raiders T-shirt and pair of Big Ben workpants.

"Yes, gumbo very tasty. Here's Tylenol." Kyong Ah grunted remembering Mrs. Loveless' "Tylenol" and wondered what curses she'd showered on the docs who reset her hip. Kyong Ah put on the tea kettle. "When you moving out?"

"*Yaah,* Omma! Let me stay here for a few more nights. I met this girl." Mickey closed his eyes and slow danced with an invisible partner, humming Tower of Power's "You're Still A Young Man."

"*Aiguh,* in bar? How long will that last? Until beer goes flat? Why should I pay for your mistakes?"

"Stop making me feel bad, Omma. Only makes me want to drink and screw up more. I know you blame me for Evan's drinking and bad behavior, too." Mickey's eyes reddened.

Tell him about tumor.

"Minsoo, when I'm gone I want you to stop fighting with your son. And no more drinking. You used to be so strong and handsome. Not too late to change your life. Promise, Minsoo-ah. Please!"

Minsoo flashed the heartbreaker smile that used to draw the butterfly girls to him when he was a football star for Oakland Tech. *Go Bulldogs!* Before he went to seed and his hair thinned. Before his three wives left him.

"Remember what Apa said?" Mickey grunted. "More kids you have, bigger the odds you'll produce some duds." He slung an arm around her shoulders.

Kyong Ah's brownie brain couldn't argue back. So she took a different tact. "Minsoo-ah, if you quit drinking, so will Evan."

"That little shit? He could give a flying fuck, I mean, damn about what I do or say. How about all the times I sobered up? Had zip effect on him. I don't drink much anymore. Goes straight to the gut." He pulled up his T-shirt and slapped his belly.

"If you stay sober long enough, Evan will, too." She coughed and struck her chest. Her lungs flapped with seagull wings.

"*Yaah,* Omma! Sounds like TB. Anyways, stop worrying about your screw-up son and grandson. When you going to get a life? I hate to say this, Omma, but stop being so, you know, Korean. Blaming yourself for everything. That guilt shit will kill you." He scratched his spiked hair.

"You and Sally make me worry."

Mickey grunted. "At least you can trust me to be for real. Unlike some people." He studied her, incredulous. "Hey, Omma, you're not high are you?"

She waved him off. "No, just a little *soju.*" She swooned, thoughts flying through the hole in her head like canaries fleeing a cage.

"Drinking by yourself? Don't do that. It's too damn depressing. That's why I go out."

"*Aiguh!* And drink with drinking women who eat all your money and ruin your life?"

"Whatever. If you're going to drink, at least wait until I get home so we can drink together. What's up with you anyways?"

Kyong Ah struck her chest, wishing her Minsoo could always be this lucid. Or maybe he only seemed that way because they were both high. "Stop chasing women. You won't find a worthy one until you fix your mistakes and become worthy, too."

"So you're saying I'm not worthy of respect?"

Sucking her teeth, she poked him in his beer belly.

"Hey!"

Kyong Ah's big eye glistened and small eye turned heavenward. "No matter what happens, remember that I love you, Minsoo."

Mickey's eyes filled. "Thanks, Omma. That's the first time you ever told me that. Directly. Now I *know* something's wrong." He should ply her with *soju* truth serum.

"I'm tired, Minsoo. Let me sleep." Kyong Ah's brow eased. Bronchial branches sighed. Her Minsoo was just as loyal as any Korean son raised back home. The more Jae Pil had beat her, the more he'd pounded loyalty for her into their son. Maybe she should consider Minsoo as a candidate for her support network. She padded back to the bedroom.

Sleep on that until sober, Kyong Ah. He's joker who is wild.

25. TRIAL

Kyong Ah's patient, Mrs. Henrietta Hamilton couldn't poop despite five days of stool softeners and gallons of liquid. Her face furrowed in pain. She refused food that threatened to add to the trucks backed up at the border. Finally, Kyong Ah greased up and hooked her forefinger around poop hard as golf balls blocking the road. Once those were out, an unbelievably long brown snake came slithering out. The furrows in Henrietta's face slid away, too. Kyong Ah cleaned up and dropped the patient off with Winny and the PTs. Thankful for the morning's blessing.

That night hoping Minsoo would come home late, Kyong Ah donned an apple print apron over a tattered Hodori Seoul Olympics Mascot T-shirt and cut-offs. She drained and ground the soaked rice a handful at a time. The food processor from Yumi and Agi jumped like a washer with too many jeans. She pounded the chopped rice with two laundry cudgels, like the ones Halmoni had used to tame abalone.

Beads of sweat gathered inside her bronchioles. Sucking on her inhaler, she cranked up Patti LaBelle's "New Attitude" on a mixtape left behind during one of Minsoo's previous campouts. Bouncing to the beat, she divided the rice in two. Kyong Ah added hot water and chopped *ssuk* to the first half, kneading it into a smooth forest green dough ball. She worked ground marijuana into the second half, producing an oregano green ball. After breaking off and shaping the dough into small eggs and steaming them, she rolled the finished *ssuk* ricecakes in chopped pinenuts and the marijuana ones in black sesame seeds.

She bagged, tagged and tucked the *ddeok* in the back of the freezer, save a few for tonight and tomorrow. Remembering the MediCannBee doc's advice, she decided to test the black sesame *ddeok* first. Refreshing her teacup, she bit into a grainy MJ *ddeok*.

Twiggy. Almost bitter.

Like the roots and weeds peasants clawed up during spring famine season back home, now relished as delicacies in exclusive Seoul Insadong District restaurants.

Too bad she couldn't just smoke it, switching Whitey for Greenie. But her *ddeok* tasted so much better than the brownies. Green tea washed it down. Kyong Ah fried garlic, red pepper, green onions and zucchini with pork for *sun-dubu* beancake stew, adding clams at the end. By the time she finished washing the dishes and selecting hibiscus print scrubs for tomorrow, a goofy grin twigged her face.

Everybody knew sushi and *mochi*. Even kimchi and *bulgogi* were household words among Oakland's BBQ and hot pepper lovers. Why not add Dream Ddeok to the tonics and herbs claiming curative superpowers that her countrymen sold from Telegraph Ave shops? *Medical Marijuana Magazine* and *Korean Yellow Pages* ads shimmered behind her third eye: hippy *halmoni* high on *ddeok*. She pictured herself wearing an *ajumah* aunty apron and goofer's grin while displaying trays of rainbow-colored *ddeok*.

Stop licking outside of watermelon and getting ahead of yourself. See how you feel in morning. And whether Cancer Goddess casts her shadow across your CT scan.

Heavy-lidded, she logged quantity and times in her notebook, massaging her tumor.

Tomorrow just eat one.

The door buzzer bleated.

What in hell time is it?

Kyong Ah clacked her dry mouth and sat up on the couch. The living room rose to meet her.

"Let me in, Omma. Got your stuff." Sally's head fisheyed through the peephole.

"Stuff?" Kyong Ah yawned and opened the door.

"Sorry it's late, but I lucked out and snagged a laptop from my friend Ricki." Sally wore a ring through her nose like a beast of burden.

Kyong Ah hugged her. "Don't say sorry. I appreciate."

"Got your printer and modem, too. *Yaah*, Omma. So you are letting Mickey crash here. Thought you swore 'never again.'" Sally pushed a pile of Mickey's dirty laundry out of the way. She set down a gunmetal grey laptop on the low rice table; it wore an ankh decal on the corner of its lid.

"Your brother just started new job. He's moving out soon. Ooh, machine so light!"

"Almost good as new. A real steal. Try it." Sally pressed Omma's finger to the "on" key; the sound of dawn awakening spread smiles across their faces.

"Beautiful. How much it cost?"

"Only $750 for everything. I left some of Ricki's programs on. Internet and word processing, right?"

"Ricky? Guy or girl?"

"Just a co-worker. Geez. Give it a rest, okay Omma? Hey, your friend's daughter get her tattoo yet?"

"*Eung.* She said Mr. Van Le did super good job. How you know him?"

"Friend of a friend." Sally's face turned a deeper shade of scarlet.

Kyong Ah's tattoo fluttered.

Is Seungsoo whatchucallit? Bi-saekssi? *Fifty percent is better than zero.*

"Let me try something." Sally punched the keyboard; up popped the Internet a thousand times faster than the Oakland Public Library turtles. "I can download a Hangeul program, too. But with my bad Korean, no promises."

"You're so smart, Seungsoo-ah." Kyong Ah went to her bedroom and counted out money from a sock hidden beneath floorboards under the shrine. She returned as Sally tossed back a black sesame seed *ddeok* down the hatch.

"Yummers, Omma! This *ddeok*'s dope."

Kyong Ah blanched. "Dope? Don't know what you're talking about."

"You know, kickin.' Tasty. Yummers. First two were so good, I had to eat two more. Been a long time, what's the occasion?"

"No more *ddeok*, okay? I made for friend's retirement party. Want leftover *sundubu jjigae?* I heat up. Here's your money." Her heart clenched as Sally downed another MJ *ddeok.*

"Keep that much cash under your mattress? That's dangerous."

"No, silly. That's first place robbers look." Her eyes smarted.

Please leave my kids something, Cancer Goddess. "

"Promise you'll marry when I'm gone, Seungsoo-ah."

A man.

Sally choked on a seed. "*Yaah*, Omma! Stop pressuring me." She scratched her broke heart tat. "What'd you put in this *ddeok?* Tastes different."

Almost like Manny's brownies. No freakin' way.

"You know *ssuk?* They call it mudwort in English."

"Teach me how to make it."

Ads of her and Sally displaying *ddeok* products throbbed behind Kyong Ah's third eye; they both sported florid *ajumah* aprons and shaved heads. Her throat and tattoo itched. She felt Mercy Goddess stagger as Cancer Goddess' threw an arm around her shoulders. A goofy goddess grin spread across Kyong Ah's chest and face.

"*Eung*, but why you want to learn Korean stuffs now? Like *yut* and *ddeok?*"

Sally twisted an eyebrow stud. "Saturn rising. Who knows."

"Saturday who? Hey, how your friends like *yut?*"

"Totally loved it." Sally lied; one of the Good Ride focus group players had freaked when a competitor landed on top of her partner's "horse." Back to research and development. "Omma, let me concentrate on setting up your computer first, okay?"

"I get dinner."

Sally was soon slurping *sundubu* and watching Omma

two-finger keys. They high-fived when pictures of *ssuk* plants scrolled up. "Don't remember your *ddeok* having this much of a kick, Omma. Where'd you get the *ssuk*? It's giving me a buzz."

"Koreana Super. You okay?"

Sally stood. "Whoa. Central Valley farmworkers must have bundled in locoweed."

Kyong Ah chewed her lip. "Want to spend night? Dangerous to drive motorcycle when tired."

"Sleepover? There's no room with Mickey's crap." Sally wove down the hall to the bathroom, a loopy smile tickling her face.

"That's okay, you sleep with me. I don't know how late your brother come back." Kyong Ah buried tomorrow's *ddeok* dose in the back of the fridge and made sure the ones in the freezer were well hidden.

Next batch, less MJ.

Kyong Ah's teeth grew dry before she remembered to close her lips. She must look as wasted as Jae Pil after *soju*-ing the night away with army buddies. Or Minsoo and Evan during their intermittent disappearances from holiday dinners.

A protective cape of *ssuk* and MJ leaves settled over Kyong Ah's shoulders. Tumor contracted nicely. Cancer Goddess must be grinning, too.

Kyong Ah lead her youngest into the bedroom. "Lie down, Seungsoo-ah."

"What's that under your sleeve?"

"Nothing. Just rash. Here, use this pillow. More comfortable."

"Maybe just for a minute. So sleepy." Sally plopped

down in the middle of the mattress; Kyong Ah covered her with the lavender peony comforter and slid a pillow beneath her head.

Kyong Ah returned to the living room and typed "mud-wort." The magic machine said, "Do you mean *mugwort?*" Kyong Ah grinned and patted the omniscient Lap God. She two-fingered "yes" and slipped through its wormhole into an herb green galaxy.

26. FAVORITES

Sally woke up sprawled across Omma's bed. Clad in a black T-shirt and plaid boxer shorts she stood up too fast and clutched her pounding head. On the way to the kitchen she found Mickey smoking a cigarette and lounging in a wifebeater tank and black jeans.

He waved the air. "Don't tell Omma about the smokes. She's quitting and pissy as hell." He scowled at Sally's shaved scalp, half-blaming himself for turning her into a tomboy and by extension, a lesbian. He suspected Omma blamed him, too. But he'd only meant to teach Sal basic self-defense to survive Oakland Public Schools.

"Yo, Dude, if she told you not to smoke in her crib, have some respect."

"Respect?" He coughed thickly. "Don't tell me what to do, Squirt. And why'd you spend the night? Get the boot from one of your babes?"

"No, I'm not like you, fartbrains."

"Whatever, grumpy." His eyes narrowed. "And when was the last time you got laid?"

"None of your fucking business." Sally twitched, remembering her unconsummated bet with Manny.

Mickey chortled. "That long?" His laugh, often infectious, irritated Sally now.

"Screw you. Got Omma cooking and cleaning for you again? Big freakin' baby."

"That's between me and Omma and none of your business, butchie." He lit up another cigarette, this time exhaling and holding it out the window.

Sally's phoenix tat pulsed neon; the vine creeping her shoulders, a deeper shade of pissed. "Hey fucker, I'll show you butch."

Surprisingly fast for a beer belly, Mickey blocked Sally and put her in a headlock. He knuckled her shaved skull, laughing and coughing up smoker's phlegm. "What's the matter with the women in this family? Can't you take a fucking joke?" He shoved her away, scrounging for a T-shirt from a pile. "Move, Squirt. I got to get to work."

"No one's stopping you, buttface."

Mickey wolfed down microwaved leftovers. "Bye, Squirt. Don't forget to lock up." He gave her a juicy smooch on the top of her head and slammed the door behind him.

"Dammit!" She wiped his slobber from her head and drilled fingers into her temples to outpain the hangover. Then she stuck her head in the freezer and rifled through frozen seafood, meat and *mandu* until she found the *ddeok* baggies. Like girlie zines hidden beneath superhero comics. Her nose hairs bristled over the black sesame *ddeok.*

Locoweed, my ass. This is weed weed.

Manny El Profe Pothead would know for sure. She pocketed pinenut and black sesame samples. She made Shin Ramyun for breakfast since Mickey the fartknocker had scarfed up Omma's *sundubu.*

Sally inspected cabinets, finding only innocent *ramyun,* crockery and kimchi bottles full of dried grains and beans. Her pawing also failed to yield contraband from bathroom cabinets or bedroom drawers. But when she opened the bedroom closet, out popped a grocery bag of black clothes and accessories labeled "Seungsoo." She sniffed the bags bearing the names of family members and Leng, Omma's running buddy at work. Whose daughter had supposedly wanted the tat. Sally scratched her studded brow.

Old lady hand-me-downs. Tat referral. Ddeok *hangover. What the hell, Omma?*

Sally needed help from a higher power.

During a lull at work, she ducked into the stockroom and phoned Yumi in Korea. "Sorry to bother you. Got a minute, Onni?"

Horns blared. Tires screeched. "We're in a taxi on our way to the adoption agency. Why, what's up?" Yumi spoke *ppalli ppalli* in the land of *ppalli ppalli* people. She wore a 2-piece heather green suit with a lacy blouse she'd picked up at East Gate Market.

"Omma's weirding me out. She's making dope *ddeok.*"

"What?" Yumi asked the taxi *ajeossi* to turn down his bouncy *bbongjjak*-style music. He complied, barely, proving who was king of the cab.

"I said weed ricecake."

"No way. You mean *daemacho?* Or *saam,* you know, hemp?" Yumi whispered, unsure how closely calls were monitored.

"I mean the mint stuff that Manny says is grown in Maui lava dust. Full of iron, minerals and probiotics."

"That's totally inconsistent with Omma's uptight behavior. Surrender control to the goofies? Not a chance."

"Well, stuff got me cloud high. With munchies and a hellish hangover."

"Sure it's not some kind of Hanyak? Remember how she used to make us drink that black mud after holiday meals? Potent."

"Give me credit, Onni. I know the difference between herb and Hanyak. Plus, I got confirmation from Manny. He's a *mota* connoisseur. Like those Napa wine snobs."

"Why'd she give them to you?"

"I helped myself to her stash before she could stop me when I was there installing her computer and printer."

"What the hell does she need a computer for?"

"That's what I'm saying, Onni. She's cranking out enough *ddeok* to open a vendor booth at Lake Merritt Farmers Market to sell to the fitness foot traffic. I don't know who her supplier is but she's been Googling mud-wort so who knows if she buys the herb online?"

"You mean mu*g*wort with a *g*, like beer mu*g*? That's your answer. Must be *ssuk*."

"*Ssuk* give you munchies and hangovers?" said Sally, now craving a jelly donut and Excedrin.

"She's past menopause, but this smacks of teen rebellion. Refusal to accept her aging." Yumi's voice tightened. "She seeing anyone? Like a young gold digger luring her into risky behavior?"

"Omma? No way."

"Believe me, I see it all the time. Women trying to recapture their youth." Yumi switched to Korean for the taxi driver. "Can you please turn the music down? I'm on a long distance call."

Sally heard the driver yell. "Why are you speaking foreigner's language instead of our nation's?" Radio Bbongjjak stayed on blast.

Yumi grunted. "Listen Sally, don't you think it's ironic? After driving Apa to an early death, she's in denial over her own aging issues?" Yumi's heart tensed around an old scar. In the war for hearts and minds, Apa had won Yumi's hands down. If only she'd grown up fast enough she might have saved him before it was too late.

Sally forced down her shoulders. "You still mad and blaming Omma for that? Yo, Onni, I know you were his favorite and all, but Apa's been gone for years."

"And yet Omma still favors you and Mickey over me. How do you think that makes me feel?"

"I don't know—bad? But wait a minute, Onni. Does Omma even have a favorite?"

"Are you that blind?" Yumi stopped short of calling out Sally's refusal to leave the safety of the closet and risk Omma's love. And her own failure to intervene and bust them all.

"Sorry, Onni. Are you there? "

Now she's pissed and won't help.

Sally shut her yap; Onni had a mean right hook and enough psych warfare smarts to make her opponent hurt for a long time in places that wouldn't show. Luckily Sally wasn't on Onni's hit list, but a recipient of her beneficence. "Don't be mad, Onni."

Yumi sighed. "I'm not half as much as I used to be. I've made a lot of progress with my anger. Agi's helped me tremendously."

Onni seemed as foul tempered as ever, but why fight about it and pay for roaming charges? "Okay, but what should we do about Omma?"

"I've got to focus on our baby. As an adoptee she needs extra love. Listen Sally, this is my last chance. I have to look out for my own family now."

"*Sikkeureo!*" The taxi *ajeossi* interrupted, saying something garbled about Korean American drug addicts and Onni's "foreign" husband; his rude *banmal* informal endings were unmistakable.

"No, *you* shut up!" Yumi retorted.

Sally had to give it to Onni; she was still Korean enough to kick the taxi *ajeossi*'s *eongdeongi*—in his own tongue.

"Onni, can you hear me? I can't handle Omma's weirdness by myself."

"Get Mickey to help."

"You can't be serious. Mickey's more hassle than help. Plus Charleena put him out and his shit's all over Omma's living room. You talk to him. He listens to you."

"You kidding? He only listens to himself. Sorry, Sally. If you'd asked me a couple months ago, I could have done something. But not now."

"Dammit, Yumi. You're the counselor. I'm begging you."

"Omma's a dope addict and pusher and you still think I'm a great counselor?" Yumi's pungent silence told Sally that guilt was curdling in her small intestine; resentment, in her big intestine. "Oh, hell. I'll think about it. No promises. Depends on the baby's schedule."

"Thank you, Onni. And I suspect Omma got tattooed, too. Not sure. She said it was a rash."

"That nails it! Some young stud is manipulating her, promising her a second youth. What kind of a tattoo?"

"I don't know. But I think she might have seen Van."

"Van? How'd she run into your old flame?"

Sally pressed a stud into her brow until it cut new flesh. "I hooked them up, but Omma told me it was for her friend's daughter. I'm calling Van to find out."

"Sure you want to root around in that pain again, Sis? Look, got to go."

"*Eung.* Call me after you talk to Omma."

"Pray for me and Agi and our baby."

"*Eung.*"

The sisters signed off. Brakes screeched as Yumi lit into the taxi driver.

"You're a disgrace to the Korean nation!"

The line went dead. The broke heart tattoo stung Sally's hand. Like Van was needling her.

27. DANGER

Mountain Elf's *maum* must have been ruled by the Hours of the Tiger, between three and five a.m. Because by four-forty-five she had managed to take the main elevator hostage and throw a wrench into morning plans to wake, toilet, wash, and prep patients for breakfast. And to make sure the devils understood she meant what she said about "*fan okey* or else," she had procured a weapon. A shiny, black plastic knife with a serrated edge lifted from the pocket of some clueless visitor that would have easily made it past the Transportation Security Administration checkers at Oakland International Airport.

"*Fan okey* or I kill you!"

"Give me that right now or they going to take you away. To place much worse than here," said Leng in Cantonese, her *Happy Feet* penguin scrubs already wrinkled.

"You kill me now!" Cheung Tai lunged, slicing Leng across the cheek, raising a thick red welt.

"*Diu nei!*" Leng swore, more surprised and pissed than afraid. She grabbed the offending hand just as Kyong Ah emerged breathless from the stairs.

"*Fan okey!* Or kill me." Cheung Tai pressed the knife

against her own throat.

Patients stumbled out of their rooms to see what the yelling was about as Leng and Cheung Tai grappled and cursed. Kyong Ah joined Leng from the left. They quickly picked up the kicking Cheung Tai by the elbows. Cut through the growing crowd of oldsters shouting, "Let her go!" or "Get her!" The aides spirited Mountain Elf into the nearest room.

"Oh. Oh. Oh." Mrs. Santos sat bolt upright in bed and watched as Kyong Ah twisted the knife from Cheung Tai's hand, snapped it in half and shoved each piece into a sock.

The aide speed-dialed with one hand. "Boy? Come up and help right away." She whispered. "5150."

"Kill me!"

Boy's voice faded in and out. "This early? Can you hang in there? I'm still waiting for Romy to clock in."

"*Fan okey!*"

"Oh. Oh. Oh." Mrs. Santos' bad leg dropped over the side of the bed.

"Wait a minute, Missus S. Don't fall and hurt yourself." Kyong Ah dropped the phone on the bed and reached an arm towards Mrs. Santos.

Cheung Tai tore off her head bandage, not realizing that the clotty Frankenstitches made her look more demented.

Leng yelled. "Need you now, Boy!"

By the time Boy made it upstairs, patients were roaming the halls in various states of disrepair. Boy bearhugged the biting and scratching Cheung Tai while Fely administered a sedative, but without the family's permission, since she couldn't reach anyone. If they were lucky, that transgression wouldn't blow back on staff.

The aides got the other patients settled and seated as Mountain Elf's *fan okey* battle song faded away.

"You're bleeding a little, Leng." Kyong Ah handed her friend a tissue.

Leng touched her cheek and muttered. "'*Sei malau.*' She's right. I am dead monkey. Look, there's Gabe and Pierre."

As the only Cantonese speaker on the floor at the time, Leng accompanied her attacker, fake smiling through gritted teeth. She patted the weeping Cheung Tai's hand as Gabe and Pierre strapped her to a gurney. Kyong shook her head as the elevator doors rattled shut on them.

Leng soon returned and ducked out to the meds room to nurse her wound with antibiotic salve. The other aides distributed the breakfast trays, which included smidges of *bagoong* for a third of the patients' *jook.* And in place of Thursday's Orange Jell-O, there was a ricecake dessert redolent with coconut and sugar.

"Bi. Bi. Bi." Mrs. Santos chanted in memory of her big brother, Carlos, who culled the sweetest coconuts for their mother's melt-in-the-mouth sweet rice dessert.

"That's right, Ate. *Bibingka.* You can thank *me.* And my Navy buddies in Oakland, Alameda and San Francisco. All the way to Vallejo and Daly City. We organized a call-in campaign for Operation Bagoong." Mr. Legaspi stirred a dab into his *jook,* storing the rest in a blue plastic glove finger. "Where'd you send the old lady? She just wanted to go home."

Kyong scowled and bit her lip. "I don't know." She pointed to the new dessert. "What's this, Mistah Rheegasepee?"

"It's Pilipino."

"I know that. How you make?"

"Sweet rice, sugar, butter or oleo, coconut and vanilla."

From the delicious fragrance it had to be bad news for diabetics' blood glucose levels. No wonder the servings were teeny. Kyong Ah fed Mrs. Santos the *bagoong*-laced *jook* first; the granny's Coke-bottle-thick glasses magnified her gratitude.

"Bi. Bi. Bi."

Kyong Ah placed a nib of *bibingka* on Mrs. Santos' tongue. The granny closed her eyes, savoring Mama island memory. Though way behind schedule, Kyong was grateful for the sugar-bought peace.

Transport brought Mountain Elf back a few days later. She looked like they'd imprisoned her deep in the forest and medicated her with powerful toadstools. The light was gone from her eyes. Her head tilted to one side. Drool gathered in the corners of her mouth. But she still possessed the prime directive. Only slurred.

"Flan. Okey. Kwill. Me."

Since it was Leng's day off, Kyong Ah fed her. "Look, Kitchen prepared *haam ha* special for you. And ricecake. Super good." If she could just get the *halmoni* to sniff, it was good as down the hatch.

"Haam? Ha?" A shrimp gear clicked and meshed in the back of Mountain Elf's head. Her hand shook. Her nose quivered. Kyong Ah placed the *jook* between her lips. When she didn't spit it out, Kyong Ah tried a second spoonful. It pooled there.

"Try ricecake. Super small bite."

The *bibingka* dribbled down her chin and a tear down her cheek. "Too. Sugar."

Patting the baggie of mugwort *ddeok* in her pocket, Kyong Ah remembered how she'd once gotten Mr. Maki, a former dementia patient, to eat spaghetti by letting him use her chopsticks so he could eat in a familiar way.

"Try this *ddeok.* Made from sticky rice, you know, *ngo mai,* like in your *nin gou* new year cake. She spirited *ddeok* into the *bibingka* dish, slicing it with a spoon. "Super good for your blood and brain. This one got no sugar. Very tasty."

"No," said Mountain Elf. But she chewed once. Twice.

She's got salt tooth like me. Mr. L was right. Sad to lose control over your food on top of body and mind.

"Great job! Want to watch TV with friends?"

"Flan. Okey."

Kyong Ah parked Cheung Tai and her wheelchair on the outer ring of the TV corral. She and Remy then pushed the tray carts back to Kitchen, telling the guys how happy the *bagoong* and *bibingka* had made the patients. Tommy treated them to tuna salad and crackers from the upcoming lunch service. When they returned upstairs Cheung Tai was purring like a napping kitten.

Not until late afternoon could Kyong Ah grab a moment to enjoy lunch in the meds room. She took a bite; her heart lurched. She choked down snot, blood, and ricecake.

Black sesame for plain ddeok *and pinenuts for dope* ddeok, *right? Or was it opposite?*

She opened her notebook. Left Lung clutched; Right shivered.

—*Pinenut = ssuk*

—*Black sesame = MJ*

—*Ate 3 MJ. Too drugged. Next time only 1, then increase by ½ until find right amount*

Kyong Ah rapped her skull to dislodge mutant cells scaling its walls, before realizing she was aping Cheung Tai's dementia knock-knock. How would *ddeok* interact with whatever sedatives and anti-depressants the docs at Flatland Lockdown had pumped into Mountain Elf? Compared to the big, burly guys they were used to tackling and sedating, she was light as moth dust. But if Cheung Tai died, the immigrant aide would take the rap for administering the final blow. MJ stayed in one's blood and hair forever.

Kyong Ah rubbed wrists that would soon sport handcuffs, her picture splashed across the front page in the *Trib*'s latest exposé on senior abuse. Kyong Ah added a new entry to her ADL notepad in secret Korean code on the time and amount of *ddeok* ingested and symptoms. Pocketing the pad, she went to the broom closet, locked the door and lit a White Knight, her hands shaking. She smoked until the hole in her head closed and Tobacco God dusted her air sacs with sacred ash.

Kyong Ah coughed into a tissue and pocketed it without looking. She pinched and returned the second cigarette, half-smoked, to its pack, wondering how much White Knights would cost in jail after she was convicted for killing an eighty-four-year-old Tinkerbelle. Prison cancer sticks would be worth every cent if they shortened her sentence.

Play with fire and you get burned; play with dope and go to dopefiend dungeon.

The aide returned to the TV corral and gently shook Cheng Tai's shoulder. No response.

Finally, Mountain Elf mumbled. "Flan. Okey. Kwill. Me." Her head slumped. Kyong Ah dug her fingers into the granny's wrist, feeling for a pulse, her own blood pounding in her ears. To rouse Cheung Tai, Kyong Ah turned up the volume on a Cantonese opera until the oldsters covered their ears and shouted in a riot of languages. She reduced the volume slightly.

"Sorry. See you tomorrow, Cheung Tai." Kyong Ah patted her hand and zipped her backpack. As the elevator doors rattled shut Kyong Ah massaged her tumor, metastasizing fear.

Please protect Cheung Tai, Kwan Seum Bosal. I beg you.

IV. DEPRESSION: *Tumor*

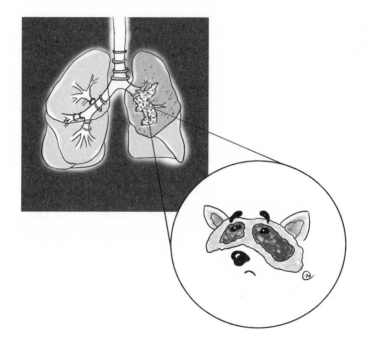

*Isn't dying enough donkey work
without having to tiptoe around
your kids' feelings, too?*
—Kyong Ah Choi

28. FLAME

Sally rang up the last customer from Good Ride's "Thrilling Threesomes" workshop. She ducked out for a smoke before doing the deed.

Call him Van. Not Nesy. Van.

"What's up, Sally? Been a long time." Drills hummed.

Speak up, babo.

Sally pushed the stud deeper into the roof of her mouth. "Hi, Van. Need your advice."

"About?"

Sally tried to adjust to Nesy's deeper voice. "It's complicated. Let me treat you to a bite after work and explain."

"I'm in a relationship now, Sal."

Sally's thorn vine tat burned across her shoulders. "Whatever. I'm not asking you out on a date. Just wanted your take on a friend's problem. But if you're too busy, no biggie."

"Can you meet in front of the Den at one tonight?"

"Sure," said Sally, too quickly.

They signed off. Sally bit her klutzy tongue. Date or no date, she'd best hurry home to shower and put on something fresh. Like her clubbing shirt. As densely black as the hole Nesy had carved in her heart. Sally's tats shuddered in anticipation of the meet. She quickly rearranged the vibrators. Straight as a pine forest.

Sally rolled up to Dragon Den on her motorcycle just as Van was locking up. Her heart thundered. The screams of a cat in heat ripped the night.

"Hey, Van."

"Hey yourself, Arrow."

Sally winced at the nickname Nesy had given her. "You look good. Still working out?"

Curse you and your bomber jacket. As much a heartbreaker as a dude as you were as a dyke.

"When I can. Shave looks sharp on you."

Sally ran her hand over her skull. "Doesn't make this big ole Korean head bigger?"

Van grinned, flashing his chipped tooth; comforting. At least that was the same. "Korean bar? Or Vietnamese?"

"Vietnamese," said Sally, although after their break-up the scent of fish sauce and lemon grass put an S&M chokehold on her. They headed up Larkin, sometimes bumping shoulders, like teenagers who wanted to put their hands on each other. Past the shuttered *phở* shops. Freaks and druggies. Dumpsters and street toilet mines.

Sally asked, "How's work?"

"Other than a stickup last week, not bad. Lone junkie. He was shaking so much I thought he was going to blast my face off." Van shrugged.

Sally shuddered. Not that beautiful face, now darkened by one o'clock shadow.

"Nelson had to Jet Li him. Lucky the chump forgot to release the safety. Locked him in the closet while cops took their sweet time responding. Had to shell out extra comp details to customers for the scare."

"Retail sucks. Tossed out a couple of white boys boosting porn DVDs in their pants. Then they jump all self-righteous and call us fags."

"Here we are." Van pushed open the padded burgundy leather door to Saigon Shack. A tiny *ajumah* mixed drinks behind a bar trimmed with bamboo and fringed with thatch. She nodded to Van and gave Sally a quick body scan and sneer like old Korean grumps did. She wore a ponytail and fuck-with-me-and-I'll-kill-you war survivor eyes. A couple Vietnamese *ajeossi* sat at one end of the bar watching a karaoke contest on satellite TV. At the other end, African American OGs in flak jackets slugged back shots while Spike TV blared overhead. Sally wondered if they were vets from the same war.

"What's your poison? OB? Tiger?"

"How about a Tiger? Let me get it since I dragged you out here."

When you could be in bed with your new honey.

"No, this is my turf. Don't even try your Korean tricks." Van ordered beers. The *ajumah* included roast peanuts, crisp fried noodles and squid to help them get their thirst on. Van's chest was ironing board flat; was he binding or had he gotten the Operation?

"Okay, Sally, what's this friend's problem you called to talk about?"

Sally drew a deep breath.

"Couple weeks ago, Omma asked me for a tat referral for a co-worker's daughter. The friend wanted some-place safe so the girl wouldn't catch HIV or anything. So of course I gave her your name." Sally gripped her glass to keep from reaching over and rubbing the stubble on Van's chin. "She call you? Did you give her a tat?"

Van's eyes flickered. "Sal, you know I don't kiss and tell. We value customers' privacy."

"Shit, Van. That's not all. Omma's mass producing marijuana ricecake!"

"Wow!" A smile danced across Van's lips. "What's it taste like?"

Sally brandished a squid tentacle. "Like rice and reefer! Like dope *ddeok!*"

"*Ddeok?*"

"Made from sweet rice like your *bánh tét.* But no banana leaf wrapping. Remember?"

Van's lip curled. "Who knew your mother was a hippie? Since you were too uptight to take me home to meet her. She wear tie-dye and rock to Jimi Hendrix at Woodstock?"

Sally's tats smoked like burning monks. "You kidding? She's an immigrant like your mom. Who you never let me meet either."

"Whose fault was that? You saying our moms don't have a right to be hippies? Anyways, my mom's a refugee who digs heavy metal.

"Stop shitting me. You said she drives you nuts with that bouncy Viet disco." Sally sniffed. "I didn't come here to fight. Just tell me. Did you tattoo my mom?"

Van thrust his chin out. "Why do you need to know?"

"Because I'm freakin' worried about her. She made me snag her a computer. All these years and she suddenly needs one yesterday. Probably for a dope edibles business. Yumi thinks some young dealer's manipulating her mind."

Van tossed back his drink. He smiled grimly. Again with that tooth whose chip was now verboten to Sally's tongue. Inhaling his ink and blood scent, Sally leaned closer, knowing a wrong move would snap the frail thread binding them.

"I'm glad things turned out for you. And your wife. Whatever her name is."

"Nancy." Van drew a long sip of beer.

Sally drilled a nail into her broke heart tat beneath the table.

What a lame-assed white bread name. Or of an immigrant's kid. Like mine.

"I did a tattoo for an older Asian lady. But she didn't have your last name."

"Korean? Was it Kyong Ah Choi?"

"No, she wasn't a Choi or a Min. That's all I'm saying. I've already said too much."

"Maybe she used a fake name so it wouldn't get back to me. She say how she'd heard about you?"

"You have to ask your mother if she has a tat. If she won't talk, she's got her reasons. Sorry, Arrow."

"Me too, Van. We were good together."

"No, we weren't. Not that we didn't try."

"Does your mother accept who you are? The T-shots and plumbing operations?"

A vein throbbed in Van's temple. "No. But she stops short of cutting me loose. Guess we've been through too much for her to let me go. Tits or no tits."

"I envy you."

Van's eyes flashed. "Fuck you and your envy. Still not out to your mom? Stop being an asshole and evolve, dude." Van drained his second Tiger.

"Who made you head monk? Just tell me one thing, Nesy, I mean Van. Are you happy?"

"Yes." Van's eyes clouded. "Not that I don't have problems. Or that there aren't psychos who want to kill me."

"Just needed to know that you're happy."

"Look Sal, maybe it's not some stud bewitching your mom. Maybe she's doing what she's doing for medical reasons."

"What are you saying?"

"Go easy on her. And yourself," Van cleared his throat. "You've got a lot of heart. Don't sell yourself short, Arrow." Again with the translation of her nickname "Sal" into English. All that they still shared. Van clapped her on the shoulder. Like a guy would.

Shit.

His phucking pheromones were screwing her up. Less fish sauce and more lime than before. But if she still wanted to jump his bones, who the hell was she?

They fought over the tab, but the *ajumah* let Van pay after giving Sally another body scan. They left and walked past Tenderloin denizens deep in self conversations. Or dozed out on cardboard beds.

Hesitant, they hugged each other outside Dragon Den's door. His scent hurt her chest. He pulled away before she wanted to let go. Then Sally's one true love put his hands in his pockets and headed off into the blackness.

29. PULSE

When Elevator God groaned open Kyong Ah's heart lurched; no Mountain Elf perky enough to block the pass.

She rode up to Third Floor and found Cheung Tai lying motionless in bed, eyes and mouth open. The aide's heart fisted. She felt for a pulse. Put ear to chest. Detected a slippery thread breath.

Thank you, Kwan Seum Bosal!

"Wake up, Cheung Tai. Super tasty *jook* and *haam ha* for breakfast."

Mountain Elf slowly blinked dry orbs and sputtered. "Fan. Fan."

"No, sleep later."

"*Ngaanh fan.* Sleep." Cheung Tai pulled the sheet over her head like a corpse.

Kyong Ah quickly folded it down. "Okay, I be right back."

Breakfast service included not only *bagoong*, but also minced green onions and dried turnips in the *jook.* Three currants and a dash of cinnamon atop the oatmeal. Kyong Ah returned to Cheung Tai's room with a tray. The granny refused to sit up and eat.

Leng poked her head in, motioning to Kyong Ah to come closer. "She sleep you whole day off. Guess all that acting bad eat up her chi. But why she sleep with eyes open since she come back from Flatland Lockdown? Looks horrible. Anyways, nice to ride elevator this morning. If we lucky, she sleep until next spring like glizzly bear."

"Everyone happy for her to shut up. But she need exercise or her body break down." Kyong Ah shook the granny's arm. "Wake up. Time to eat."

"*Ngaanh fan.*" Mountain Elf turned her butt towards them.

"You have to eat. Or nurse feed you by tube. Please sit up." Leng raised the bed to a sitting position.

"*Haam ha.* Your favorite." Kyong Ah held the *bagoong* smelling salts beneath the granny's nose. She folded a smidge into the *jook,* hoping the gruel would flush out the last of any residual dope from the *bibingka* mishap the other day. Mountain Elf made a sour prune face and shook her head. But she did not slap the spoon away and let Kyong Ah slip it into her mouth. Taking her time, she eventually finished half a bowl. Leng left to return breakfast trays to Kitchen.

"*Fan okey.*" If she chanted the magic number of times, she'd wake up at home, free of these devils.

"Right." Kyong Ah changed Cheung Tai's diaper, dabbing zinc ointment on red spots.

"*Fan okey.*" Mountain Elf yawned and stretched.

Same song, but less combative.

Kyong Ah coughed and drank an inhaler puff.

"What's that?"

"Help me breathe easier. Too many cigarettes. You don't smoke do you?"

"I don't know." Shame and confusion flooded the granny's eyes.

Poor thing. People, pleasure and vices all washed away.

Kyong Ah and Cheung Tai took a backdoor route that avoided the dread elevator trigger zone. In the Rec Room seated teams played volleyball with balloons. The colored globes bounced off the heads of patients unable to raise their arms fast enough.

"Want to play?"

"*Fan okey.*" Cheung Tai's gaze froze on the folded cot where she'd slept in her Panic Room domain. "What's wrong with me? Why I here?" The granny rapped her knuckles against her skull, asking, "Why I stupid?" for the ten thousandth time.

Kyong Ah took her hands. "You're not stupid. You fall down and hurt head. But you're getting better. Want to draw? Or read magazine?"

"Magazine? *Fan okey.*"

"Right. Read first."

Later, Kyong Ah returned Cheung Tai to her bed.

Good thing you didn't put Cheung Tai into MJ coma and your eongdeongi in jail. But she's calmer. Maybe dope ddeok shrinks tumors and rage.

Smokers Lounge beckoned. But Kyong Ah took her break with Leng in the Meds Room.

"Cheung Tai kind of recognize Rec Room. Like she is standing on bridge that half washed away."

Leng darned holes in her husband's socks. "I hate to

say, but people not supposed to live this long. That's why I tell my kids to put poison in my seaweed soup if that happen to me. What's good of living downstairs when nobody upstairs?" Leng rapped her skull like Cheung Tai.

Kyong Ah grabbed Leng's wrist. "What your kids say?"

"Stop being drama queen. You told us million times. Don't worry, we take care of everything."

"Everything? You mean healthcare? Or seaweed soup?"

"Both, I hope. Hey, you talk to you kids about surgery stuffs?"

"Not yet."

Leng sucked her teeth. "*Aiyah!* What you waiting for?"

"Surgery is not for weeks." Fingering a knight-in-waiting in her pocket, Kyong Ah made a mental note to procure prescriptions for sleeping pills and painkillers.

"Forget surgery. Play game. If you had to choose which kid to live with right now, who is it?"

"I don't want to live with my kids."

"*Aiyah!* Can't you just play game? Say first kid's name pop in you head when I count to three. Ready? *Hanna.*"

"Wait!"

"*Deul.*"

"I'm not playing."

"*Set.*"

Kyong Ah rasped. "Yumi, my oldest. Maybe Minsoo, my son. I don't know, maybe Seungsoo, my youngest."

"Think harder. Why?"

"Yumi's oldest and got house and is most responsible. Probably knows how to get MediCal. But she hates me. I not last one day under her roof. Anyway, she and husband adopting new baby. Better she put her energy into new life than old hag."

"Don't say that. What about you son?"

"Minsoo? He's good cook and loves me, in his own way. He means well, but cannot keep promises. He is slob and likes booze too much. Living with him like working here. Only no pay. I got to get him out."

"And youngest?"

"She just got me good deal on computer. Doesn't stab me like her big sister. But she's still big baby. No house, no husband. Live in small, super messy studio. And work at porno store. If she take care of me, she lose chance to find love during her best baby making years. Then she be alone forever."

"Husband? I thought she was gay girl."

A rusty nail punctured Kyong Ah's kidney. "I'm not sure. But it's my fault. When she see how me and her *apa* fight, she say why bother with men? Anyways, what American kid wants to live with mother if they can avoid?"

Leng patted Kyong Ah's shoulder. "That not so hard, right? Like Winny and PTs say, 'more you practice, easier it get.'"

"I still don't know who to tell."

"*Aiyah*, you just told me. You son if you had to. But probably you youngest."

"But others will get hurt feelings."

"Maybe not. Maybe they do happy dance behind you back that they not one who get choosed. When you going to tell them?"

"I got lots of stuffs to do first." She wondered if she could find Yoneda San's exit secrets on her new computer.

"Don't wait too long. Hear me, Kyong?"

"*Geulsse.* Maybe." Kyong Ah fondled Whitey; he crumbled in her pocket.

30. BAIL

Kyong Ah tore open the envelope from Flatland; she choked on her *ddeok.*

Aiguh!—$14, 444.44! Equals bad luck multiplied. For the biopsy alone. No surgery and no treatment but nearly $20,000 in debt.

She paced the kitchen, provoking a coughing fit. Expelling a bloody glob, she dispatched it down the garbage disposal. Maybe if she coughed hard enough, she could hoik up her tumor.

The whirling blades and water calmed her.

You got rabbit-speed computer. Get your eongdeongi *to work.*

She sat down with her celadon cup of green tea and typed combinations of "lung cancer," "treatment" and "cost" and oozy lung cross-sections and numbers breast-stroked across her eyes and face. Two-fingered pecking gobbled three hours before she found a rough estimate of $50,000 a decade ago. But the figure was not broken down by procedure. Nor did it include drugs or complications. HMOs seemed reluctant to give a definite dowry price until they sized up how much they could wring from each suitor.

Squirreling away a few thousand dollars had cost Kyong Ah years of meal trays, sponge baths and I&Os. Her nest egg would barely cover what she owed on that first ER drop-in. Chewing her lip; she made a crude estimate by dividing the 1997 cost of treatment by three and padding for inflation. That meant $40,000 each to hire Knife, Raygun and Poison Generals to roust Cancer Goddess. But how to magic bunny hat the money?

Where's Minsoo? He should be home and in bed for work.

She grunted.

Stop worrying about him.

Kyong Ah ate two MJ *ddeok* and brushed her teeth. She lay down and massaged her tumor.

Please enjoy ddeok, *Cancer Goddess. Then find someplace else more comfortable to rest.*

She drifted off to sleep.

Bullets whizzed close in her shooting range dream. She hurled rice balls at a Korea-shaped lung target. A bald man to her left flung scalpels past her ear at a liver target. Why did women always get stuck with loser weapons? What she wouldn't give for Goguryeo Kingdom founder King Jumong's magic bow and arrows. Was he born of egg or woman? And who should claim kingdom bragging rights—a magic three-legged crow or Jumong's omma and her powerful uterus?

The "guns down" order thundered overhead and she went to check her target, half hoping someone would surprise her with a merciful shot she wouldn't see coming. When she pulled down the tattered target, ddeok tumor goop teeming with mutant genes ran through her fingers. On a hill faraway, a monk struck a bronze bell, vibrating the hole in her head.

Kyong Ah woke up coughing.

Depressing. Ddeok is just busywork illusion that you can succeed in tricking Cancer Goddess.

She turned on the light and squinted at her singing cell. No glad tidings came at this hour. Kyong Ah picked up. "Hello?"

"Halmoni? Sorry for calling so late. But there's no one else. Can you come bail me out?" Kyong Ah's tall, lanky grandson, wearing the spiky black hair of his father and cinnamon skin of his mother, had begun to attract the unwanted stares of predators.

"*Aiguh!* Evan? Where's your *apa?*" Kyong Ah rose and stumbled into the living room.

No Minsoo. Out tomcatting again, that no-good bum.

A crazy shouted obscenities behind Evan, who cupped his hand around the phone. "He won't answer."

"What about your mom Juanita?" Kyong Ah prayed they'd somehow reconnected.

"You're all I've got left. Please, Halmoni. You gotta get me out."

"*Ssibal!*"

"What?"

"I said SHIT, Evan! I already go through this thousand times with your father. What you do now?"

He lowered his voice. "Cops say DUI. But they been gunning for me. DWB, you know, Driving While Brown."

Kyong Ah's neck cramped. "DUI? Alcohol or drugs? If your parents won't get you out, how can I?"

"Please, Halmoni. If you can't do it, promise you'll ask

Sally Komo."

"You hurt anyone?"

"No, just totaled my car. Well, I might have grazed someone. Promise you or Sally Komo will get me out."

Kyong Ah's BS-o-meter stung. She'd spoiled Evan with gifts and his favorite foods since birth. But this time Cancer Goddess had torched the protective sheaths of her nerves. Devoured her ki. Spent any lingering patience for the knucklehead.

"Don't talk back to cops, Evan. They already heard every kind of BS from *meongcheongi* like you. Hear me?"

"Please, Halmoni!"

The line went dead. Kyong Ah called Minsoo. No answer. She barked a message. "Where are you? Your son's in jail. You bail him out!"

Who to call now?

She knew that even if Minsoo had answered, he would have told her to let his screw-up son rot. If Yumi was back from Korea, she'd blame it on Kyong Ah. Evan was right; it was either his *halmoni* or his *komo.* The two suckers.

What happened? Evan had been such a cute baby, always climbing into cabinets and exploring. During his *dol* one-year-old birthday party he'd chosen the twenty-dollar bill, portending a rich man's future. Kyong Ah's spirit sagged; if they'd added a beer can or cocaine vial, he probably would have grabbed them instead.

Kyong Ah returned to bed, tossing like a dried anchovy on a hot skillet, worrying about how to raise money for treatments and now, Evan's bail. Despair fed tumor and dampened her desire to stick around.

Long life didn't live up to the hype. Not when you'd birthed idiot descendants like these. Sleep? What's that? Get to work.

Kyong Ah got up, sucked her inhaler and resumed stuffing gift bags. Yumi the thorn bush's bag was easy to fill; in went a rose cashmere sweater with pearl buttons, silk blouses and rayon floral print dresses. Then a tailored, chocolate-colored wool suit and red V-neck sweater. Sally the pincushion's bag was also a no-brainer. Black oversized sweaters. Black sweatshirts. Black knit hats and scarves. Black, black, black. Girlie Yumi and Blackout Sally had each inherited a swatch of their omma's style after all.

Kyong Ah kept her black funeral suit and an ankle length black dress with a princess cut that still looked good on her. In case her deaf kids wanted to display her in a box and not cremate her nice and cheap as she'd said a zillion times. Too bad they couldn't wash her body, dress her in an unbleached cotton Hanbok, fold her in a straw mat and bury her on a hill overlooking the sea. As the village aunties had done for Halmoni. Simple. Economical. Environment-friendly, too.

Kyong Ah put a wine-colored velvet scrunchy and a purple sequined sweater in a bag labeled, "Minsoo's Girlfriend." He could give it to the next pageant queen, perhaps the one he'd apparently been spending the last few nights with. She wondered if Charleena had taken him back.

Please, Kwan Seum Bosal.

She stuffed more work scrubs in a garbage bag that Leng could alter or pass along. The floral kind that cheered the gardeners among her patients, oldsters who could still tell the difference between a daffodil and a dahlia. Like

Mr. Yoneda. She held back hibiscus, rhododendron, and lilac print tops with matching solid-colored pants, even though she'd probably have to quit soon.

Not bad. Tomorrow, do Minsoo and Evan's stuff.

Kyong Ah opened the window to let in the dawn.

When Mickey hadn't come home by the next morning, Kyong Ah phoned Sally from work.

"*Yaah,* what time is it, Omma? I got in late."

"On a date?" Kyong Ah touched her tattoo, hoping it was that nice man Van Le.

"Sheesh, just an old friend."

"Evan called me last night to bail him out of jail. He crashed his car."

"Shit. DUI?"

"*Eung.* He said cops were harassing him. Discrimination."

"And you believe that?"

"Am I that big of *babo*?"

"Why's the knucklehead bothering you instead of Mickey?" The fact that her dope-*ddeok*-manufacturing omma thought her DUI nephew had screwed up somehow reassured Sally.

"They not talking. I leave message on Minsoo's phone."

"So fool's down to his *halmoni* and *komo.* That's jacked."

"Seungsoo-ah, I don't want scary stuffs to happen to him from criminals. No matter what *byeongshin* retard he is."

"Forget it, Omma. If I call a bail bondsman, we'll have

to put down a deposit up front. But if Evan screws up and doesn't show up for his court date, we're out the money. I don't have any spare cash lying around. Do you?"

Tattoo smoldered. Tumor twisted at its waist. "No, I got bills to pay. I already go through this with Minsoo. Evan turning out like him. Only more stupid. But leave him in jail?"

"That fartbutt knows we're the only semi-softies in a family of hard asses. I feel bad he's in jail. But did I put him there? Did you? Go to work and stop worrying."

"Thanks Sally. I love you."

"How come you keep saying that, Omma? You're freakin' me out."

"I don't know. Life so short. Want me to stop saying?"

"Of course not." Sally sighed loudly. "When all this settles down, I'll drop by to install your Hangeul program."

"Thanks, Seungsoo-ah. I appreciate."

"*Allasoh.* I know."

"Bye." Kyong Ah hung up, a bit less worried about Evan than before. She hoped the weight hadn't shifted to Sally's shoulders.

31. CLOT

"Ba. Ba. Ba." Mrs. Santos leaned forward as Kyong Ah parked her beside Mr. L.

"Not just *bagoong*, Ate. *Pancit canton*, too. Thanks to me. Let's see if those Chinese guys cooked it right."

"Goong. Goong. Goong." Mrs. Santos hoped they had used the yellow noodles with the coconut flavor she preferred.

"And pan pan cit cit." Mr. L rapped his cast. "By dinner I'm out of this dump. Not another night in your lumpy bed. I can snore without a damn roommate poking me with his cane."

"What your doctor say?"

"That my ankle's strong enough for my daughter to get me out today."

Murmurs swept the hall as Dong and Bing emerged from the service elevator pushing carts of ochre-colored noodles stir-fried with chicken and dried shrimp. Bell pepper and carrots. Onions and garlic. Friday Purple Jell-O shimmied alongside.

"Easy as *lo mein*," said Dong. "Boy gave us his mama's recipe."

"Pan. Pan. Pan."

Mr. L raised his fork like Lady Liberty's torch. "You can thank me, folks! Never surrender!" He sucked his noodles up. "Not as tasty as my Lorena's. Needs more garlic. But ballpark." A catnip grin spread across his face. "Going to miss me, Korea?"

Kyong Ah suppressed a smile, wondering what the old *ddong* disturber had looked like twenty years ago. "Let young guy prune tree next time, okay Mistah Rheegasepee? You going to miss your friend, right Missus S?"

"Pan. Pan. Pan." Mrs. Santos struggled to nod affirmation.

Kyong Ah coughed. Pain clawed Left Lung.

Up ddeok *intake tonight.*

Mr. L waved his fork. "When you going to do something about that awpul cough?"

Kyong Ah spit into a tissue, pocketed it and applied sanitizer to her hands. She struck her chest. "Not contagious. Only allergies."

"Ba. Ba. Ba."

"I know, Ate. Goong. Goong. Goong."

Kyong's tumor tugged; tomorrow she'd have to find Mrs. Santos another friend to stimulate her vocabs.

The next morning, bagoong perfumed the hall as oldsters attacked their *jook* with vigor. When lunch featured a watery chicken *adobo*, Kyong Ah chuckled.

You fooled me, Pockmark. Surprise me again and let Mistah Rheegasepee's shrimp revolution last.

"Doh. Doh. Doh." Mrs. Santos managed a half smile on the lazy side of her face. If only she could return to her smock full of crayons and get away from this place smelling of dying old people.

"*Adobo,* right Missus S? Vinegar and garlic making me hungry, too."

"Doh. Doh. Doh."

Kyong Ah wrapped Mrs. Santos' hand around the fork and lifted a bite of chicken to her lips. "You look tired today. Why not take a nap after you finish? Then we can dance."

Later that afternoon Kyong Ah found Mrs. Santos lying in bed with terror constricting her pupils. Electricity crackled her hair. The tremor that occasionally visited her lower lip radiated down the right half of her body.

"B--." Fear gathered behind brain stem.

"What's wrong?" Kyong Ah caught a skittish pulse.

"P--." The small gold cross the granny wore pulsed.

Kyong Ah pushed the call button. She dialed Fely's cell, which went straight to message mode. "Fely, come right away. I think Missus Santos is having stroke!" Kyong Ah hung up. "Don't be afraid, Missus. Be right back." She rushed out to alert Leng to get a nurse.

Kyong Ah returned to find Mrs. Santos' forehead half tropics and half desert.

"H-. H-. H-."

"Can you smile for me?"

The granny's cheeks hollowed. Spirits gathered in a bamboo orchid grove. An ancient ancestor with Mrs. Santos' limpid eyes freed her long white hair from its pin.

"Try to raise arm. No? How about other one?"

The right side of the granny's face trembled but both

arms remained toy soldier stiff. Kyong Ah pressed the buzzer again and again.

"He."

"He?"

She's too sweet to worry about Hell.

"Yes, help's coming."

"In-. In-."

"Iná, *have you come for me? I'm scared.*"

Kyong Ah massaged Mrs. Santos' rigid cheeks.

If only Mistah Rheegasepee was here to interpret.

"Nod your head if you can hear me."

Mrs. Santos' body shook. Her lips parted. Air escaped. Blood overwhelmed aspirin and anticoagulant helpers. Knotted behind eyes brimming with memories and regret.

Should have gone to Italy and Vatican City two summers ago. Should have taken drawing and cooking classes with Anatess. Should have married Vicente. But who would have taken care of Amá?

Fely rushed in with a stroke kit. "Let's start you on anti-clotting activator now. Doctor Chu's on her way. And so is the ambulance."

"You're going to be okay, Missus. Dance partners forever, right?"

She'll have to build up vocabs all over again.

Mrs. Santos' mouth trembled and drooped. Her eyes held Kyong Ah's. A whimper escaped.

"You're super brave. You're going to make it."

Mrs. Santos lurched forward. *"Iná!"*

Kyong Ah hugged her patient as life shuddered from her swallow body. A breeze lifted the lavender curtains.

Then they fell still.

First Fely and Kyong Ah and then Gabe and Pierre from Lifeguard Transport tried to revive her. Kyong Ah wept. They didn't crush her ribs with compressions, because she had no family members to insist on the pointless procedure. When paddles and shots failed, they stopped.

Fely noted the time and pulled her hand over Mrs. Santos' eyes. "Where's Doctor Chu? Better if she calls the family."

"Family? No one ever came to see her," said Kyong Ah. *This is how single women die. With strangers.*

Fely held Mrs. Santos' hand. "She's got a niece named Ofelia down in San Jose. Hasn't made it up here yet, but maybe this time she might."

Gabe hung up his phone, shaking his head. "Got another urgent. We can check back with you after that. Depending on where she's headed next."

"Go ahead. We need to reach her niece first," said Fely.

Doc Chu rushed in and stopped when she read their expressions. "Fill me in on the details." They did. Fely asked the doctor to call the niece. Kyong Ah struck away tears.

After the doc left, Fely asked, "What's the matter, Kyong?"

Kyong Ah lowered her voice so Mrs. Santos couldn't hear. "I just feel sad for Missus Santos. She try so hard after her first stroke. And her friend Mistah Rheegasepee just left yesterday."

Fely gave Kyong Ah a long hug. "You had a special relationship with her, right? Take a break. Want me to ask someone else to take over?"

Keep moving. So melancholy has no place to roost.

"That's okay. Let me prepare her."

Did you decide to end it, Missus Santos? Because you had no one to care for you when your Medicare days at Golden West ran out?

Mrs. Santos' paper-thin skin felt warm. Kyong Ah eased the granny's right shoulder down. She went through the clothes in the closet and drawers, selecting a long flannel nightgown printed with rosettes and ruffled at the bottom, as if she'd passed away in her sleep without pain. Kyong Ah hung the nightgown on the closet door and folded the other garments into bags as she'd been doing with her own stuff. She snapped on fresh gloves remembering Halmoni's burial instructions so many autumn tides ago. She smelled spring water and incense.

Cleanse each part thoroughly so spirits see how loved this person was before crossing over. Wrap body in fabric strips, placing softest layer closest to skin. Only rich yangban can afford silk for first cocoon layer, but cotton is noble, too. Use homespun if you must, but only after you've beaten it soft with ironing cudgels. What matters most is love and skill of person performing ritual.

Kyong Ah gently rolled Mrs. Santos' body and sponged away the sour smell of fear, occasionally pausing to massage her own tattoo and tumor, as swollen as the earth during Korean rainy season. She put a fresh pair of underpants on Mrs. Santos. What self-respecting oldster wants to make their final journey wearing a diaper? That's when Kyong Ah realized that Mrs. Santos must have put on her panties singled-handed during that mystery poo incident an eternity ago. After slipping the rosette print nightie on her, she combed Mrs. Santos' hair, dabbing a bit of baby lotion on her face and neck.

Kyong Ah got rid of the dirty laundry and checked the room to see if she'd missed anything. Then she pulled up a chair and sat beside Mrs. Santos, whose skin was starting to take on the faintest of blue undertones, signaling life force's farewell and death's alchemy. Kyong Ah covered the small hand with hers.

Hope you felt no pain, Sweet Lady. Travel safely to your Heaven. Where they will understand your words perfectly.

A wave of sadness descended over Kyong Ah. She knuckled her sternum to push down the sorrow, bowed her head and wept. She released her patient's hand, wiped her eyes and fetched Leng to help move the body before it got too stiff. The aides transferred Mrs. Santos to a wheelchair, arranging her head and limbs to look like she was sleeping in case they ran into patients. She was so light. They took her around the back to the viewing room with the canary-yellow chintz curtains, a vase of artificial roses, and a Bible. Recent additions were a Koran and a small statue of a seated Buddha. These were rotated based on the road traveled by the departed.

They passed Cheung Tai sitting at a window with sunlight dancing across her face; Leng's knuckles whitened around the wheelchair handles; Kyong Ah's shoulders clenched.

"*Fan okey*," said Cheung Tai without malice, her eyes intense. Like she knew to which *okey* Mrs. Santos was headed.

Kyong's tumor grew damp, throbbing with a wanton proliferation of killer cells. Who danced and jumped up and down like *mudang* possessed by thunderous spirits, drums and gongs. Like the shaman who once lay hands on Kyong Ah. When Halmoni exhausted savings to purchase her escape from Smallpox Goddess. In the land of azalea mornings. Bustling fish stalls. G.I. Joe black market cigarettes.

32. HAUL

Grief radiated between Left and Right Lung as Kyong Ah drove home. Depending on how intensively she'd been involved in a patient's care, their spirits could take a while to navigate through her waterways. Her chest was already soggy with a dread that usually didn't call until weeks later. How had frail Mrs. Santos pushed the door open so soon?

Not now, Depression Goddess. I can't carry you and Cancer Goddess, too.

Monsoon sorrow forced Kyong Ah to stop in front of her building, half blind. Rivers of sadness swirled to the sea. Like Mrs. Santos' ocean tide eyes. A sharp rap on the window forced Kyong Ah to suck up snot and wipe her face.

Fridge and Flaco!

She'd first met the Goodwill drivers at work a few weeks ago when they'd stuffed Golden West clothing discards into their Goodwill van. Flaco wore life on his leathered face and Fridge in his cranky knees. But now in the turmoil over Mrs. Santos' death she'd forgotten she'd arranged for them to help her haul the gift bags to a storage place tonight. That must be their battered pickup truck, ribbed with tree branches and plywood. It sat across the street from her apartment building on the park side where neighborhood kids were playing a loud game of basketball. A group of oldsters practiced the five animal forms of Qigong at the other end.

"What's the matter, Miss?" Fridge asked with alarm.

"Not contagious. Only allergies. Sorry I'm late. Almost forgot. But I got snacks, too."

"Snacks?" Delight lit Fridge's face.

Flaco elbowed his partner. "Let's finish the job first, *vato*." Flaco's railroad-tie arms sported tattoos, including a winged heart one like Sally's. Except his was pierced with a gruesome knife and wept red tears.

"Sorry no elevator."

"Fridge needs to drop some tonnage anyway."

"All muscle, man." Fridge bulked his guns.

Kyong Ah parked the car, returned and let them in. "How many trips? I think storage place close at eight."

"Just show us what you want loaded, Miss."

Kyong Ah pointed to the gift bags lining the hall and stacked in the closets. They refused her offer to help. She locked the door and followed them downstairs.

"Want to drive? Or ride with us?" said Flaco.

"Nice to ride along if not too much trouble."

"No trouble at all," said Fridge, sniffing at the fried chicken wings and veggies and fish fried in egg batter snacks she'd put together for them.

After hitching a net over the load, Fridge drove and Flaco rode shotgun with Kyong Ah sandwiched between. When they reached the storage facility on High Street, half of Oakland was there pushing carts loaded with TVs as bulky as Fridge. Sofas with sectionals. Battered washers and dryers. Jalopy computers and monitors. Banker boxes flapping with paper. Stored to make room for bigger pieces. Or until repossessed lives could be freed.

Fridge and Flaco snagged a cart. Kyong Ah paid three months advance rent to a young lady with butt-cutter ebony hair whom Fridge flirted with while she eyed his partner.

Inside, each aisle bore an Oakland road name. Like Nimitz Freeway and Hwy 580. Kyong Ah turned left on International Boulevard and opened a locker the size of the meds room at work. Fridge excelled at lifting and Flaco at cramming stuff into skinny spaces. Kyong Ah asked them to stack by household. Her kids would have to deal with whatever remained in the apartment. A bed. Kitchenware. Dustball memories. She still needed to write a will to go with the keys. A wave of grief for Mrs. Santos swelled; Kyong Ah closed her eyes and let it wash the insides of her lids.

After securing the locker, the three returned to the truck. Kyong Ah unwrapped the snacks so the guys could use the Styrofoam trays as plates.

"Scrumptious. Don't you want any?" Fridge wore smashed rice on his chin.

"No, I'm not hungry."

"How about a wing? Yo, *vato*, you got food on your mug," said Flaco, the pirate's eye patch on his Raider's T-shirt peeling.

Fridge's tongue swirled around his lips like a street sweeper. "I do love me some Korean barbeque."

"Really? Where you go?"

"Telegraph Ave, near where the old Sears used to be. But only once for my sister-in-law's birthday. Kind of expensive."

"Sister-in-law?"

"Yeah, she's from Korea. Like you, right? Fell in love with my brother when he was stationed there."

"If you like to save money, go Koreana Super. They got meat already soaked in sauce. Just cook. Or ask your sister-in-law for recipe. Easy. See? Address on this container." Kyong Ah winced. Of all the times she'd been to Koreana Super, she had not seen her old patient Mr. Bak. She feared the worst but sent out a prayer anyway.

Please protect our countryman Bak Seonsaengnim, Kwan Seum Bosal. Please heal his throat and keep him cancer-free.

Fridge pocketed the cellophane. "Not that it's any of our business, but who the bags for?"

"Just family and friends." Kyong Ah sighed. The smoke encrusted cab scratched her tumor; she hacked into a tissue. "Allergies."

"If you say so, Miss," said Fridge.

"You ought to see someone for that cough, Señora."

"You smoke? Stop before too late." The ashtray overflowed.

Fridge squirmed. Flaco's face stiffened as he said, "Shouldn't your family be helping you? Not that we mind the work."

"Or the food." Fridge scratched his belly.

"Just thought Orientals were super family people. Like us Mexicans."

Fridge stink-eyed Flaco. "Hey, man. Trying to say us

Black folk don't care for our own?"

"Why you always got to twist shit around? Watch the road, man."

"We like to be called Asians, not Orientals."

Kyong Ah couldn't remember why big shot professional Yumi had jumped down her throat about that. "I don't want to bother my kids. They super busy. Thanks for helping. Junky house make junky mind. How much I owe?"

Kyong Ah disembarked and gave Flaco the money through the window, including a *gordo* tip.

"Wow, call us whenever you need help, Miss!" said Fridge.

"Thank you, Gentlemens." Kyong Ah waved as they pulled away, cranking up the bass on some lowrider song thumping their radio. Brown men serving as her limbs and back, as she and her co-workers did for their oldsters. Getting rid of the bags felt liberating—like a monk stepping off a Jiri Mountain cliff to freedom.

A demon cough ambushed her on the stairs. She sucked her emergency inhaler so she could make it up to her other inhaler, *ddeok* and green tea waiting in her kitchen. Mutant cells choked air sacs. Lungs smoked like tire necklaces. Hanging on to the rail, she managed another three steps then had to sit, feeling her face for stiffness.

No stroke, please.

She lifted each arm; they still worked.

Call 911. No, want fat ambulance bill? Call your kids like Flaco said.

But Yumi was in Korea and Minsoo hadn't even called

back about Evan. She dialed Sally, got the message tape, hung up and phoned her haulers.

"We forget something, Señora?"

"Take. Me. ER?"

"Emergency? Be there in a minute."

Kyong Ah slid down the stairs on her butt as a neighbor returning home let Fridge and Flaco in the front door.

"Where's your hospital, Señora?"

"Flat. Land."

Fridge and Flaco sat Kyong Ah between them and took off with Flaco patting her back.

"Bags. My kids."

"Save your breath, Señora. Tell us later."

Kyong Ah's cell rang in her hand. "Sally. I."

Flaco took the phone from Kyong Ah. "Hello? Is this Señora Chuey's daughter?"

"Who the heck is this?"

"Friends of your *mamá.* We're taking her to Flatland ER."

"What's the matter? Let me talk to her."

"Hold on." Flaco held the phone against Kyong Ah's ear.

"Bags. Key."

"Omma, put the man on again."

Fridge shrieked the truck around a corner. "Tell the daughter we'll be at Flatland ER in five minutes."

"I heard. Meet you there."

"Give me your name and number." Sally yelled over her shoulder. "Manny! Omma's in trouble. Gotta go. Sorry."

"We're her haulers," said Flaco.

Sally's jaw went slack. "What's she hauling?"

"Stuff."

"Stuff? Let me talk to my Mom."

Kyong Ah wheezed. "Love."

Tears ran down Sally's cheeks. "Love you, too, Omma. I'm almost there." She donned her helmet and gunned her motorcycle.

Kyong Ah prayed that ER had grownups on duty this time. That Doc Gokul's records on her hadn't been sent to collection.

Should have written will. Said goodbyes. Shouldn't have cut it so close. Missus Santos, you were trying to warn me.

Kyong Ah wanted to tell Fridge and Flaco to give the storage locker key and address to Sally. Before coughs mugged her.

33. C-WORD

"Her name is Mrs. Chuey," said Flaco as Fridge squeezed her hand.

"I need to hear that from her." The same ER nurse Kyong Ah had seen eons ago quizzed her about name, the date and time. Kyong Ah answered between coughs and sucking her inhaler.

"Let me borrow that for a moment." Nurse Ricard pocketed the inhaler. "Are these gentlemen friends or family?"

"Haulers and friends," interjected Fridge while Kyong Ah coughed into Flaco's bandana. "I'm Al Brown and this is Gene Valenzuela. We helped her move stuff to storage. After we left, she got sick and called us back. Got her here soon as we could."

"That's my mom!" Sally waved her arms through the windows before a beefy guard made her surrender her ID and face jewelry, pass through the metal detectors, and sign in. "Don't worry, Omma. I'm here now."

"She going to be all right, Nurse?" Flaco scratched his tat while the daughter checked him out.

Nurse Ricard squeezed patient's shoulder. "When did

this episode start? Didn't we see you several weeks ago? You're a nursing aide, right? Busy as a beehive tonight, but I'll get a doctor as soon as possible."

The scent of her coconut-oiled hair calmed Kyong Ah's racing heart.

As Omma coughed into tissues, Sally pulled the two guys aside. "Thanks for rushing my mom in. I'll take it from here."

The burly guy shook Sally's hand. "No sweat. Let us know how she's doing."

The skinny guy glowered. "You should keep a closer eye on your mom."

"Got it covered." Sally's cheeks burned as the big guy scrutinized her face jewelry and the skinny guy, her shaved head.

Fridge stepped over and touched Kyong Ah's arm. "Take it easy. Call us again when you need heavy lifting."

Choking, Kyong Ah tugged Sally's sleeve. "Pay. Them."

"No, that's okay, Miss. You already paid us for hauling."

"No need. Just get well, okay Mrs. Chuey?"

"Please. Pay."

"Right. Don't worry, Omma."

Sally paid and took the big guy's number, avoiding the accusation in his partner's eyes.

This time Kyong Ah only lay in the hall two hours before Nurse Ricard got her a room, put her on a drip, X-rayed her chest with a portable machine, and over her protests, attached a catheter. At least no Mackerel pronouncements.

"Go home. Rest. I okay."

"Save your breath, Omma. Not leaving until they let you out. Or Mickey relieves me."

"Don't. Tell. Anyone."

"Too late. Already left messages to call me."

"I sleep. Come. Later." Kyong Ah fake yawned, closing her eyes so Sally would leave before a doc came in and snitched.

Sally's eyes narrowed. "Who were those guys again?"

Not the peach fuzz pimps Onni suspected. But what's she been telling these strangers about us?

"Fridge and Flaco. Goodwill. Help move junks."

"What's this about the nurse seeing you before?"

"Promise. Make doctors. Pull plugs. No veggie."

Finish paperwork before anything worse happens. Your maknae *is too weak to choose quick, merciful death.*

Sally sucked her lip stud off, swallowed by mistake and coughed. "You should talk to Yumi and Mickey first."

"My decision. Not. Theirs. Please. Hospital. Too expensive."

Sally's eyes reddened. "Why's your freezer full of marijuana *ddeok?* What other secrets are you hiding?"

"Promise. Con. Pee. Den. Chul."

"Confidential? From Yumi and Mickey? And me, if I hadn't caught you?" Sally pushed her nose stud in so deep she gasped. "Where's the damn doc?"

"Flatland. Always. Slow. Promise."

"Don't think I can keep a secret? Being discrete is part of my job."

"At sexy store?"

"Yes, at the sex store. You making dope *ddeok* for a

boyfriend dealer?"

"Dealer?" Kyong Ah nosefarted and winced. She coughed up and swallowed mucous salty with blood. She sucked a backup inhaler the nurse had missed. "Medicine. Not. Get high."

Kyong Ah nodded off to sleep. Drifting in and out as machines sucked and whirled around her and nurse ghosts vampired away her I&Os. Her *maknae* went on the prowl for a doc. She got chicken flesh when she heard a brittle voice nearby.

"Fan okey! Sei malau!"

Worlds collide. Ssibal! *Trapped with your crazy patients.*

A large, dark hand touched her shoulder. "We didn't expect to see you so soon."

"Dr. Gokul? Cheung Tai?" Kyong Ah opened her eyes, her breathing easier thanks to magic drips and vapors.

"Who?" The doc and Sally asked simultaneously.

Sally rose and shook his hand. "Hi, Doctor. I'm her daughter, Sally.

Dr. Gokul nodded. "Glad to meet you. Despite the circumstances. Were you calling someone, Mrs. Choi?"

Kyong cocked her head; a man brayed like a donkey nearby. How close was Lockdown? Had they moved Cheung Tai? No, she must be hallucinating.

"Just bad dream."

Dr. Gokul nodded. "How did this episode start, Mrs. Choi?"

Kyong Ah slowly recounted her attack.

"From your tests and the diagnosis of Dr. Fong, your admitting doctor, we think you suffered congestive heart failure."

Kyong Ah frowned. "Heart? Not lungs?"

"A lot of water is backed up in your lungs, signaling that both heart and lungs are having difficulty doing their jobs pumping air and fluids. On the positive side, your X-rays show the mass in your lungs may have shrunk a bit."

"Mass? You mean tumor?" said Sally.

Shrunk? Sugo! Ddeok *heroes, you are total champs!*

Dr. Gokul frowned. "Mind if I speak with your mother alone for a moment?"

Shaking her head, Sally left.

"Mrs. Choi, you haven't told your daughter about your lung cancer yet? Of course it's your decision. But it's much harder to make this journey alone."

Kyong Ah folded her arms. "Promise not to make her worry. She's my youngest."

"She spent last night here with you, right? Why not accept her as part of your support network?"

Kyong Ah struck away treasonous tears. But she did not object.

"I'll take that as a yes. Let's call her back in, shall we?"

Sally returned as summoned. Stone faced. Like she hadn't been eavesdropping.

"You've still got water on your lungs, though less with the diuretic that Dr. Fong put you on last night. We may need to move up surgery, pending stabilization of your current condition."

"Surgery?" Sally's shoulders shot up.

Kyong Ah pressed her moist lung and coughed.

If Cancer Goddess croaks another beggar and gives you their time. Maybe MediKeoji will drop alms in your bowl.

The doctor observed the daughter's full eyes and continued. "To remove the tumor in the upper lobe of your mother's left lung. Depending on outcomes, we'll follow up with chemotherapy and radiation treatments."

"Chemotherapy and radiation? So you're saying she has lung cancer?"

"Unfortunately, yes. But we can improve her chances with treatments. Our department has a good, solid track record."

"Why all the hush-hush, Omma?" Sally struck away tears.

"I told you I got no money for that, Doctor. And I got lots of work to finish first."

"Perhaps your daughter can help. The nurses will move you upstairs as soon as a bed becomes available."

"No, I want to go home now. I can't afford this."

Cheung Tai was right. Fan okey *or kill me.*

"Chemo and radiation, eh?" Sally blew her nose. "Doctor, what about medical marijuana?"

Kyong Ah sat up on her elbows and shot Sally a death-ray look. "I'm taking Korean herbs. Maybe they're eating away cancer."

"The sooner the surgery, the better the chances of success. Medical marijuana is outside our purview and the jury's still out on its effectiveness in cancer treatment. But some studies report it can help alleviate pain and bring back appetite." The doctor looked from mother to daughter. "No one's proved that it cures cancer. In your mother's case, smoking of any kind is absolutely out. Mrs. Choi, do you need me to write a letter to your employer for medical leave?"

"Yes, but please give it to me so I can show to boss at right time."

The doc looked at Sally. "I told your mother we have cancer support groups and information posted online. I've got other patients to see now but feel free to call or e-mail me with your questions."

Sally took his card and chewed her lip until he left. "Lung Cancer? Wait until Yumi finds out. She's going to kick your *eongdeongi!*" Sally's face twisted. She threw her arms around Omma's neck, crying into her hair.

Kyong Ah wiggled free. "Promise not to tell."

"You're kidding, right? Yumi and Mickey will skin and debone me if they find out you told me but not them. Or if, Heaven forbid, there's a complication before they find out. Don't do this to me, Omma. Or to yourself."

"Let's see how MediCal app and surgery goes first. Trust me, Sally. This is best way. I know. We take care of lots of cancer patients and families at my job."

"MediCal app? There's no shame in having cancer." The C-word sizzled across Sally's virgin tongue. "You're acting like you caught an STD or something."

"STD? You mean sex disease?" Kyong Ah grunted. "I should be so lucky." She heard Dead Husband howl at the joke.

"You're going to beat this thing. Lots of people have. We can look for info online." Sally ran her hand over her stubble head. "*Yaah,* is that why you needed a computer?"

"Go back to work, Seungsoo-ah. Don't lose job because of me."

"No. Yes. Maybe just for a few hours. What should I tell Yumi and Mickey when they call?"

"Say I had bad stomach flu. Or whatever. I can't ride back of your motorcycle. I take Veterans Cab home. Don't worry. Please find out if Evan still in jail."

"Evan? Forget his sideshow, Omma! *You're* the main event," Sally choked. "I love you."

"I love you, too." Kyong Ah closed her eyes. Guilty and relieved her *maknae* was in on the secret.

34. NO!

Kyong Ah weaseled her way out of Flatland to save money she didn't have. Clutching a bag of diuretics, beta blockers, aspirins and inhalers—and sleeping pills—she pulled herself up the rails of her apartment building stairs and unlocked the door.

Bless you, Fridge and Flaco!

Even with Mickey still bunking there, her place felt freer. She was light as a monk with only a begging bowl. She just had to get him out.

Work first. Ddeok second.

Withdraw cash from savings and apply for Medi-Cal—check, check. Buy computer, donate junk, store gift bags—check, check, check. What next? She pulled out the DNR packet from Nurse Ricard, now called "Advance Health Care Directive." As if anyone was fooled by the phony name.

Kyong Ah checked NO to CPR, breathing machine, and dialysis. NO to blood transfusion, artificial feeding, and hydration. NO to surrendering her I&Os to others. NO to life support machine gods. NO to seeing death mirrored in her kids' eyes.

Sure, she had helped stretch Life's taffy for her old-sters, glad to be of service. But now was her taffy turn. YES to being strong enough to talk with family and friends, perform her own ADLs, make her own decisions, and not be a burden to family.

She chewed her lip over the designated health care agent and alternate. From Leng's go-with-gut exercise and yesterday's crisis, Sally had rock-paper-scissored herself into first place. But should Yumi or Minsoo be the alternate? Kyong Ah shuddered like a threadbare beggar in a blizzard.

Isn't dying enough donkey work without having to tiptoe around your kids' feelings, too? Ssibal. *Longer you wait, less you control.*

No matter what Doc Gokul said, *ddeok* needed more tumor nibbling time. Kyong Ah remembered the Medi-CannBee dreadlockers with hair thick as marijuana buds and nosefarted.

Dope can't save hair from chemo. You'll soon be bald as Seungsoo. And you don't have enough money for ammo so Poison and Raygun Generals can drive Cancer Goddess from your valleys.

The phone rang in the damp midnight of desire. Skin glistening, Kyong Ah rose, her joints popping and brain spinning.

Let me go, Jae Pil, you bum.

She shoved Dead Husband off. "Yumi-ah? You already back from Korea?"

"We're at Inchon waiting for our flight." Yumi smiled and waved at Agi and their new daughter seated nearby. "Sally left a message to call right away. So what couldn't wait for us to get home?" China Air made a final boarding call for Jinan, Shandong.

"Seungsoo said what? I can't hear you." Kyong Ah held her head; the dinner *ddeok* handicapped her against viper-quick Yumi. But maybe Sally hadn't blabbed the full story. Or Yumi wouldn't be so evil. "I'm fine. Don't worry. How's the baby?"

The baby called out. Yumi's lower lip trembled. A tear slid down her cheek. "Omma, she's gorgeous." Yumi's scowl returned. "But what's this about you smoking marijuana?"

"I'm not *smoking* marijuana." A bud of guilt smoldered in Kyong Ah's gut.

"So why is your freezer crammed with it?" Yumi's eyebrows cut sharp.

"Empty rumor. Stop bossing me. I'm *omma* and you're *ddal.*"

Silence crackled through submarine cables. Yumi sucked her teeth. "What's this about you going to the hospital? For what? Who's your doctor?"

"Nothing to worry about." Kyong Ah sucked her teeth, hoping Sally hadn't surrendered her oncologist's name. Doc Gokul was no match for Yumi; she'd vacuum-suck his brain for incriminating evidence.

"Don't think I have ways of finding out?"

"What, from Sally?"

Kyong Ah smacked her head. *Babo-ya!*

Yumi thumped her trump card. "You're seeing a younger man, aren't you? Some guy covered in tattoos."

Kyong Ah heard Agi say, "Sweetheart, watch your tone. And volume."

"Tattoo man? Where you get this nonsense from?"

Meany hissed. "Some young dealer making you sell drugs? Like Evan?"

"*Ssibal!* Is Evan eating *and* selling drugs?" Tumor punched membrane retaining walls. Cancer Goddess powdered Depression Goddess' cheeks with coffin dust rouge.

Eldest daughter leaned into the knife. "Why did I even bother to call? This is the last thing me and Ji-Eun need now."

"Ji-Eun?" The baby fussed. Kyong Ah's tumor shimmied like a blob of Joker's Wild Jell-O. She feared attaching to the child; it wasn't fair to the baby.

Yumi will blame you for your death. So what? Let her make it into a lesson for her child. "Don't smoke and kill yourself like your foolish halmoni did."

"Hug Agi and Ji-Eun for me. Have safe flight." Kyong Ah's lungs spasmed. She grunted, "I love you." She hung up before Yumi could make her want to take it back.

Kyong Ah went to the bathroom, peeing a spring snow melt from the diuretics and aspirins for her congestive heart failure. She went to the living room.

Where the hell is Minsoo?

She went to bed praying for sleep's return, Evan's release, and Yumi's safe passage.

Kyong Ah dreamed that she mistakenly checked YES! on her DNR to all the boxes that should say NO! And vice versa. And signed away all her rights to her kids. She screamed behind an anesthesia mask while Doc Gokul sliced open a skin flap door to her chest. Heart flailed as a rib spreader stretched her open. Doc G thrust his hands inside, pulling out fistfuls of screeching, raccoon-eyed mutant cells. While Yumi and Mickey leaned over the operating table brandishing DNR forms bearing their two-inch tall signatures.

Yumi's eyebrows curved like scythes. She wore an unbleached Hanbok for mourning. "If you'd treated Apa better he'd be here to take care of you."

Minsoo wore a blue shower cap and a blue apron on top of his overalls. His plastic gloves were slick with motor oil. "Tell the doc to soak your lung in turpentine. Knocks out the greasiest stains. Sure to kill your cancer, Omma. Yooms, you're Omma's health proxy. I'm late for work. Go ahead and decide whatever you think's best.

Kyong Ah wept. "I love you, Yumi. I love you, Minsoo. But that's not the same as trusting you with my death. Can't you understand? Where's Seungsoo?"

Minsoo snapped his shower cap. "Omma's lips are moving. She's trying to say something."

Yumi shook her head. "She's a delirious dope fiend, Mickey. Just like Evan."

Mickey pulled off his mask. "Stop badmouthing my boy."

Kyong Ah tried to sit up. "Evan? Where's Seungsoo?"

"Who knows? Can't we hurry this along?" Tapping the floor with her ppalli ppalli ballet flat, Yumi cursed her watch.

"Is Seungsoo out on date? With man or woman?"

Kyong Ah woke up gasping for air.

Talking to Porkypine is same as shouting through bullhorn to Meany and Meathead. Whatever you want done, do it before surgery and you're too weak to fight their bad decisions.

Sally rang. "Hey, Omma. Hospital said you left already. Why didn't you call me?"

"Don't worry, I took cab home. But your sister called from Inchon airport to talk bad to me. You promised to keep my illness conpeedenchul so everyone not get worried. I trusted you, Seungsoo."

Sally gulped scalding coffee. "I kept it vague. I hope you told her the truth, Omma. I wish you and Onni would stop fighting."

Detect-o-meter spiked. "Whatever. You say I smoke marijuana? And got baby boyfriend and tumor? She treats me like idiot. Swear not to tell her anything unless I give permission first."

Sally flopped like a rag doll. "*Yaah*, Omma. Why are you putting me in the middle?"

"Look, Seungsoo-ah. Let her be happy with new baby. I just make her mad." She tried the Leng test. "If you got in trouble who would be better helper, Yumi or Minsoo?"

Sally sputtered coffee down the front of her orange Koreans Against War & Racism T-shirt. "Isn't it obvious?"

"Tell me anyway."

"Mickey bipolars between mean drunk and mush head. I'd choose Onni."

The hole in Kyong Ah's head constricted painfully. "Bipolars?"

And Yumi will take advantage of your weakened state for revenge.

"Thanks, Seungsoo-ah."

"What'd I say? Onni loves you," Sally ventured, "but she just has a hard time showing it. Promise you'll talk to Yumi and Mickey about your tumor right away."

"*Geulsse.* Maybe."

"Please. I love you, Omma."

"I love you, too, Seungsoo-ah."

They hung up, both teary-eyed. Kyong Ah fried ancho-vies and peanuts, spicing her kitchen with hope.

That settles it. Seungsoo will be both health agent and alternate. Pray that if Seungsoo consults Yumi and they come up with something that violates your wishes, you'll be past caring. Be grateful you've raised at least one child who might help you die with dignity. Even if she has pincushion face. And is resbian.

35. PEASANTS

After taking a couple days off with the "flu," Kyong Ah returned to work. It took forever to ready her patients for breakfast, push the carts and distribute trays. When she passed Mrs. Santos' old room, the sight of the still empty bed unfurled repressed *han.* She sat down and let her soggy lungs weep.

After the storm passed through her body, the aide wiped her eyes and sucked on her inhaler.

"What's wrong? You breathing sound bad," said Leng, dragging a couple of meal carts.

"Water on lungs. I feel better now."

"*Aiyah!* Why you come to work?"

"To tell Pockmark I got to take leave for surgery."

Leng pulled Kyong Ah into a broom closet. "Flatland schedule you? What you going to tell Pockmark?"

"I got no idea."

"Tell him you have cancer, Kyong. This is SNeeFah. If he can't understand, he's bigger asshole than we already know. Not you fault."

"Except for smoking."

"Pockmark ever see you smoke? Then say stomach.

Too much spicy Korean food."

"No, I'm bad at lying. Just tell truth."

"Okay, lung cancer. Then what?"

"I got to take off time for treatment. Surgery, chemos, radiation."

"How long?"

"Not sure. Everybody different. What if he fire me? Flatland made me sign scary papers to do surgery. Should I cancel? If I survive, I can never pay off."

"What if Pockmark say he need worker every day?"

"I ask him to keep job open and hire temps till I return. I work here sixteen years, longer than him. Take good care patients."

"You deserve healthcare, too. Just like our patients. Want me go with you? You talk. I stare at him all mean."

"Thanks, but too much hassle for you. And he'll say no, anyway." Kyong Ah sat up, listening to the sound of absence. "Where's Cheung Tai? Dreamed I heard her at Flatland when I was there. Hope she not get 5150'd again."

"She check out of here day before yesterday. Maybe run out of Medicare coverage. Hope her family find some nice Oldsheimers place to stay. Wherever she at, those people and their elevator going to be super busy."

Kyong Ah wrangled a meeting with Pockmark—"to discuss a problem on Third Floor," she'd said, so Leng could come, too.

Pockmark ran his fingers through his combover, motioning for the two peasants to sit in the squat chairs opposite him. Kyong Ah made her face blank; Leng's eyes narrowed and her perm bristled.

"Make it quick. I'm late for my daughter's piano recital. Before you start, we're operating within strict dietary and budget constraints. We've done all we can to alter the menu. My hands are tied."

Kyong Ah's mouth went slack.

I'm dying and he's still whining about shrimps?

"That's not it, Boss. I'm sick. I need time off."

His jaw hardened. "You know how short-handed we are. For how long?"

"I got surgery in a few days."

"Sorry to hear that. What's wrong?"

Kyong Ah swallowed a cough. "Tumor. Left lung. Docs got to cut it out."

"Benign?"

"No." She felt naked and crossed her arms for protection.

"Sorry to hear that. Did the doctors tell you what stage it is?"

"Stage One, but they don't know until they operate."

"Which hospital?"

"Flatland."

"You know, for people who got no coverage," said Leng, sharp as a cue ball banking off the side.

Pockmark cut his eyes at Leng. "Flatland's got a top rate oncology department." He cleared his throat. "But I hope you're not here to ask me to hold your job open for you during treatment."

Kyong Ah swallowed a cough, praying to last night's *ssuk* and MJ *ddeok* to power her through. "I can't quit, Boss. Treatment is super expensive. How about I work when I feel well and you hire temps on other days?"

Leng jumped in. "I can train temps, so no problem for patients."

Pockmark shook his head. "Look at the issue from Golden West's perspective. Once we make an exception for you, we have to do it for everyone."

"I work here sixteen years, Mistah Whang, even before you bought. I take super good care of our patients. I never caused any problem."

"What about voting for the wrong side in that union drive? And helping that troublemaker Legaspi fellow with his stupid shrimp campaign?"

So much for secret ballot. Diu nei, *Pockmark, you* ssibal nom.

"Union? I don't understand. Anyway, how can I refuse Mistah Rheegasepee when he ask me to wheel him here? Anyway, I not come to fight. Let's talk as people who work together long time. After surgery and treatment start, I have better idea of what can be work schedule."

Pockmark shook his head. "Think recovery is that predictable? After what you've seen here?"

As rain clouds gathered behind her eyes, Kyong Ah fake smiled and nodded as if charming honey down his gullet. "Think about it, okay, Mistah Whang?"

"I'll let you know my decision in two weeks." His eyes climbed her chest until they reached her eyes, which narrowed.

Control yourself, beggar.

"Leave us for a moment, Leng."

Leng growled like a pissed-off chow chow. "Why?"

Kyong Ah coughed. "That's okay, Leng. Thanks."

Standing, Leng scowled. "You got to do right thing,

Boss. Especially since Golden West not pay for our health-care."

Pockmark harrumphed and closed the door after Leng. "If you quit soon, you might be eligible for MediCal. Have you applied yet? Takes three months or longer to get processed."

"I did a few weeks ago."

"Did you say you worked here?"

"Of course." Fatigue washed over Kyong Ah. She shouldn't have let Leng leave. Her judgment was as slippery as Cheung Tai's dope *ddeok* pulse. She coughed blood into a tissue and disappeared it into her pocket.

"Well, if you tell MediCal you've quit, I'll try to make a call to move your application along. No promises. But I beat it."

Ocean waves lapped on a distant shore. "Lung cancer?"

"No, something else." He sniffed.

Kyong studied her boss intently.

Prostate. He doesn't want to talk about how Cancer Goddess shriveled his balls.

"When was it?" she asked.

"Three years before I came to Golden West. Been in remission since. They've got better drugs now. Surgery is less medieval." He ran his fingers through his combover.

"You go to Flatland?"

"No, of course not. I went to Summit, then UCSF."

"Good for you Po-oss. But even with MediCal, I'm still going to owe tens of thousands for treatment. Please. I need this job."

"Got it." Pockmark stood, signaling the meeting was over.

❧

Leng was waiting outside. When Kyong Ah reported what Pockmark had said, Leng hissed. "Booshit. He's fart-talking dogshit. Don't quit, make that cheap *chau-hai* hire temps or lay you off—and call MediCal, too. Then at least you can get unemployment. If he want keep his unemployment rate low, pay for our healthcare, asshole."

"I hope you not on *ddong* list now. He remember everything."

"He's bluff. See how he watch you face when accuse of voting union? I told you he's big potato from Cultural Revolution horseshit. He's pigeon-eye dead monkey."

"I got to push back surgery until find out if MediCal going to approve me."

"Can't you kids help? Sooner take out cancer, more better and more cheaper. What you tell patient in same situation?"

Kyong Ah drew a wheezy breath. "Surgery first, worry later."

"Right! What Winny and PTs always say? Try walk right away, but one step at time."

Kyong Ah let tears sting her cheeks as Leng hugged her.

36. GRAVEROBBERS

The anesthesiologist with carrot curls escaping her scrub cap put the mask over Kyong Ah's face. "Count backwards for me, starting with ten."

"Ten."

"Nine."

Eight.

A lucky round number. That fell sideways. Making two sleepy eye dashes.

She was a grave mound. The moon hung low, puppeting ghost shadows across her chest. Sharp shovels sank in, piercing grass skin. Soil flesh. Nerve roots. This must be how Earth felt every planting and funeral season.

Hurt. Hurt. Hurt.

The moon glinted off the gravediggers' raised picks. Ribs gasped open. A bone cracked. Left Lung wept. Cell soldiers of opposing armies unsheathed swords and fought along the banks of Sorrow River.

"Nurse? Saw. Spreader. Pick."

"Careful now."

"Jackhammer. Bait. Tackle."

"Is it steamy in here? Or is it me?"

"Bag that lymph node for Path. And that one. And that one."

"Trench it. Deeper. Gotcha!"

"Sure? She's too poor to be dug up more than once."

"Heart's working hard. Tag team for lungs."

"Scalpel. Stop that bleeder! What's that shadow?"

"Where?"

"To the right. No, further down. Four o'clock. That wasn't on the map."

"Stop the bleed first. Deal with mapmaker later."

"Heart rate's dropping."

"Get out of my lungs!"

The graverobbers kept digging. Deaf. Relentless. Beneath moon witness. As ocean wind raised blood and lymph waves. Dressed in hemp mourning clothes, Singer Jang Sa Ik's ghost lead her funeral march, his wails cutting a steep road to Heaven. Drums and gongs and paper flowers accompanied them. Borne by oxcart, she wore a straw mat cape. A sea mist engulfed them.

Halmoni grunted and hoisted herself into the cart. "Hold my hand, Granddaughter."

"You've come, Halmoni? Did Minsoo bail Evan out of jail? Has Yumi's new baby cut her first tooth? Will Seungsoo find someone to love her?"

"Release worry. Any work left unfinished will be completed by others. If meant to be. You can see loved ones from the other side. And speak with them—if they summon you for counsel. As you've done all these years with me."

"So scared, Halmoni. Where's Omma?"

"Who knows where she wandered off to? You're stuck with me again. I'll never forget that ginseng you dug up for me with *your bare hands. Kept me going for another month at the end, didn't it, Granddaughter?"*

"Ashamed to say, but when I tried to steal a bigger one from a ginseng vendor's table he boxed my ears. Yet not before smaller root had climbed up my sleeve."

"*Sesangeh! Lucky he didn't do worse. What a smart girl! Helping your sick* halmoni *cannot be called stealing. You're experimenting with healing herbs again, right?*"

"See how far it got me."

"*At least you tried. That's what counts. You've been on your own, taking care of me and others since you were little. It's in your marrow. But now is the time for you to let go and let others care for you.*"

"I can't, Halmoni."

"*Think it was easy to let you watch over me?*"

"Honestly? Lying here with strangers' hands invading my chest? No."

"*But I did. What's stopping you?*"

"I don't want to be burden."

"*You keep repeating that like monk chanting for enlightenment. Why do you have such little faith in* saekki *you raised? Without stitch of help from that wind-smoking cheater? His betrayal bonded their loyalty to you.*"

"No, they blamed me for all they lacked. I was the one left standing there to blame. Dead Husband's memory only grew more precious. Hard being the oldest one alive. Miss you."

"*Sesangeh! How can descendants of mine be that thick-witted? Maybe you should have softened their hard heads with my fish-taming cudgels.*"

"Speak louder, Halmoni. Closer. Through hole in my head. And lung."

"Aiguh! *Hold my hand tight, Granddaughter. Here we go.*"

Kyong Ah found herself tracing stone village walls with her fingers. She pushed open the wicker gate to Halmoni's shack and ran to hug fat-bellied earthenware jars brimming with magic sauces and pickle treasures. She clenched her fists as Halmoni braided her hair so tight her eyes widened. They walked the beach, reading fortunes inside the curl of each ocean wave. Time took wing as Husband's stubbled face scratched her cheeks and his rough hands fevered her thighs. Year-old dol *parties tornadoed until she couldn't remember which child chose money versus pen or arrow versus silk thread. She clapped in delight at Yumi, radiant in the cloud-white gown of her first wedding. Minsoo, nuzzling the Homecoming Queen's neck. Sally standing on tiptoes on the bathroom stool pretend shaving with Jae Pil's razor—Aiguh! Was that the first sign?*

Gravediggers reached the edges of the operating theater.
"*Staple, staple. Stitch, stitch.*"
"*Watch the bleeding.*"
"*Over the hump now.*"
"*Not over until it's over.*"
"*Bag please. Pickles for the med school kids.*"
"*Unusual shape.*"
"*Like her country, she says.*"
"*Weird. Anyone else smell smoke?*"
"*Like a burning cane field.*"
"*With a hint of hemp.*"
"*Really? I don't smell anything.*"
"*The Caucasian nose is clueless to all but the strongest odors.*"

"I smell AB Type blood on your sleeve."
"Cheater, you read that on the blood bags."
"Put everything back the way we found it."
"Plus the new tubing."
"Minus her uninvited guest."

Pain. Each breath leapt a chasm that Tumor used to bridge. Nerves, vessels, cells panicked. Straining to remember how they held hands. Before Knife General.

Outside the moon sighed; inside the lamp haloed around Sally's shaved skull. "Omma, you awake? Thank God!"

"Sally. Don't hug. So hard. Hurt."

Thank you, Halmoni and Kwan Seum Bosal. Go in peace, Cancer Goddess. Far away. Please.

"Sorry. The docs say sooner you get moving the better." Sally tucked Omma's greying hair behind her ears. She offered water from a paper cup. "I'll tell the nurse you're awake."

Kyong Ah waved it away. "Sleep. First."

As soon as Sally left, Kyong Ah threw up in the green plastic container on the nightstand. Covered it with a tissue. Noted the IV, monitors, and catheter radiating out of her. Gingerly lifted her gown and peeked at the dressing and knife-and-shovel tracks. Sexy as Mr. Bak's rust grin and DMZ razor wire. Starting to sting. Tattoo's Left Lung had faded from salmon pink to milk white. Trembling, Kyong Ah massaged her inner arm.

Bless you, Tattoo. For appeasing Cancer Goddess. Missus Santos had her cross; I've got you.

Grief for Mrs. Santos rode the seam where Cancer Goddess used to nest.

Nurse Bones entered with Sally. "Glad to see you awake so soon." The nurse checked vitals and monitors. "So far, so good. I'll get a breath therapist in here so you can get your respiratory system back on track. Ready for lunch?"

"I don't think I can keep anything down. Sorry." Kyong Ah pointed to the container.

The nurse examined the puke container and replaced it with a clean one. "How about chicken consommé and crackers for starters? Got to get you eating and that plumbing moving. Your daughter says you're an amazing cook and might be able to contribute a veggie recipe to my healthy Texans cookbook. Makes me happy as a clam at high tide. Lots of Koreans in Dallas these days."

"Wow, Koreans in Texas." Sally imagined Omma's people sporting ten-gallon hats and armadillo boots.

Kyong Ah thanked the nurse before she left. "How long I sleep, Seungsoo-ah?"

"Two days."

"You're kidding, right? You didn't take off from work whole time, did you?"

"Don't worry, Omma. Yumi and Mickey will come relieve me soon." Sally stretched like a sleepy black cat.

"Go to work. Nurses take care of me."

"Does it hurt to breathe?"

"A little."

"Then save your breath for the therapist, Omma." Sally fake smiled; her pupils constricted with worry.

Kyong Ah hoiked and spit into a tissue that she crumpled and slipped under her pillow.

Still bloody. Don't celebrate yet.

Her lips flatlined.

Do whatever they say so you can fan okey. *Don't make your kids clean up your I&Os.*

V. ACCEPTANCE: *Wings*

"Sucker basically drops a WMD on you."
—George Watts

37. ROCK-PAPER-SCISSORS

Kyong Ah's surgery scar burned her awake. Her eyes cracked open. Blurry at first, her three kids loomed over her. Yumi's hair sharpened into a tight ponytail. Minsoo wore a black Santana T-shirt and jeans, and smelled of stale smoke and motor oil. Seungsoo chewed a stud on her lip and scratched the backs of her hands.

Am I already in grave, Halmoni?

No; the nose-hair-curling smell of disinfectant, tug of sutures and discomfort of the catheter testified that she was still at Flatland.

"Why you all here? *Yaah*, Yumi-ah, what about your new baby? Minsoo-ah, Evan out of jail yet?"

Yumi looked meaningfully at Sally, whom they'd decided at the pre-meeting would kick off the intervention. Sally cleared her throat. "Omma, we're all here because each of us is super concerned about your health. We want to do everything we can to help you get better."

Mickey grabbed his mother's arm. "*Eung*, Omma. Why didn't you tell us you were sick? And here I am living with you. Why am I always the last to know?"

Yumi gave him the stink eye. "What Mickey and Sally

meant to say was if you'd let us know what was going on maybe we could have helped and you wouldn't have ended up here."

Kyong Ah tried to sit up to face her accusers directly, gritting her teeth. "You're all so busy. Why worry you needlessly before doctors know for sure?"

Mickey nosefarted. "Oh really? Then why'd you tell Sally and not me?"

Sally punched Mickey's arm. "How many times do I have to repeat myself? I only found out Omma was here when her haulers called. Please tell Yumi and Mickey the rest, Omma. Don't put me in the middle."

"Haulers? Freakin' strangers?" Mickey growled, feeling his pockets for cigarettes.

Yumi tapped her foot. "You better tell us the whole story, Omma."

"What's to tell? Docs are waiting on lab results."

Yumi grabbed the chart hanging at the foot of the bed. "It's all here." Waving it triumphantly, she smirked as if she could read the docs' illegible code.

Kyong Ah pulled a pillow behind her back and sat up higher on her elbows.

Damn Flatland. What happened to HIPAA? Bet private hospitals don't tattle on patients like this.

She hissed in pain. "*Ssibal,* give me that! It's conpeedenchul. Seungsoo-ah, remember?" She shot her *maknae* a look.

"Remember what?" Mickey grabbed Omma's shoulder.

"*Aiguh!*" Kyong Ah sharply inhaled. "That hurts!"

He snatched his hand away.

"Yumi, give me chart. My body. My informations."

Sally's armpits blossomed with sweat. "Omma, just tell them what Doc Gokul said."

Stool pigeon.

"Don't worry. Hospital will take care of everything."

Yumi interjected, her eyes matador red. "Right, based on your Advance Health Care Directive. Do not resuscitate. And Sally is your sole health agent."

Sally's tats burned. "They made me tell them about that, Omma. In case their names were on it. Please tell them about your condition now."

Kyong Ah exhaled painfully.

Babo-yah, what's big secret? Who are you fooling, lying here with dressing bulge over your cut lung? And fighting with Yumi is sucking up too much ki.

"Docs took out tumor from Left Lung. I got non-small cell cancer. Stage One. From smoking, Minsoo and Seungsoo. Check Internet for how looks." Kyong Ah coughed blood into a tissue and disappeared it inside the pillowcase.

Mickey rubbed his salty eyes. "I knew it. All that coughing. Why am I always the last to know?"

Kyong Ah grabbed his hand. "I need you to respect my wishes. As long as my mind is working, I make decisions about my health. If mind goes, Sally decides. Watch your kids well, Minsoo and Yumi. Don't worry about me. Either I get better or I don't. Anyways, I'm nursing aide and seen people die all kinds of ways. Luckies go in sleep. Unluckies rot in veggie garden."

Her eyes red, Yumi returned the chart to its place. "Have you applied for MediCal? They take their sweet time to decide. Did your doctor schedule you for chemotherapy or radiology?"

"Maybe chemo. Already applied to MediCal."

"When?

Kyong Ah touched her forehead unsure whether to divulge how long she'd known about Cancer Goddess' presence. "I don't remember exactly. Anyways, I probably make just enough for them to reject me. Can you find out eligibility cutoff, Yumi-ah? I appreciate."

Yumi pulled her ponytail tighter. "Right now I'm swamped. But let me see what I can do."

Mickey slung an arm over her shoulder. "You'll make time, right, Yooms? And kick in for Omma's care with me and Sal since we don't make that much."

Yumi removed the offending arm. "Omma, if you don't get MediCal soon, we might be able to raise enough between us to cover a brief stay at a SNF after you get out of Flatland. Then, pending how you're doing, you may need to move in with Sally."

"I hate it!"

"Come on, Omma. I'll fix up my studio." Sally scratched ditches into the backs of her hands, mentally listing the contraband she'd have to hide before Omma bunked at her place.

Yumi sucked her teeth. "You can't stay by yourself, at least in the beginning. Since Mickey is moving out, right?"

"Yes, tomorrow night. Wilfredo's going to spot me a place on his couch while I look for an apartment. But I'll still pick up groceries and help cook when you're at Sal's."

"Really, Minsoo?" From his sour expression, his sisters must have leaned on him to move out, knowing what a pain in the *eongdeongi* he'd be to her and her stitches.

What a relief!

Kyong Ah lightly touched the dressing covering her new surgery scar. "How's Evan?"

Mickey scowled like a palace guardian god. "Don't worry about Evan, Omma. He's in an outpatient drug rehab program."

"Really?" A wave of fatigue washed over Kyong Ah.

Please help him succeed this time, Kwan Seum Bosal.

"I appreciate. But don't worry about me. I went through worse stuffs during war and martial law back home. And getting started in this country. Just remember. I love you."

Kyong Ah let them kiss her cheek one by one. Minsoo with thick, smoker's lips. Seungsoo with bumpy studs. Yumi, for the first time in eons. Although Yumi's was a dried up little peck, Kyong Ah felt beggar grateful.

38. SNUFF

Daughter inched mother in wheelchair forward in the admitting line at Rosewood Convalescent Care, the SNF Flatland had unloaded Kyong Ah on to post-op. Its halls smelled of false teeth and sheep.

"Don't wait with me. Go to work before you get fired, Seungsoo-ah."

Sally sucked a stud, checked her watch and winced. "Sure? Call if there's any problem. Mickey will come visit tonight." Sally waved from the elevator.

A grimacing greybeard wearing a leaky bandaged leg stump and a Mexican cowboy hat waited ahead of Kyong Ah.

Diabetes. Next stop, hospice.

Rosewood had more black and white patients than Golden West. Its aides were African, Latina and Asian immigrant women, with a few African Americans, too.

Kyong Ah tried to catch an aide's eye as the woman hurried past; no luck. She pressed the edges of her surgery incision, weepy from transport. After the admit nurse let a stomach surgery and two prone hip fractures cut in front, Kyong Ah rolled forward. "Ma'am, I need to use restroom now."

"No, wait. Be with you in a moment."

What's the care like if they can't even check me in? What did Boy say about Covehaven affiliates? Something about speedup + overbooking = more profits.

Kyong Ah returned to the line; her bladder swelled to bursting. She wheeled up beside an ankle fracture auntie now in front of the nurse. "I got to go to bathroom. Be right back."

Pursing her lips, the nurse shook her head. "You need to be admitted first."

"Then do it now. I been waiting over hour."

"Please be patient, Mrs. Kim. We're getting your bed ready."

"My name is *not* Kim. It's Choi, Kyong Ah Choi. I go pee and come right back."

The nurse snapped. "I said you need to wait."

"Whatever." Kyong Ah turned around and headed for the closest room.

A granny looked up from her *People* magazine. "What is this? Grand Central Station? Flush the toilet when you're done."

"Sorry. I appreciate." Kyong Ah waved and closed the door, clenching her teeth as she got on the toilet.

Ah, what a relief. Tip: don't give oldsters too much to drink before transport. Especially if they're not wearing diaper.

On the way back to the nurses' station, Kyong Ah pulled her wheelchair over to give right-of-way to a *hal-moni* whose droopy face and misaligned body looked like she'd had a stroke.

Poor Missus Santos.

Wiping away a tear, Kyong Ah tapped where Tumor and Cancer Goddess used to lounge. She pulled out her cell.

"Hello, is that you Fridge? I need you and Flaco to give me ride home."

"Mrs. Chuey? Where are you?" In the background someone yelled that orders of *burritos mojados de carnitas y carne asada* were ready.

"Rosewood Convalescent near Fruitvale and International."

"That's not far. Be there in seven minutes."

"I got to ask you another favor. Can you carry me to my apartment up three floors of stairs? Remember?"

"Sure, no problem."

Kyong Ah found the service elevator and made her way down. A Goodwill truck soon rolled up. The sight of Fridge and Flaco gladdened both lungs.

"Please return wheelchair to lobby."

Flaco lifted her into the Goodwill cab. "Where's your kids?"

"At work like you guys. This place is loser. Too many patients. Too few staffs."

They pulled away without incident.

You'd love Rosewood, Cheung Tai; no guards to block you from freedom and fan okey!

At Kyong Ah's, Fridge and Flaco alternated carrying her up the stairs. She unlocked the door, wheezing. She clapped her hands; Minsoo's stuff was gone. For once her dear son had kept his word.

"Please wait one minute." Kyong Ah shuffled to the bedroom, closed the door and lifted the loose floorboard beneath the shrine. She made a mental note to refresh the tobacco, fruit, and rice wine offerings so Cancer Goddess wouldn't get pissed off at stale tributes and return to prove her power.

She returned to the front room and paid Fridge and Flaco, wondering what rites the *mudang* in West Africa and Mexico performed to smoke out Cancer Goddess.

"Thank you. Take it easy, Señora."

"Good luck, Gentlemens. I really appreciate."

Kyong Ah went to bed, pulling the lavender comforter over her head and enjoying the first real rest she'd had since before surgery. Until her cell rang.

"*Eung*, Minsoo-ah? What time is it?"

"Late. Where the heck are you?"

"Home."

"That's what I thought. Let me in. I'm at the door."

"Wait. I'm slow. My stitches." Kyong Ah groped her way down the hall.

Dressed in fatigues, Mickey looked like he'd returned from weekend maneuvers. "Why didn't you stay at the SNuF?"

"No way. Those guys suck."

"Tell me about it. Chumps sicced a goon on me."

"No more arrests, Minsoo-ah. How's Evan doing? You hungry?"

"Sit down, Omma. I'll cook. Don't know why I let Yumi and Sally talk me into moving out. You need me here."

"*Ramyun* and seaweed on top of fridge."

Minsoo went to the kitchen and poked around in the freezer. "What's this, your dope stash? Why am I always the last to know?"

"No touchy!" Kyong Ah shouted from the other room.

After the microwave beeped Mickey emerged, his cheeks lumpy as a squirrel's. "Omma, your *ddeok* is delicious."

"Minsoo-yah! It's my medicine to fight cancer. Hard to grind rice after operation."

"I can grind it for you. Here, I heated up a couple extras."

"Kuurrh."

Mickey grinned as Kyong Ah plucked black sesame seeds from his chin. Omma and *adeul* soon slurped *ramyun* with seaweed and crunched *kkakdugi* kimchi while watching *Guardian Angel,* a drama about an orphan that made Kyong Ah's surgery scar weep.

"At least I never abandoned you kids," she mumbled.

"What?"

"Nothing." She fingered the edges of her dressing and lay down, sucking in a sharp breath.

Minsoo cleaned up afterwards, a first. Later, he gently shook her shoulder. "Tell me what you want from Koreana Super. Sally and me will share cooking. Yumi said Sal should look for a health aide to help out for a couple weeks."

Kyong Ah gave him a grocery list. "I *am* health aide. Anyways. I got to save money for chemos."

"Need me to pick up any of your meds? Docs prescribe any painkillers?" he said, too animated.

"No, hospital already gave me what I need."

Better hide White Man's Medicine so he doesn't help himself to that, too.

"Want me or Sal to crash here tonight?"

"You are good son, Minsoo. No, go home and rest. I

don't need."

"No big deal, Omma. I'll stay until Sal gets off work."

"Okay, I sleep now." Kyong Ah tossed as Minsoo watched some loud, pirated Korean action movie.

She got up in the middle of the night to pee.

Ah.

She lifted her nightgown and checked her bloody dressing, making a mental note to change it in the morning. She took a towel to protect the bedding.

Almost tripping on the way back, she reached down and felt the big head.

Stubble, not spike—Seungsoo.

She felt half guilty, half relieved her kids were watching over her.

Kyong Ah woke up to the smell of *doenjang* soup. Another first.

Sally called out. "Ready to eat, Omma? Doc give you any special dietary restrictions?"

"Just eat lots of veggies, fruit, and protein."

"If you'd stayed at Rosewood, they would've taken care of all that."

"I tried but that place is too scary. And moldy bathrooms. Who knows what you catch. Maybe Legionnaires *byeong,* you know, sickness."

"How about Golden West?"

"And have coworkers do my ADLs? No way, Joe-say."

"ADLs? Okay, why don't we hire someone? By the way you're out of *ddeok.*"

"What? That Minsoo!" She snatched her coffee cup to throw it but slowly put it down. "Help me check computer about treatments and cost. Please get my mail from downstairs."

"Done. Better check out the one from MediCal."

Kyong Ah opened the too thin envelope.

Have mercy, Kwan Seum Bosal.

Her heart dropped. "*Ssibal!* MediCal *kaesaekki* already reject me? Did Pockmark call and make things worse?"

"Get Yumi on them. Make her your power of attorney on finances. She's a whiz."

"If I need, I want you to do. You not yell at me like I'm stupid. Or steal my *ddeok*."

"Please, Omma, think it over." Sally tried to keep the whine out of her voice.

"Help me change dressing. We got to store *ddeok* at your place so Minsoo not steal it."

In the bathroom, Sally helped Omma pull the gown over her head. "Shit, Omma. This is why you need to be at the SNuF. I might hurt you."

"It's SNiPeh. Look worse than is. Just pull off little at time." Kyong Ah clenched her teeth as her *maknae* peeled away the rusty dressing. Daughter's hands shook; mother knew from training aides not to yell and scare the newbie.

Omma's melons sagged lower than Sally remembered, filling her with sadness. She dressed the wound as her mother directed. "Dammit, Omma. You either need a homecare aide or to move in with me. At least I've got an elevator."

Kyong Ah grunted noncommittally.

Cancer Goddess, please have mercy. Don't make me turn my youngest into old maid caring for me.

39. CUDGELS

That weekend, back at Kyong Ah's apartment, mother handed daughter a pair of worn cudgels. "Ready? Beat rice until turn into flour."

"Like this?" Sally pounded the coarsely ground rice on a stone platform.

DAT dat DAT dat DAT dat.

"Watch."

Dat da dat da dat da.

Kyong Ah remembered Halmoni beating clothes clean and smooth; Kyong Ah's sickly gnat strokes were no comparison. "Start with less. Do more even." Kyong Ah returned to her chore—grinding marijuana with a mortar and pestle. Her neck and brow glistened.

"Rest. I'll do yours after I'm done with this."

"No, this is my PT. You do rice. That's hard part."

"No wonder you stopped making *ddeok.* Too much freakin' work." Sally paused to wipe her face. The rice was still lumpy.

DAT dat DAT dat DAT dat.

"Who taught you?"

"Your big-*halmoni.* She was little but had arms of iron.

She could tame squid, octopus, laundry, rice—any opponent. People say she fought off wolf trying to steal my
uncle when he was baby. I'm wimp compared to her."

"You're the strongest person I know, Omma." Sally
felt the oak grain and imagined a *halmoni* with Popeye
arms landing bats between yellow wolf eyes.

DAT DAT DAT.

"Are these Big-Halmoni's?" Great-Halmoni of cudgel
fame must be where Omma got her OCD DNA from. Always
working. Always itchy. Sally picked up the pace; her brain
backfired and surged forward.

"No, got these after I broke my old ones."

"How?"

"On your *apa*'s shoulder. I was aiming for his head.
You don't remember?" Kyong Ah growled and replenished
her bowl with another bud, crushing it with the pestle.

"I remember lots of screaming, but no bats." Sally
cranked up Mary J's "I'm Goin' Down," double-timing the
bats to the bluesy beat.

DAT-DA DAT-DA DAT-DA DAT-DA.

Sally panted from exertion. "What'd you fight about?"

Nostalgia webbed Kyong Ah's lungs.

*Don't speak ill of dead. And maybe they won't speak ill of
you.*

"I forget," said Kyong Ah.

"His outside women?"

"Seungsoo-ah, when you have kids, don't raise them
alone like me."

Sally nosefarted. "Kids? First I'd need a partner.
Anyway, not sure I want kids. How about I just teach
Yumi's kid to skateboard?"

"What about that nice tattoo man Van Le? My friend's daughter really liked him."

Sally thrust her chin at her mother. "Okay, Omma. You let me see your MediCannBee card when we picked up your supply. Why can't I see your tattoo?"

Kyong Ah put down the pestle, pulled up her sleeve and twisted her arm.

"Happy?"

Sally bit her lip.

"Winged lungs? Should have known. I thought it was a broke heart. Like mine. I'm envious. Yours is so original."

"Make me look like convict." Kyong Ah lowered her sleeve and dried her eyes. "My turn to ask question."

"Shoot."

DAT DAT DAT DAT.

Kyong Ah picked up the pestle. "Were you and Van Le *aein,* you know, lovers?"

"What gave you that idea?"

DAT DAT DAT DAT.

"His eyes turn super dark when I mention your name. Same like you. It's over?"

Sally checked the rice. Finally, a respectable powder. She scraped it into a bowl and refilled the platform. She pushed the stud against the roof of her mouth, opening up a ki lesion passageway. "Screw it. I got something to tell you. That you're not going to like."

Kyong Ah's pestle hovered like a seagull. "What? That you are resbian? I already know." She crushed the bud and wiped away tears, accidently dusting her face with ground herb.

Half relieved, half cheated, Sally swore beneath her

breath. "But how?"

"Just tell me if you are, you know, bi-*saekssi*. Don't sugar pill me. Is that why Van Le leave you?"

"Sorry to disappoint you, but I'm not bi. Your daughter's a lesbian. But Van and I were together for a time."

"How? He's guy."

Sally scratched her phoenix tat, then the thorn vine riding her shoulders. "When he was Vanessa. Now he's transsexual—in the dude direction."

"Trans-*saekssi? Aiguh!*" Kyong Ah slumped, striking the table and raising puffs of rice and weed powder. "You're cursed in love. Like me and Minsoo. And used to be Yumi. All my fault." She rubbed the hole in her head. "Did he have whatchucallit operation? Can't he change back?"

"Forget it, Omma. Nesy, I mean Van's in another relationship."

"With guy or girl?"

"Someone named Nancy." Sally stopped scratching her tats when she noticed Omma doing the same. Like they were each other's funhouse trick mirrors.

"Was he guy or girl when you were together?"

"How long have you known I was a lesbian?"

"I don't know. After you stop letting me meet your friends. But you always were different."

"Like how?"

Kyong Ah shut her eyes so memory could flicker behind her lids. "Remember when you cut your face fake shaving with Apa's razor? And how you save money for Batman costume at Halloween? Never Batgirl. Never Catwoman. Never makeup and high heels like your *onni*. I told myself you just, you know, tomboy. Copycat your brother."

"Some lesbians prefer the princess stuff. They're called lipstick lesbians, Omma."

"You not ripstick resbian. You baldhead resbian. Why not bi-*saekssi?* Why always do things hard way?"

"What, and pass? No, I love women, Omma. This is who I am. Disappointed?"

"No," Kyong Ah lied, looking Sally straight in the eye. "You do like Frank Sinatra 'My Way.' Because me and your *apa* fight too much. Sorry."

"That's got absolutely nothing to do with it."

"No need to go easy on my feelings, Daughter. But promise me one thing, Seungsoo-ah. Find someone to love you. Living by self is too hurt."

Sally grimaced. "No biggie. I'm used to it now."

DAT DAT DAT DAT.

After they'd finished kneading, steaming and bagging the *ddeok,* Kyong Ah lay down for a nap. Sally surfed the Internet for treatment costs to help Yumi, who was overwhelmed with the new baby.

Goddamn depressing. Omma's right; she can't afford any of this.

Sally got up, heated and popped a *ssuk ddeok* in her mouth for inspiration. Then she put together a rough budget but stopped before sending it to the others without Omma's permission. Sally looked toward the bedroom where her mom was sleeping. One false move could end their frank "are you resbian?" and "I broke my favorite bats on Apa's back" pajama party secrets.

☯

In the morning, Kyong Ah brewed *nokcha* while her youngest snored over the laptop.

Who knew Porkypine would prove so filial?

Kyong Ah sat down and quietly moved the laptop; the screen lit up with Sally's budget. Treatment would cost enough to help Seungsoo or Minsoo put a down on a house. Rusty despair grinned inside Kyong Ah's chest. Cancer and Depression Goddesses beckoned.

Jump in the river and swim to the other side before you're too weak to succeed.

The ankh decal on the laptop lid throbbed. She closed the machine, put her head down and wept.

Halmoni, help me!

Sally sat up, rubbing sleep from her eyes. "Omma, I'm not finished with that budget yet. Yumi said she and Agi could help pay, though it'll take Mickey a while to save much. I can help, too, if it's spread out in installments. *Yaah!* You're bleeding."

Kyong Ah pulled the clotted top away from her chest.

"Shit, Omma! That looks terrible!"

"Not bad," Kyong Ah lied. "Help me change before you go work. Wash hands first."

"Okay, but shouldn't you go in and get this checked out?"

"No, not serious enough. I got to put some money down first. Then Doc says maybe try chemo next. Maybe not need radiation. Remember well, Seungsoo-ah. If brain still working, I decide. Promise if my brain stop working, then you do exactly what DNR say."

Shaking her head, Sally reluctantly hooked her pinkie around Omma's. While crossing fingers of her free hand behind her back. Then she fetched dressing and disinfection ointment and Omma walked her through the procedure.

After Sally left for work, Kyong Ah took out pen and paper. What to leave Evan that he couldn't sell for drugs? She rubbed the hole in her head. An ocean breeze raised chicken flesh on her skin. She put pen to paper and the hole in the back of her head closed like a baby's fontanel.

I, Kyong Ah Choi, being of strong mind write this will.

I leave to my children, grandchildren and work friends gift bags with their names at storage place. Here is key and business card. If any cash is left under board under shrine in bedroom, divide into three among my children. Give celadon teacup, teapot, babsang and purple ibul to Yumi. Give TV, VCR, DVDs, Korean dramas, pink ibul and Korean pillow to Minsoo. Give yo, computer, printer and kitchen stuffs to Seungsoo. Give pink slip and car and boom boom box to Evan. Give cleaning deposit to Yumi for Ji-Eun's college fund.

Yumi, good luck to you and your family. When you make mistakes, let them be different from ones I made with you. Minsoo, thanks for taking care of me. Stop drinking and be good example to my grandson so my spirit can rest in peace. Evan, you be good, too. Thank you for everything, Seungsoo. Please find good person to love you.

Please cremate me and drop my ashes in ocean from Golden Gate Bridge—on facing Oakland side.

Respect my wishes. As you would want your children to respect yours.

I love you.

☯

Kyong Ah signed off. Touched her surgery scar and tattoo.

Ready. Almost.

40. PLATINUM

Kyong Ah was last to join the half circle tethered by portable IV catheters to drip machines dangling bags at Flatland's Infusion Unit on the 7th Floor. Carboplatin and Paclitaxel were her delegated poisons.

At the first station sat an African American hulk of a man named George wearing a burnt orange jogging suit. He looked vaguely familiar and wheezed like a punctured tire. *COPD?* His wife wore the hint of a rod behind her smile.

School principal?

A Chinese man named Albert occupied the second station, his face gaunt. His snowy eyebrows strained as if trying to fly him free of this dungeon. He was missing a foot.

Diabetes? What did he do with the empty mate of his shoe?

Beside him sat Marie, his jittery wife.

Lakshmi, a young South Asian woman with razor short hair and enormous eyes sat at the third station.

Breast cancer?

She wore even more face jewelry than Sally. A young man with a cherry-bomb red Mohawk sat beside her. A magnetic field crackled between the couple.

Kyong Ah lightly tapped the port on her hand. No nausea or pain yet. Nurses Shirlee and Celia visited the hostages periodically. Tropical fish swam laps in a tank. Travel posters graced the walls. Sunny white cliff houses trimmed in blue overlooked a turquoise Greek sea. The Great Wall dragon snaked over maple mountains. Egyptian pyramids pointed to heavenly mysteries. Lady Liberty welcomed the weary. Trips still possible if the Poison Generals won. Kyong Ah visualized lying on a mat beneath a thatched roof during rainy season.

Heal me raindrips.

Sally snored at the ceiling, her jaw slack. Kyong Ah touched her elbow. "Go to work. Nothing for you to do here. I got another five hours to go."

"Maybe." Sally wiped drool from her face. The last few weeks were a blur from cleaning her disheveled apartment near Lake Merritt and moving Omma in. Running a godzillion errands, she'd turned Manny into a surly bitch from covering her absences.

Albert moaned to his wife in Cantonese, a perfect language for complaining. As Korean was for seizing your enemy by the throat.

How much time does he have left? Not long. What odds do people wager when they see me? Better than pancreas, brain, or bone marrow cancer tribes? Worse than breast, throat, stomach, or liver tribes? Or do tribes share equal powers of devastation?

"Seungsoo-ah, go now."

Sally rubbed the ache in her neck. "How you getting home?"

"Veterans Cab. Don't worry. Nurses say side effects

won't happen until tonight."

Sally yawned. "Got your set of keys? Call me if there's any problem. Mickey's still on probation at work."

"*Allasoh.* See you later." Kyong Ah caught Sally check-ing out the girl with the face jewelry on her way out. They nodded and smiled. Mohawk bristled.

*She must be bi-*saekssi *ripstick resbian.*

George caught Kyong Ah's eye, waving his tubed arm. "I'd shake your hand but you know how it is. I'm George. This is my wife Esther." George was bald from chemo, age or heredity. His lady wore a lilac twin sweater set and a purple straight skirt.

"Glad to meet you. I'm Kyong Ah Choi."

"Your first time?"

"How you know?"

"Your vibe. Plus you still got hair." He slapped his head, making a tight drum skin sound.

His wife peered over stern glasses. "Don't go scaring the lady, George."

"That's okay. He not going to scare me more than when doc say I got cancer."

"Isn't that the truth? What kind?"

"George!"

"That's okay, Missus. Lung. Too much smoking."

"Mine's colon. Too much eat, drink and be merry-ing."

"How many treatments you had?"

"This is my fourth."

"Gets easier or worse?"

"Zigzags to keep you off balance." George nodded at his machine. "Sucker basically drops a WMD on you. Equal opportunity. Kills bad and good guy cells."

Kyong remembered patients who had not recovered from aggressive treatment. "How long take before you feel side effects? And how long until you feel better?"

"You'll be twisting on the Devil's rack by day's end. Took me about two weeks to get over the first session. Then a week. Then three weeks."

Esther harrumphed. "Add a week or two on to what he said. Everyone's different."

"Sleeping Beauty your daughter?" George rubbed his skull.

"Yes."

"My Esther's been a champ."

"Then why don't you listen to me?"

"I love you, too, Honeybee. Big C took out Pop and before him, Big Pop. Both when they hit sixty-five." He thrust his chin at his drip bags. "But me and platinum are trying to beat the odds."

"Platinum? No wonder it cost so much. My parents and grandparents all die before sixty-five, too."

"Cancer?"

"No. Hard life in Korea."

"Do tell. Pop fought to save your people in the Korean War. Left a couple toes over there to frostbite. Don't know what's worse." George lifted his shirt to show off his colostomy bag. "No toes or wearing this shit bag until I'm done."

Esther pinched him. "Stop it, George! Nobody wants to look at that foul thing."

Kyong Ah pressed her tattoo, grateful colon wasn't her cancer's clan.

"Stop blabbing and let the lady rest, George."

"I got to do my talking now. Who knows what shape I'll be in when the kill juice kicks in? Anyways, haven't seen you at support group meetings."

"Um."

"Helps to talk with people going through the same thing as you. Meetings are Mondays and Wednesdays at seven p.m. And Thursdays at two p.m. You can bring your daughter, too." George smiled with perfect dentures.

What a nice man. Bet he doesn't cheat on his wife.

The nurses came to check on them and resupply infusion bags. The fish played hide-and-seek while a game show ran on the TV overhead. Lakshmi and Mohawk each fiddled with their own device. Albert snored while his wife knitted a scalloped baby blanket with turquoise yarn. George and Esther played bid whist, slapping the cards down loudly. That's when it came to her; she'd last seen George lying half out of his mind on a gurney the first night she'd spent at ER. And here he was with his support system, upbeat and tethered to hope.

Never know what tomorrow will bring.

Kwan Seum Bosal alighted above Kyong Ah's head and sat cross-legged on a lotus. Dragonflies hovered over her shoulders and hummingbirds, her knees. Monks chanted from the throats of mountain caves. The goddess remembered how she'd lost her eyes and learned to see.

Kyong Ah was the last to get unplugged and have her blood drawn for tests. Nurse Shirlee gave her pills for side effects and a list of signs to watch for. She pushed Kyong Ah's wheelchair to the taxi zone. "Visualize your chemo wiping out those cancer cells. Unless there's a problem and you need to come in sooner, we'll see you at your next appointment. Good luck."

"Thank you. I appreciate." Kyong Ah smiled at the white jade Guanyin Mercy Goddess pendant Nurse Shirlee wore on her neck. Kyong Ah stroked the wings on her tattoo.

Go, Poison Generals. Banish Cancer Goddess and her attendants.

41. SHAVE

Camped over at Sally's in case of complications, by dinnertime Kyong Ah's stomach pitched like a shrimp boat in a typhoon. She rushed to the bathroom and threw up on her feet, just short of the toilet. Gasping, she hung over the bowl and retched out the rest. She rinsed her mouth and cursed the green ghost staring back from the mirror. Then she washed her feet and wiped up the floor.

Time zigzagged between bed and toilet. Ache and puke of the strained soups Sally left her. Until she set a metal bowl beside Sally's queen mattress and flopped down. The room staggered with messy shelves of graphic novels, DVDs and CDs. Go-bots and pictures of Sally with short and shorter hair. Celadon cup and vase gifts from Kyong Ah. Laptop and Kyong Ah's meds bag.

Poison Generals, release me. Fan okey. *To Big House or Small House. I don't care.*

She crawled a twilight circle, too exhausted to track her I&Os for days on end. Finally, when she could stand without the room spinning, she headed for the kitchen. Searching Sally's cupboards, she found Shin Ramyun, dried seaweed, granola, tuna fish and rice crackers. Her tongue felt furry as Wolf's back.

Don't get dehydrated.

She boiled water. Sat slumped over the kitchen table. Got up and checked the chaotic drawers praying for green tea.

Messy as Minsoo. Yumi's only tidy one.

Kyong Ah found half a can of coffee.

Getting warm. Bingo!

A black bag. She peered inside.

"Ssibal! Sesangeh!"

Three plastic pricks: Wednesday Green, Saturday Pink and a Sunday Joker's Wild Blue. With a strap for only Kwan Seum Bosal knows what. Kyong Ah's face turned Monday Red. If her *maknae* was a lesbian, why so many pricks? Did Sally wear the dildos? Or her playmates?

"Yaah!"

Wednesday Green leapt from her hand and buzzed the floor. She caught and turned it off. Rinsed, dried and thrust it back in with its pals. After closing the bag she slipped it back in where she'd found it, beneath a roll of foil and a glass contraption that looked like a water pipe. A grey bag beckoned from beneath a package of blue sponges.

Don't look. Aiguh! Ssibal!

A DVD featured a strapped woman wearing another.

Now you know, nosey. Seungsoo wears them.

Kyong Ah slipped the DVD back in the bag beneath the sponges. She shook her head wearily.

At least she's getting sex. More than you with Dead Husband.

She drank hot water and limped back to bed, hoping she'd turned the corner on the nausea and Sally's scary toys.

When she woke up, every hair on her head hurt. Her nails and hangnails hurt. The roof of her mouth hurt. Her membranes hurt.

Go, Platinum. Vanquish Mutants.

Raccoon battalions howled, choking canals with cell corpses. Poison General exploded white phosphorus bombs. Tattoo Lungs bled phagocyte white. Lumpy as the tumor glop the gravediggers had harvested from Left Lung. Tattoo Wings crumpled. Halmoni bone dust sighed from a hill overlooking the sea.

The phone rang.

Shut up!

She knocked it off the mattress, closed her eyes and curled into fetal position. Like a girl skeleton tucked into a small grave.

"Omma? What's going on?" Sally flipped on the lights and covered her nose.

Kyong Ah pinched her eyelids against the harsh bulb. *"Mwoya?"*

"Mickey come by?" Sally opened windows to free stomach acid fumes.

"Mickey?" Kyong Ah's skin glowed a pale metallic.

Sally felt her mom's forehead. "Forget it. Want some *jook*, Omma?"

Kyong Ah made a sour face. "No. Sleep."

"The nurses said you have to keep drinking and eating in small amounts, as much as you can. Got you some pop-sicles. I'll start the *jook*."

"Bagoong. Mistah Rheegasepee."

"Who?"

"Fan okey."

"You're not making sense."

"Missus Santos. Sorry. Sorry. Sorry."

"Right. Omma. Got it covered." Sally microwaved a bowl of *jook* and started a *ramyun* for herself. She left messages for Yumi and Mickey reporting on Omma's progress and asking when they could relieve her.

Kyong Ah crawled in and out of sleep. Who knew you could throw up three licks of a melon popsicle? Deep in the night, she hugged Pillow Monster.

Teach me your pillow trick, Yoneda San. Before I'm too weak to pull it off.

Her arteries and veins glowed platinum. Her heart and lungs slowed to dream tempo.

An entrance. A clearing. Yoneda San pushed a wheelbarrow of tools. Pick and rake. Pruning shears and shovel. He stopped and removed his gardening gloves. Held his fingers together like the wings of a crow. He motioned for her to do the same. Shaking his head at her first attempt, he turned his hands over so she could see what mercy hands looked like from the palm side. How heart, life, and fate paths crossed or separated. She tried to mimic his hands. And how he bent his elbows to press the pillow to stop air. Finally, he nodded, smiling faint as the first fallen leaf sentry signaling autumn's advance. His gnarled fingers told her to practice until small sleep grew into BIG SLEEP. Luckily, her hands and arms were friends with heavy labor. But how to repay him for sharing his secret? She nodded knowingly.

☯

Cancer Goddess' cell soldiers surrendered through sweat, puke, and dreams, clogging blood and lymph pathways. Sally, Mickey, and Yumi babbled over Kyong Ah's potato face. Sacrificial hairs covered her pillow. During pilgrimages to the bathroom, she avoided eye contact with the evil mirror.

On Day Seven, she stood up without the room pitching. Sweating like a fiend in withdrawal, she reheated a pot of *jook* while Sally was at work. Watched it simmer. Ladled it into a rice bowl, adding a dab of soy sauce. She raised her spoon.

To bagoong *and Mistah Rheegasepee. To White Knights and Bak* Seonsaengnim. *To you, Missus Santos, wherever you now dance.*

She swallowed. Reached for an empty bowl. Wiped away puke and sipped water. She waited for an hour, tried again. Retched again. Repeated the ritual until she was able to keep down a spoonful. To which she added another. Waited. Then another. And another. She returned to the mattress and watched the black cat clock's eyes and tail click back and forth. Sally would be on break by now. As relieved to be at work as Kyong Ah was to have the apartment to herself so she could puke in peace. The place smelled of stomach acid and greasy comic book covers. Shin Ramyun and mystery lubricants.

Get out. You're spoiling your maknae'*s love life and chance of finding mate. Even with woman. Even with scary penises.*

Kyong Ah grimaced.

As long as she has someone to love her.

But the thought of scaling three flights of stairs to her apartment tugged her stitches. That's when she got a red-bean popsicle of an idea. She called her landlord.

"Hello, Mistah Lew? This is Kyong Ah Choi, your tenant in Apartment 303. I'm having problems with these old knees. Can you let me know if a first floor apartment becomes available? Thanks. I appreciate."

Kyong Ah hung up and took a sip of water and spoonful of *jook.* She gathered fallen hair soldiers for the trash and screwed up the nerve to stare the bathroom mirror in the eye.

Yaah, you look like refugee! Crater cheeks. Mangy dog scalp. What if it doesn't grow back?

She found Sally's razor; hefty, decisive. Must be for the head; Sally's pits bloomed as wiry as ever. Kyong Ah soaped her scalp and slowly shaved what remained of her hair, using an extra mirror for the back.

Finally got your haircut. Now you're stark. Raving. Bald. Cancer POW for world to see.

Like Nurse Bone's half-flat chest. Yet the shave felt better, braver than those pitiful strands. She turned left and right.

Like your youngest. All you need is porkypine jewelry.

She rinsed the razor and returned it to the cabinet. She watched TV while practicing Mr. Yoneda's crow wing hands. For the first time since chemo, a twang of hunger strummed her tummy.

One day at a time.

42. FEVER

Kyong Ah won her pressure campaign to move to the first floor studio that became available in her old building. Minsoo and Evan moved her stuff down from the third floor, bickering until she forbade them to say another word. They continued with growls and shoves. Apparently Evan had missed some court-mandated rehab meetings. At this rate, he'd be in jail when time came to scatter her ashes. She wondered how they'd spend holidays when she was gone. She doubted Yumi or Seungsoo would invite the idiots over for Thanksgiving turkey, Christmas kalbi or New Year *ddeok mandu* soup.

"*Geumanhae!* Stop it! I'll do it myself. Evan, shape up. Be nice to your *apa* or you'll spend Thanksgiving by yourself at Denny's or soup kitchen. You, too, Minsoo! Why can't you give me peace of mind before I'm dead?"

"Stop talking like that, Omma, you're going to outlive me," said Mickey, his smoker's cough thick with phlegm.

Evan covered his ears. "Stop, Halmoni! You're freaking me out."

Kyong Ah pulled his hands down and barked. "Evan, you go to rehabs! Don't make my dead spirit wander through hell restless because of you. Promise me you'll sign up for college classes at Raney again."

"Maybe. I don't know, Halmoni."

"No maybe. Yes or no."

"Alright, alright."

"Alright, alright what?"

"Alright, I'll sign up for classes tomorrow."

"That's great, Son," Mickey slapped him on the back. "Auto shop?"

Evan paused, making a face.

"*Ssibal,* don't nag him, Minsoo. He already made promise to his *halmoni* who is fighting cancer. Right, my favorite grandson?" Her big eye and small eye looked into his heart and softened.

"Yes, Halmoni. I promise." Evan and his *apa* gave her hugs that squished air from her lungs.

Mickey grinned. "Hey, why don't I make lunch? What do we got? How about a pot of my scrumptious *yukgae-jang?*"

After a tasty meal, Mickey and Evan finished setting up and left. Kyong Ah flopped down on the bed like a flogged donkey.

Next time hire Fridge and Flaco.

She massaged her stitches. Maybe she should check out George's support group for baldies. She drifted off to sleep.

Kyong Ah wheezed up and down cloud hatted mountains. That flattened into an unforgiving desert of snakes and sand that swallowed travelers. Hot, hot, hot. A bell around her donkey neck became a fist on the door.

☯

"Omma, you there? Open up, it's me Sally."

Kyong Ah groped along the wall towards a sliver of light under the door. She struck the door to let Seungsoo know she was there. Fumbled the locks open.

"Omma, you're burning up!" Sally found the hospital instructions by the bed and called the oncology hotline. "I just stepped on the thermometer, but I can tell my mom's burning up with fever. She got chemo last week. Yes, Dr. Raj Gokul's patient. Yes, we're headed to ER."

"Sleep first."

"Sleep at the hospital. *Yaah,* why'd I let you talk me into moving out of my place so soon?" Sally stuffed a change of clothes, toothbrush, and Omma's meds in her backpack. She grabbed the car keys. Guilt and fear hamster-wheeled her brain.

"Thirsty."

Sally raised water to Omma's lips.

"Ride piggyback, Omma. Don't argue. Want Doc G to kick my *eongdeongi?*" Sally hooked her arms around her mother's thighs.

Reverse childhood.

Omma's front fevered *maknae*'s back.

An ER doc whose face and scrubs said he'd been working two days straight put Kyong Ah on meds while the nurses applied ice packs. Vampired blood. Stole urine. X-rayed viscera. Conferred in whispers. Kyong Ah slipped in and out of consciousness. Until a blur focused into a scowl.

"Yumi-ah. Where's Agi?"

"Home watching Ji-Eun." Yumi felt her mother's forehead; still somewhat warm.

"When can I see baby?"

"Not until you're stronger. Kids have too many bugs. That's why it's best for you to stay with Sally. But I'll let you see her picture."

Kyong Ah smiled weakly at the big-faced baby with the rosebud lips. Her thick hair saluted punk rocker straight. Fear and disbelief crouched in her eyes.

"So cute. Sleep through night yet?"

"Up every couple hours. We're fried. Don't know how you managed raising us all." Yumi held a spoon of ice chips up to Kyong Ah's mouth. "You should have stayed at Sally's longer. That's exactly where you're going when you get out."

"No. Too much trouble."

"For who? Bringing you back to ER was hard on Sally. Budget's tight but maybe we can help you two get a bigger place. What's happening with MediCal? They won't answer my calls."

Go away Meany.

Kyong Ah shut her eyes against Yumi's hard looks. She fell into a dream.

A donkey carried her up and down a mountain range. It nosed open a twig gate to a shack overlooking the sea. Halmoni emerged, more bent than ever, holding out a bundle of dried grass that the donkey nibbled.

"Hurts me everywhere, Halmoni. Am I dying?"

"Sleep, child. Answer will come when you awake. Or don't."

"Costs too much money to stay alive."

"*So work until you're in ground. Like me. You're not one to let events decide themselves. You'll find way.*"

"*Don't know if my strength will ever return.*"

"*When you feel better, why not babysit for Yumi? Improve your status by doing something she values. Then take in another baby or two to put money in your hands.*"

"*More she sees me, more she kicks me. Babies? Taking care of oldsters is all I know.*"

"*Would you say same thing about babysitting Seungsoo's baby?*"

"*Is she pregnant? With turkey baster?*"

"*What? I don't understand.*"

"*Nothing. My brain is dizzy from white man's poison they're feeding me for medicine.*"

"*That's old healer trick. But must be right amount so doesn't kill you. Even too much salt ruins tasty soup. Anyways, why not let your kids help so they can feel less guilty when you're gone?*"

"*Maybe. I'm practicing old patient's crow wings farewell ritual.*"

"*Better not be* nom *from enemy land who had crush on you. After our history? Careful. Listen well, Granddaughter. Death hates to be outsmarted.*"

"Omma! What the hell? Trying to kill yourself?" Sally snatched the pillow Omma was pressing against her face.

"*Mwoya?*" Kyong Ah coughed and gulped, flushing her lungs oxygen red. "Don't worry. No, don't call nurse. I'm okay."

Sally sat on the edge of the bed. "You're soaked."

Kyong Ah shivered. She tucked her crow wings beneath the sheet. They felt strong enough to fly up a mountain and ride a pillow to the other side. The pilot run filled her air sacs with gratitude.

"I dreamed I climbed mountain. And saw your great-*halmoni.* Air was so thin." The fear on daughter's face told mother loud and clear.

No matter how terrible the pain or veggie the brain, your maknae *won't be able to let you go.*

Maybe she should ask Leng, familiar enough with Death to be on a first name basis. No, she couldn't put her friend in such a risky position. Better to charm Doc Gokul, or better yet, a baby doc into writing stronger scripts for sleep and pain so the bye-bye responsibility would be hers alone. And she'd better squirrel away enough anti-nausea meds to keep her from throwing up the Big House sleep elves.

"You're moving back in with me, Omma. Yumi says you're here because of moving out too early."

"Your know-it-all sister. That's not reason. I'm here because of chemo side effects."

"Whatever. You're staying with me. I mean it."

"Maybe for couple days. Then I go home. I can only sleep in my own bed."

"Save your breath." Sally swallowed. "You're stuck with me."

Kyong Ah had barely settled back at Sally's when she got a call from Flatland.

"Mrs. Choi? It's Nurse Bones from Doctor Gokul's office. We've got a bit of bad news for you."

Kyong Ah's chest tightened. "More cancer? Don't sugar pill me."

"No, it's about your financing. Billing just informed us that we can't provide your next treatment until they receive a cashier's check for at least half of what you owe."

Kyong Ah's lungs shriveled. "My kids said they already made a payment."

"Apparently not enough for us to proceed. I'm so sorry. Maybe the payment hasn't been logged in the system yet. I'll keep checking to find out."

"Why you not tell me earlier?"

"I got a burr under my saddle and I'm mad enough to strangle Billing myself. We've already received your chemo meds."

All that work building up her strength and appetite. She stared up at Sally's ceiling. A spotted spider worked her web.

How many times has your careful work been torn apart, Sister Spider?

"How much money you talking about?"

"You have to speak to Billing for specifics."

"They got meanies there. I rather get bad news from you guys first." Mutant cells did a funky end zone dance. Sleeping pills sprouted chorus girl legs.

You don't want me, Poison Generals? I don't want you either.

Kyong Ah's hands crow winged.

"I'll talk to Doctor Gokul as soon as he gets back from leave to see if there's anything we can do from this end. Timing is crucial to success. We hate to push back treatments."

"Flatland do this to your other patients or just me?" Kyong Ah asked, as if shared membership in Club Cancer made such indignities more tolerable.

"Oakland needs single payer. But no way with Bush-whackers at the wheel. Don't get me started. Let's focus on your recovery. Doing your breathing exercises? Eating your anti-oxidant vegetables, fruits and beancake?"

"Yes, I'm nursing aide, remember?" Kyong Ah caught herself using the present tense. Like she still had a job and occupation.

"Hang in there, Mrs. Choi. We'll get you back in here as soon as we can."

Kyong Ah closed her cell.

All that puking for nothing. And now cheated out of the privilege of puking. No money, no generals.

Her lungs clenched. She lay down and held the bottle of sleeping pills over her heart. So they could bond to her like newborns. As Minsoo and Seungsoo had.

43. PRACTICE

Stuck back at Sally's again, Kyong Ah caught an episode of *Dae Jang Kum,* hoping the sumptuous palace banquet prep scenes would arouse her appetite. She quilted a blanket decorated with sea creatures that she'd begun for Yumi's baby when her cell rang.

"Leng? How you been?"

"Kyong, guess what? Pockmark sold out to Covehaven!"

"*Aiguh!* Boy was right. What happened?"

"Boss got beat at Reno blackjack table trying to win money to repay his gambling debts. Maybe to Macao gangsters. Maybe to Hong Kong Triad. Who knows? Anyway, Covehaven own us now. Everybody have to re-interview for job."

"Terrible! When? That damn Pockmark."

"In next couple weeks. If we mess up interview— *piang!* Out on street looking for job. At this age. You lucky you got out in time."

"If I survive, I need my job back."

"At this *gausee* place? Don't be clazy. Listen to me. This is Pockmark gift to you that he not mean to give. Maybe you can get unemployment without having to quit. And qualify for MediCal. Kyong, what's wrong?"

Kyong Ah sucked in snot. "They cut off chemos until I pay. MediCal just rejected me. I don't know. Even if I reapply with new layoff info they still might not approve me in time. I'm good as dead. And bald, too."

"*Aiyah*, don't talk like that! Hair will grow back. Know it's hard, but try to be positive. Help you recover faster."

"That's just lie we tell our patients."

"Hey, that lie is true. You feel like eating yet? We go diem sum. My treat."

"Maybe later. I don't want to throw up your money."

"You still eating that Korean medicine ricecake, right? Maybe take care of you until MediCal come through. Sorry I not call sooner." Leng's voice cracked. "My old guy Jimmy's not doing so good either. All those days marching in cheap PLA boots screw up his feets and bones."

"So sorry. Anything I can do, Leng?"

"Pray to Guanyin Mercy Goddess for us. I pray to her for you, too. I got to go. I come visit you one of these days."

"Take care of yourself, Leng. Don't work too hard."

The women signed off, one returning to threading elastic through a flannel pajama pant waistband and the other to quilting a blanket she prayed she'd live to see the baby outgrow.

Later that evening, Kyong Ah swallowed fast, pocketing the rest of an MJ *ddeok* when the doorbell rang. Yumi and Agi waved through the peephole. Kyong Ah's heart quickened as she opened the door and Yumi handed her the new granddaughter.

"*Eomeo!* She's heavy. What cheeks! What yummy fat legs! *Annyeong,* Ji-Eun-ah."

The baby's eyes flew from Kyong Ah to Yumi. Her mouth turned upside down. She shrieked in terror.

"What's wrong, Baby-yah? Bald *halmoni* too ugly? Look at Omma and Apa instead." Kyong Ah returned the baby to Yumi. Ji-Eun seized Yumi's pinkie like flotsam from a shipwreck.

Kyong Ah put on the kettle for tea and opened the fridge. Almost empty. Then the freezer.

Ssuk *is pinenut, MJ is black sesame. Or is it opposite?*

Rather than testing whether Yumi would be a happy or meany *ddeoljaengi* pothead if accidently stoned, Kyong Ah closed the fridge, fanned sesame rice crackers across a plate and returned.

"Her hair so thick." Kyong Ah ran her hand over her own skull. "One day maybe she'll remember meeting a bald lady monk."

"You really look like Sally now, Omma."

"No, Sally looks like *me.*" Kyong Ah chuckled at her own joke until her teeth sounded like a grinning squeegee. She wiggled her pinkie and the baby grabbed it.

Only Kwan Seum Bosal knows if you'll be around to see what she chooses during destiny game at her one-year-old party. An eternity from now.

Kyong Ah winced.

Yumi stood the baby up in her lap. "Her full name is Ji-Eun Amihan Min De La Cruz."

Kyong Ah drew in a wheezy breath. "Long as shooting star's tail. Amihan is Pilipino, right Agi?"

"Yep. After my mom's mom."

"Thinking about calling her Ji-Am for short," said Yumi.

"Or Jam Jam," said Agi, his coo tickling a smile from the baby.

"Jam Jam? I like it. You staying home from work with her, Yumi-ah?"

"For another month or so. Then Agi's going to take over for a month."

"Daddy helping out? So nice."

So American.

"Isn't she beautiful? Why didn't we do this sooner?" Yumi played peek-a-boo and the baby laughed. Kyong Ah raised her eyebrows and Agi, his shoulders. Because Yumi had to discover motherhood late, the Frank Sinatra "My Way."

"Oh, before I forget." Kyong Ah fetched the baby quilt that she'd barely finished. Tropical fish swam across ocean blues and seaweed greens. Despite the wheezies and countless breaks, she'd cudgeled it lamb soft.

"Beautiful, Omma." Yumi smiled with Jae Pil's dark eyes, hurting Kyong Ah's heart. Yumi fingered the blanket. "Remember that purple cosmos quilt you made for me? What ever happened to it?"

"Who knows with all the moving around we did?"

Poor Yumi-yah, longing for what is gone and not appreciating what is in hand. Perhaps you'll remember me almost as fondly as you do your apa *after spiders spin webs in my mouth. Dead are easier to cherish than living that do bad stuff right to your face.*

Agi went to heat up a bottle for the baby. Harshness crept into Yumi's eyes.

Kyong's shoulders bent.

Oh, oh, here it comes. She enjoys kicking me when no one's around to see.

"Why didn't you stay with Sally after chemo instead of scaring us all? And what's this about you trying to smother yourself with a pillow?" Yumi's neck veins throbbed.

"That what your sister said? She's wrong. Ever try to sleep in hospital? Pillow blocks out noise and lights."

Yumi's eyes filled. "Agi's mother is already gone. Jam Jam doesn't need to lose her only surviving *halmoni*."

As if picking up their negative vibe, the baby began to cry. Kyong Ah made bunny ears with crow wing hands. After a moment Jam Jam rewarded her with a giggle that made her want to give Cancer Goddess the slip and stick around.

"Let's not fight, Yumi-yah. Let me enjoy granddaughter."

May your daughter be more forgiving of you than you are of me. May memory of my mistakes grow soft as this quilt.

"Adoption people say anything about her parents?"

Yumi winced. "Her mom is a sixteen-year-old who wasn't ready. The father's a mystery. They treat single mothers like criminal sluts over there, Omma."

Kyong Ah nodded. *"Eung."*

Like you did me, after I threw Apa's stuff in street. For cars to cudgel soft.

Kyong Ah chuckled remembering tire treads on Jae Pil's belongings.

Yumi looked like she wanted to say more. Kyong touched Left Lung and shuddered.

Go ahead, Daughter. You won't have such a handy punch-

ing bag when I'm gone.

As if they shared the same bloodline Yumi's eyes narrowed like her adopted daughter's. "I'm sure you'll beat this illness and be at Jam Jam's college graduation. But have you thought about where you want to be buried? There's a plot waiting at Evergreen beside Apa. He asked me to make the arrangements near the end." Her eyes watered. "Like I said, no need to decide right away. But just so you know. Oh, by the way, Agi and I never made it down to Namwon or Dolsando to look for family graves. Maybe next time. Guess Evergreen will have to serve as our family cemetery here."

Kyong Ah sighed and knuckled her chest with her fist. "That's alright, Yumi. Make Evergreen give you your money back. I want you guys to scatter my ashes from Golden Gate Bridge. Your *apa* and I traveled together for a while. But we walked separately even longer." She paused. "Not everything was bad. He gave me you kids. But fog or sun, Golden Gate is best place to fly from."

"Let me know if you change your mind. Like I said, it's already taken care of."

Agi returned and gave the bottle to Yumi who said, "Want to feed her, Omma?"

"No, watching you three together makes me happy." Kyong Ah kissed the baby's forehead. The baby sucked rhythmically, closing her eyes. Her head grew damp. Yumi wrapped her in the quilt like a *mandu* dumpling. Kyong Ah kissed her silk cheek.

Jam Jam-ah. Release sorrow of past. Beautiful Country lets you start over.

"When's your next treatment, Omma?"

"Hospital will let me know when it's scheduled." Kyong Ah struggled to keep her lying face smooth. One *soju* night that big-mouthed Minsoo had let slip that he was pissed at Yumi for not kicking in more money so she could restart chemo sooner. Then Kyong Ah had had to apologize to her son for cursing him out for bothering Yumi about it.

"Promise me you'll stay with Sally until you've really recovered from treatments." Yumi dried her eyes and packed up the baby's bag.

"Enjoy your baby. They grow up so fast." Kyong Ah coughed hard to dislodge the phlegm and regret. "I love you. And Jam Jam. And Agi."

"I love you, too. Omma." Yumi hugged her omma breathless. Harder than any time since before her parents had split up.

Kyong Ah honked her nose into a tissue. And left well enough alone.

After they'd gone, Kyong Ah discovered that Agi had washed and dried the dishes. That nice man somehow found prickly Yumi pleasing. Perhaps they'd grow old together. She fetched the half-eaten *ddeok* from her pocket, plucked off the lint and chewed thoughtfully.

Well, you got to hold Yumi's new baby Jam Jam. One soul enters, one soul exits. Don't be greedy.

Kyong Ah splayed her fingers to uncramp them from the crow wings they'd unconsciously made whenever Yumi spoke. Like Braxton-Hicks contractions that prepared moms for birth, Yoneda San ones prepped Jam Jam's *halmoni* for bye-bye.

44. RE-UP

Kyong Ah pushed Pillow Monster from her face. Gulped in the dense night air and sat up disoriented.

Still trapped at Sally's. Disrupting your maknae*'s life.*

She massaged the shrieking pain in Right Lung. Her chest lurched.

Right Lung? "No, no, no!"

"*Yaah,* Omma. Another nightmare? What time is it?"

"I'm okay. Go back to sleep."

Sally groaned and flipped over, pulling the covers.

Heart thundering in her ears, Kyong Ah waited until Seungsoo's snores returned. She tiptoed to the bathroom, sucked her inhaler and turned on the light, rubbing her skull and pressing the bruises beneath her eyes. She lifted Sally's oversized black T-shirt and traced her surgery scar.

Before tumor surgery, Left Lung had felt like a dagger was leaning into it; now Right Lung felt like the dagger was twisting. If Cancer Goddess had outsmarted Doc Gokul's saws and shovels and border crossed into Right Lung, who could stop her from setting up camp in Brain's panic room and Bones' hallways? Or wherever White Knights and Sorrow had opened paths?

Kyong Ah's lips flatlined. Grief crab-walked her chest and regret, her marrow. But no tears this time. Just a leaden weariness. Then jaw squared; cheekbones sharpened. If she let her kids pay to restart chemo, they'd soon exhaust their savings on a gamble with bad odds. But not rushing to treat Right Lung meant predicting the optimal time to pull the plug for a successful mission and the least heartache for her kids. She had to move out of Sally's ASAP so she wouldn't get caught in the act of performing the Kevorkian. Plus she didn't want to stain her *maknae's* place with suicide's bad *aek* and *sal*.

Sleep first. Plan later.

In the morning, Kyong Ah served fish egg soup to Sally for breakfast.

"Yummers. What are you doing today, Omma?"

"Maybe go for walk. But can you drop me at unemployment office first so I can apply? They lay off everyone at Golden West. Car keys on TV."

"Sure."

Kyong Ah handed Sally a shopping list, a permission note, her MediCannBee card and cash.

Although afraid they'd kick her out for wheezing too much to sound available for work, Kyong Ah scored a nice caseworker at the unemployment office. If everything checked out, they'd send her an award letter soon. Then she'd give MediBeggar a copy as proof of income and ask them to reboot her app.

She returned to Sally's via Vet's Cab and flopped down. After napping, she inventoried her pills. Practiced her crow wings. Took a jam jar of water for a walk. Poured it over a shapely azalea bush.

Thank you, Yoneda San. Ssuk *ricecake and azaleas are gifts our peoples share.*

She continued around the block, periodically sitting on a curb to catch her breath and massage the new growth in Right Lung and surgery scar in Left. She remembered ballroom dancing with Mrs. Santos. Would Mrs. Santos have ended it if she'd known the second stroke was imminent? Not likely. She would have needed the capacity to kill. What about Mr. Legaspi? All that bragging about surviving this and that battle; he must have killed many enemy soldiers. What would happen when he got too sick to savor Life's *bagoong*? He'd surely go out DIY executioner style. But maybe he'd entrust the final decision to his daughter.

Kyong Ah had seen and touched Death's Face many times. That was the task written in invisible ink at the top of her job description. To not shrink from Death but to push it's probing fingers away as long as possible. Fight failure of heart and lung, kidney and courage. Slow the final descent after the first fall. Soothe screamers and ravers. Find spots in the sunshine for the depressed and withdrawn. Turn, turn, turn away flesh-eating bedsores and percussive bruise blossoms. Staunch the flood of blood and piss. Expunge gangrene, sepsis, and bone rot.

Some days she had stalled Death until nurses, docs, and EMTs arrived. With compressions and breaths, sound and touch. Rocking and praying. Other days she alone bore the job of honor guard alongside a patient's last step into the first step of the lonely journey. She eased fear and shock from faces into death masks of serenity and relief as shells stiffened. She washed effluvia and surrender down the hazmat chute and respectfully dressed them for family members' final visits. Before releasing then to transport and funeral home magicians.

Yes, she knew Death intimately. And still it surprised her.

Pain twisted Right Lung. White Knight memory scratched her throat; how about one for the road?

Work first, enjoy later.

She added fresh columns into her notebook for breathing and walking exercises. Tracking her ADLs lifted her mood and made her feel productive. Less like a useless sack of stones. She tallied the times she noticed pains in Right vs. Left Lungs. She took a nap and woke up scratching her inner arm. Her heart dropped at the sight; Tattoo's Left Lung was pale, almost white, and Right Lung, blotchy.

Magic Vermilion Wings, thanks for absorbing Cancer Goddess' blows. Help me.

That's when she got a needle sharp idea. She pulled out her cell.

"Van Le? This is Mrs. Chang. Don't know if you remember, but I got tattoo from you of lungs with Magic Vermilion Bird's wings."

"Of course I remember. How's that cough, Mrs. Chang?"

"Still got. But tattoo faded. First on left side. Now on right, too. You know why?"

"Shouldn't have faded period. But if it did, both sides should have done so at the same time. Come in and I'll take a look. Depending on what's wrong, I can throw in a discount if you need them re-inked."

"Okay. How about later tonight?"

"Good. See you then."

After they signed off, Kyong Ah found a couple Korean suicide sites online whose young depressives made her weepy. But those sad kids posted smart end-it tips re killer cocktails and sequencing. Smoother than the fiery pesticides the farmers used to down when their kids abandoned them, chasing the Miracle on the Han River. Rasping, she surfed tattoo sites and found a blog for breast cancer survivors. That gave her a pink ribbon of an idea.

That evening, Sally set down grocery bags. "Hey, Omma. MediCannBee folks were out of your Maui Wowie. They recommended this Morning Glory strain for you. Want me to soak the rice for *ddeok?*"

"*Eung.* Your kimchi fried rice is ready. Can you take me over to Van Le's to fix my tattoo after dinner?"

Sally's brows leapt. "Why?"

"Colors faded. I got appointment tonight."

"Omma, how many times I got to tell you it's over between us?"

"See how weird tattoo looks?" Raising her sleeve, she winced, as Right Lung twisted. "Van said he can fix. Eat first." Kyong Ah narrowed her eyes so her *maknae* wouldn't detect craftiness hiding there.

Sally shoveled down dinner. Switched out several studs. Sniffed her pits and changed to a clean black shirt.

The City's lights beckoned as Sally drove Omma's Hyundai over the Bay Bridge. Studying the Pacific's dark waters, Kyong Ah prayed her kids wouldn't get busted when they released her ashes from the Golden Gate. With all the jumpers, hidden cameras, and restrictions, death had grown fiendishly complicated.

"Seungsoo-ah, how about you get tattoo, too? On Internet many *omma* and *ddal* get tattoos for good lucks to fight breast cancer."

"That what you want, Omma?" Sally gunned the gas. Like she needed another scar from Nesy. Yet the vision of Van's drill poking her was a turn-on.

Kyong Ah waited for Sally to lock the car so they could enter together. She wanted to read their faces. They walked in. Before Van could open his mouth, Kyong Ah grabbed his hand.

"Thanks for seeing us so soon, Van Le. My name not really Chang. I am Kyong Ah Choi. And this is my daughter Sally. You know her, right?"

"Yes. Please have a seat." His eyes softened at her but darkened at Sally. Kyong Ah's *nunchi* pulsed.

He still has feelings for my baby girl.

Van scowled at Kyong Ah's tat. "Sorry. Don't know how this happened. We use the best inks. You didn't wash it too soon, did you?"

"No. I do exactly what you tell me." Right Lung torqued, but she rushed ahead. "I got lung cancer. I believe your tattoo helped me survive surgery on Left Lung and chemos. But it got wounded during battle."

"Sorry to hear about your illness. Glad the tattoo was of service. What do you need Mrs. Chang, I mean, Choi?"

"Please make color like before. Then give one to my girl, too. She's my support group. Like breast cancer moms and daughters. Right, Seungsoo-ah?"

"Sure. After Van fixes yours." Heat climbed Sally's cheeks.

"Thank you. I appreciate." Kyong Ah kissed Sally's blush, sucked her inhaler and got comfortable. She removed her headscarf since this was the one place outside the cancer ward where she'd look perfectly normal. He didn't blink.

What a nice young, well, man.

Kyong Ah tried to sneak a peek at his chest, imagining how he might look as a girl. Until the drill and ink made her swoon. That's when she remembered Sally's drawer of kitchenware and toys and realized that her youngest must have turned the family *yut* sticks into some kind of porno store game. Kyong Ah sighed loudly.

Sally leafed through design albums, periodically peeking at Van. Kyong Ah alternated between clenching her teeth against the drill and watching Sally and Van eye each other when they thought she wasn't looking.

Help my Seungsoo find love. Please Kwan Seum Bosal. You began as a man and ended as a woman so you understand.

Mother and daughter switched chairs. Kyong Ah watched lungs and wings emerge on Sally's upper left arm, opposite the one emblazoned with the phoenix and broken heart. Now Kyong Ah had another set of wings. Powerful enough to push down sorrow. Summon breath and life.

Sally's eyes salted. "Omma, how do you write 'Omma Forever' in Hangeul? Can you copy her Korean, Van?"

"I'll try. Go ahead, Mrs. Choi."

Kyong Ah wiped away tears and wrote in Hangeul on

Van's sketch pad. He practiced a few times; Sally chose her favorite one. Which reminded Kyong Ah of Joseon Dynasty banners flying into battle. Van began drilling letters in a semi-circle above Sally's fresh lungs. The buzz was hypnotic.

At the end he gave them instructions for care. Sally and Kyong Ah jostled to pay the bill.

"Forget it. Your money's no good here, Mrs. Choi."

Van nodded at the broken heart tat Sally had gotten to commemorate their break-up. "Nice work. BY's, right?" He studied her eyes.

Sally let the color climb her cheeks and did not look away. "Right. Unique as a fingerprint, I guess." The phoenix and vines Van had given her strummed her arm and shoulders.

"You are super nice, Van Le. Just like my Sally. She take good care of me." Kyong Ah smiled coy as a new bride. "By the way, you got girlfriend?"

"Omma!"

Van Le grinned. "Don't mince words, do you, Mrs. Choi? Glad to finally to meet you." He smiled, showing off the chipped tooth that hurt Sally's heart. Mary J's "I Can Love You" swiveled to the top of the playlist.

Kyong Ah hugged Van, whispering in his ear. "Be nice to my Seungsoo. She's good person. Make a good, whatchucallit? Partner." Van shook his head, a faint smile on his lips. Kyong Ah shook his hand and left to give them some space.

"See you," said Sally, gingerly traced the border of her new mother-daughter tat.

"Any time. Hope your mom feels better soon." Van

smiled his chip. They hugged for a deliciously long time. Sally stumbled out. A California poppy sprouted in her heart as she drove them back across the bridge. She'd pay off the bet with Manny tomorrow and figure out a way back into Van's life. Or some-lucky-body's. With Omma's blessing.

"What'd you say to Van, Omma?"

"That's conpeedenchul. He's my tattoo doctor."

"*Yaah!* You're shameless. And about as subtle as an eighteen-wheeler truck." Sally grinned at her puffy new tat, praying it would wing fresh luck to them both.

Kyong Ah turned up the radio and dug her fingers into her hands. To outpain the pain twisting Right Lung. She prayed the tattoo would give her time to finish the things she still had to do. Her eyes grew moist.

At least you gave your maknae *your blessing and love, a nudge. Please Kwan Seum Bosal. Don't let her and Minsoo die alone.*

45. GIFT

The tattoo tune-up opened up Kyong Ah's air and ki passageways. As they worked on a new batch of *ddeok*, Sally handed her a brochure. "Look, Omma. Training for minority- and women-owned businesses. You're both, a twofer."

"Doing what?"

"Dope *ddeok*, of course."

"I'm too sick and got no capitals."

"What if we did it together?"

"You finished two years at Raney College. You can do better than kitchen work."

"I'd help until you're back on your feet."

"What about sexy store job?"

"I'd keep it, of course. Check out the first workshop, okay? Lots of people your age begin new careers now."

"They'll take away my unemployment. When's class start?"

"Month from now."

An eternity.

"They refund money if got to cancel?"

"Let me worry about that."

"I'm ready to move back to my own place."

"Bad idea, Omma. Don't want you to end up in ER again. Want Yumi to kick my ass? Just wish that freakin' MediCal would hurry up so you could restart chemo. Let's see your tat."

"Perfect. How about yours?"

"Ditto." Sally blew on her new tat, making the wings more lustrous.

Kyong Ah waged a relentless campaign to move back to her own apartment until she wore her kids down. Sally helped cart Omma's stuff back, while leaving behind some *ddeok* in the freezer, out of temptation's way. Mickey continued to help out with dinners. With Yumi's editing input Kyong Ah reopened her MediCal app with Rashida Leonard. Whose rough cough sounded four tobacco fields worse than when they'd last met.

Have you claimed another couch, Cancer Goddess?

After returning home from MediCal, Kyong Ah found her first unemployment check in the mail. She pumped her fist. Napped. Deposited the check in the bank, cashing part to reimburse Seungsoo and Minsoo for expenses. She used the rest to make a payment on her Flatland bill and managed to wrangle an appointment with Doc Gokul to check out Right Lung.

She tossed and turned half the night wondering if she should bring Sally along. Before dread unlocked the gate for Dead Husband.

Wolf licked her earlobes. She swooned. Ovaries flared; womb plumped. Wolf's loofah tongue raked her skin.

"Can't breathe. Stop stealing my breath!"

"*Close, you're very close to joining me. For eternity, Wife. You heard our daughter. Everything's ready for you. I'll show you around. I'm quite popular. Let me demonstrate why.*"

"*No, leave me alone!*"

"*You're almost mine. Why wait?*"

She exhaled. Opened her fist and stroked the beast's furry head, scratching behind his ears. "*Jae Pil-ah, for old time's sake, please be honest. Can you see how and when I will end? Be truthful.*"

"*Truthful?*" Wolf sighed. "*No, I don't know. But I can help you in other ways. Stop fighting me. Just let me love you. Now that you've reached the end, can't you see that no one could ever take my place? Though many have tried.*"

A magpie trilled. Cicadas sang drunken love songs. An owl blinked. Kyong Ah sighed. "*So you can't help me. Thanks for not lying. Yes, let's stop fighting. I release you. Now you must release me, Jae Pil-ah. You have Yumi to look after your grave.*"

"*And you have Seungsoo and Minsoo. But Yumi hasn't visited me for so long.*"

"*She's got a new baby now. A girl.*"

"*Really?*"

"*How do you not know?*"

"*I've been busy.*" He purred. "*Anyways, let them all come visit us. From now on let's spend Chuseok and New Year together.*"

"*Jae Pil, I don't need anyone to visit me at graveyard. Children either hold us in their maum or they don't. What's done is done. They'll scatter my ashes off Golden Gate Bridge. American style. Goodbye, Jae Pil.*"

"*Don't be so hard, Woman. How about good luck hump for road?*"

"Let go of me. Farewell."

Kyong shook herself awake and out of his clutches. She sat up. Coughed. Soaked a tissue with her blood.

That Jae Pil. What a scoundrel. But he's right. End feels soon. Take your maknae *with you to Doc Gokul's.*

Kyong Ah bowed deeply before her shrine to Kwan Seum Bosal. She then wheezed her way to the bathroom. Coughed into a fistful of fresh tissues. Examined the bloody sputum. A thicker, bluer shade of red than Left Lung's distress flares. She leaned into the mirror.

You're dying. Vermilion Bird can slow Cancer Goddess. But not stop her. Don't piss away what time you have left.

Kyong Ah flushed away the blood. Returning to bed, she massaged her lungs. Sad, yet somehow settled.

Mother and daughter sat in red leather chairs across from Doctor Gokul to hear the verdict on the X-rays and CT scans.

"The cancer has metastasized to your right lung and a troublesome mass has appeared in your left lung near where we operated. I am so sorry." The doc's cheeks were gaunt.

"I knew it." Kyong Ah closed her eyes and pressed Right Lung; Cancer Goddess pushed back.

"No way!" Sally burst into tears, mopping her face with a magenta and black paisley bandana. "The cancer wouldn't have spread if she'd continued her chemo treatments right away. This is jacked!"

The doctor's large hands fumbled helplessly. "Treatments might have helped slow the process, but this looks like a particularly virulent cancer."

"I reapplied for MediCal and they should approve it in three months," Kyong Ah said, quietly.

"You always told me not to sugar pill you, Mrs. Choi."

"Right, Doctor. I've cared for many cancer patients."

"You may not have enough time for your MediCal to be approved. Even if you could re-start treatment immediately, we can't predict the outcome." His dark eyes told her nothing could help.

"This is bullshit! How can Flatland deny my mother chemo?"

"*Yaah,* please don't swear at doctor, Seungsoo-ah. This is my fate."

Too much han. *Your father. My White Knights and foolishness.*

"It's your call, Mrs. Choi. If you need a couple of days to think about it, that's perfectly fine. Did you get a chance to check out some support group meetings, Sally?"

Sally scratched her Omma Forever tat. "Not yet. How bad, Doctor?"

His eyes moved from Sally's to Kyong Ah's. "Stage Three bordering on Four, I'm afraid."

"No!" Sally teared up and pulled out the bandana again.

"*Eung.* How much time I have?"

"We can't predict the exact time. But from past experience I'd estimate zero to six months. You and your daughter should talk to a caseworker immediately about hospice care and other options. I'll write you hospice and homecare orders. We'll do our best to line up medications and an oxygen tank for you, based on what you and your family decide."

Right Lung contorted. Left Lung throbbed. Marrow tingled. Oncogenes twirled in a mad, mutant dance.

Hospice means backdoor to Big House. Hear that, Cancer Goddess? You're taking me to Sorrow River. Ddeok *and tattoo, surgery and chemo only slowed you.*

"Thank you for everything. I really appreciate." Her blood thickened and slowed. She smelled freshly dug soil. Black and damp with nutrients. Swooning, she looked up at the doctor for mooring. She frowned.

"What's wrong, Doctor? You don't look so good."

His dark eyes flashed and turned midnight black. "No sugar pills, right?"

"Right."

"Seem to have contracted stomach cancer. Like my mother."

Left Lung tugged around old wounds and new clusters. She felt Seungsoo tense at her side. "I'm so sorry. Flatland taking care of you?"

"No, UCSF. My alma mater. Don't worry. I've already briefed my colleagues here on your case, and I'll continue working with you as long as possible. That's how we do, right, Mrs. Choi? As long as body, mind, and spirit are willing."

"Yes, but please take it easy." She patted the hand that had wielded daggers in her defense.

"Thank you. Let us know as soon as your MediCal comes through. Then Nurse Bones will contact Billing and make sure to set your treatment in motion. Take care."

As Cancer Goddess expanded her domain and sucked away her breath, Kyong Ah began to rely on oxygen tanks.

She used Monster Tank with a long tube when she was at home and the portable Baby Tank for when Sally, Minsoo, or Evan took her on outings to Lake Merritt, the Berkeley Marina or Yumi's. Kyong Ah soaked up Jam Jam's every sound and move, wondering if the baby would retain any *halmoni* memories. Yumi did not offer her house as hospice site or to pick up more expenses than her less endowed siblings did. But she did sheath her dagger tongue and for that Kyong Ah was grateful and returned the favor.

While her kids paid for her oxygen, Kyong Ah hawkeyed her sleeping and pain pills and rehearsed exit scenarios. She strengthened her crow wings while watching Korean dramas, adding pillow exercises when Sally and Mickey weren't around. While many of her former cancer patients had stopped eating and had to be put on drips as the disease progressed, Kyong Ah's MJ *ddeok* nurtured her appetite, though for admittedly smaller amounts. But she had to grant herself lots of time to do even the simplest tasks, like washing a few dishes or running a brush around the toilet bowl. Some days she sucked up the pain to complete tasks; other days she zonked out on painkillers to compensate for working too hard the previous day.

One morning, Kyong Ah woke up feeling almost like her old self, strong enough for a small project. Should she get a Korean cookbook for each offspring and stash them in the gift bags in storage for after she was gone? Left Lung throbbed.

Run errands with Baby Tank out to storage place? That's how you got in trouble before. Let go of that attachment. Time to subtract, not add to task list.

Instead, Kyong Ah called Sally at work with a shopping

list to make *ddeok* and fish soup for the coming week and a treat for tonight. Then she remembered to stash a couple Depends near a small packet of mercy pills in the bottom drawer of the dresser so Sally wouldn't get stuck cleaning her parting I&Os.

That evening, she talked Sally through how to make crab *jjikae.*

"This is kickin,' Omma." Sally sucked meat out of a blue shelled crab leg.

"Good. Promise you teach your kids how to cook Korean food when they grow up."

"Kids?"

"And you guys all get together for big holidays when I'm gone. Tell Minsoo and Evan what to bring so they not come empty handed and bum off you girls. Minsoo puts too much salt in his stews. But I appreciate him and Evan bringing us meals and giving you break. Your brother's good cook."

"True that. But we got to get him to teach Evan a couple chicken recipes so he can lighten up on the Popeyes'. That stuff's a heart stopper."

Kyong Ah clucked her tongue. "*Eung.* But it's Evan's way of sharing." She grabbed Sally's hand. "Remember to pull plug."

"*Yaah,* got it, Omma! For the zillionth time. No veggie. Ashes over the bridge. Oakland side."

"Good. If you forget what to do, check list in first book on top shelf. List not there yet. But it will be at right time."

"Your Korean American dictionary? Alright, alright. But you look fantastic, Omma. I think Doc Gokul was wrong about your prognosis. Wait till MediCal kicks in and knocks out the cancer. You just got to hang on until then. You're going to beat this thing. Then your Dream Ddeok business is going to kick *eongdeongi.*"

"Maybe." Kyong Ah smiled, not mentioning the number of patients she'd seen perk up the week, day or even hour before their end. Memories of Halmoni and Mrs. Santos and so many other spirits crowded her chest. Like villagers dancing in the snow beneath the lunar new year's first full moon. Even as Cancer Goddess and Kwan Seum Bosal floated among them, their billowy sleeves fluttering. Kyong Ah marveled at human beings' capacity to deliver final thanks and farewells.

"I love you, Seungsoo-ah."

"I love you, too, Omma. See you tomorrow night, too. Mickey's got a hot date. Hope he doesn't blow it. Call if you need anything."

"*Eung.* You should be going on dates, too, Seung-soo-ah. I'm so sorry for dragging you down."

"Whatever, Omma. See you tomorrow night."

After Sally left, Kyong Ah chewed a *ddeok* thoughtfully. The more breaths she drew, the darker the circles beneath her *maknae*'s eyes grew. Then again, her crazy illness had brought her family together in ways impossible to pull off before Cancer Goddess descended. Could she have predicted a truce with knife-tongued Yumi? Or that Minsoo and Evan would share time cooking for her? Or that her baby lesbian Seungsoo would grow up and serve as her nursing aide with such compassion?

Thank you Cancer Goddess for giving me opportunity and enough time to learn. Thank you Kwan Seum Bosal for mercy and compassion to soften road and lighten load. Please watch over my family after I've passed over.

Kyong Ah laughed. Then coughed. Then winced from the pain and exertion. She laughed again. Soft as a secret.

She found her hands stiffening into crow wings prepping for flight. She relaxed them and considered summoning the pleasure of her White Knights. They beckoned from a hiding place inside a bag of dried seaweed in the back of a kitchen cabinet. Kyong Ah inhaled memory of forbidden smokes she and girlfriends enjoyed behind docked fishing boats. Great days of youthful anticipation unfurling towards a limitless future.

Kyong Ah bit her lip. Shook her head. Waved off the knights, Dead Husband, and every other interloper she hoped to leave behind in the next life. Right Lung's pain twisted and Left Lung's leaned. She coughed up a thick bloom of blood. She double-checked to make sure her will and the storage locker key and card were in the right place. After putting on a relaxed, plum-colored cotton Korean top and pants, she slowly drank down the pills she'd prepared. She sighed with sadness and gratitude. The green tea in her favorite glazed celadon cup was refreshing as Rock Mountain Island spring water. After voiding her bladder, she pulled on a diaper and then panties over it, smiling at the memory of Mrs. Santos' miracle.

Kyong Ah lay down on her bed. Big eye swelled like an ocean wave; small eye relaxed in meditation. She pulled Pillow Monster close.

Thank you Yoneda San. I can take it from here. Halmoni, please sing seagull loud so I can find you.

GLOSSARY

Note: Unless otherwise identified as indicated below, words defined in this list are Korean.

Additionally, words marked with an asterisk* employ spelling from before the institution of the Revised Romanization of Korean (국어의로마자 표기법.)

C: Cantonese
I: Ilocano
J: Japanese
K: Korean
S: Spanish
T: Tagalog
V: Vietnamese

adeul	아들	*son*
adobo		*stew of meat or seafood marinated in vinegar, soy and garlic (T)*
aek	액	*bad luck*
aein	애인	*sweetheart, lover*
agassi	아가씨	*miss, young lady*
*-ah/ iah**	-아/야	*suffix that turns first name into diminutive*
*aiguh**	아이고!	*Oh dear! Good grief! What a disaster!*
aiyah	哎吔!	*Oh dear! Good grief! What the heck? (C)*
ajumah	아줌마	*auntie, an older woman*
ajeossi	아저씨	*uncle, an older man*
*allasoh**	알았어	*I know, informal*

amá		*father, papa (I)*
annyeong	안녕	*peace; informal greeting, from peace be with you*
apa	아빠	*papa, informal*
ate		*elder sister (T)*
baahk gaap ngaahn	白鴿眼	*pigeon-eyed snob, elitist (C)*
babo	바보	*fool*
babsang	밥상	*table for dining when seated on floor*
bagoong		*fermented shrimp, anchovy or fish paste (T)*
bánh mì		*Vietnamese baguette sandwich (V)*
bánh tét		*sweet rice and stuffing wrapped in banana leaf and steamed (V)*
banmal	반말	*informal speech; rough talk*
bbongjjak	뽕짝	*popular music from 1930s with "bbongjjak-jjak bbong-jjak" beat*
bibingka		*ricecake dessert made with coconut and butter (T)*
bonghwang	봉황	*phoenix*
bulgogi	불고기	*"fire meat," barbequed marinated beef*
byeong	병	*sickness, disease*
byeongshin	병신	*cripple; un-PC slang for fool*
chauhai /	臭閪 (蟹)	*smelly cunt*
nei ge mama ge	你嘅媽媽嘅	*yo' mama's (C)*
daemacho	대마초	*weed*
dambae	담배	*tobacco, cigarette*
ddae	때	*dirt, grime*
ddal	딸	*daughter*
ddeok	떡	*ricecake*
ddeoljaengi	떨쟁이	*pothead*
ddong	똥	*shit*
diu nei	閪你	*screw you (C)*
doenjang	된장	*fermented soybean paste*

dol	돌	one-year-old birthday party
eomeo	어머!	Oh my!
eongdeongi	엉덩이	butt
eung	응	yes, informal
fan okey	返屋企	go home (C)
fongpei	放屁	fart (C)
gangpae	깡패	gang
gausee/ lou	狗屎/ 佬	dogshit/ dude (C)
geulssae	글쎄	well, let me see
geumanhae	그만해	stop it
gooksoo*	국수	noodle soup
gordo		fat; can be an affectionate nickname or an insult – fatso, fatty (S)
haam ha	鹹蝦	fermented shrimp paste (C)
halaboji*	할아버지	grandfather, grandpa
halmoni*	할머니	grandmother, grandma
han	한	grief, regret, grudge
hanna/ deul/ set	하나/둘/셋	one/ two/ three
¡híjole!		Wow! Gosh! Jeez! (S – Mexican)
ibul	이불	comforter
iná		mother, mama (I)
jai	仔 (자)	son, offspring (C & K)
jaji	자지	penis
jaugau	走狗	running dog, lackey (C)
jeot	젓	fermented shrimp, anchovies or fish guts, etc.
jjigae	찌개	stewpot
jjimjilbang	찜질방	public bathhouse that includes hot tubs, saunas, massage tables, heated floors, etc.
jook*	粥 (죽)	rice gruel (C & K)
jujak	주작 & 朱雀	Vermilion Bird of South in Korean and Chinese constellations
kaesaekki	개새끼	son of a bitch
keoji	거지	beggar
keojitmaliya	거짓말이야	it's a lie

ki	기	energy, spirit, breath of creation
kkakdugi kimchi	깍두기김치	radish root kimchi
kkeojeo	꺼져	screw you
komo*	모	paternal aunt
komtang	곰탕	rich soup of boiled beef bones and oxtails
kut*	굿	shamanistic ritual, exorcism
-lah	啦	ending to soften, simplify or emphasize preceding statement (C)
leche flan		caramel custard (T)
lola		grandma (T)
lo mein	撈麵	stir fried noodles (C)
lumpia		fried or fresh spring rolls (T)
maeuntang	매운탕	pepper pot soup, often of fish
maknae	막내	youngest child
mắm ruốc		fermented shrimp paste (V)
mandu	만두	dumplings stuffed with meat and vegetables
manong		older brother, term of respect, including for early Pilipino immigrant pioneers (I)
masee	馬屎	horseshit (C)
matyeh	乜嘢	what (C)
maum	마음	heart-mind
meongcheongi	멍청이	fool, idiot
mochi	餅	ricecake (J)
mo muntai	冇問題	no problem (C)
mota		slang for marijuana, weed (S)
mudang	무당	shaman
mwoya	뭐야?	what? informal form
ngaai hou	艾蒿	mugwort (C)
ngaanh fan	眼瞓	go to sleep (C)
nin go	年糕	ricecake (C)
ngo mai	糯米	sweet/ sticky/ glutinous rice
ngow nguk chow fun	牛肉炒粉	beef fried wide rice noodles (C)

nokcha	녹차	green tea
nom	놈	guy, informal; can be rude
noraebang	노래방	rented "song room" where people take turns singing pop tunes with mic over recorded tracks
nunchi	눈치	mind-reader ability, quick-witted; picks up unstated vibes
omma*	엄마	mom, mother, informal
onni*	언니	big sister of a girl or woman
pancit		stir fried noodles with meat or seafood and vegetables (T)
phở		noodle soup with meat or seafood and vegetables in rich broth (V)
piang	砰!	bang! (C)
pinakbet		mixed vegetable stew with bitter melon, often flavored with bagoong (I)
ppalli	빨리	hurry
profe		prof, professor, informal (S)
pupusa		thick corn tortilla filled with beans, cheese and or meat (S - El Salvador)
ramyun*	라면	instant noodles
saam	삼	hemp
saekki	새끼	offspring, young, guy; could be used as a curse word
saekssi	색시	bride, wife, girl; barmaid
sal	살	evil spirit
samcha	삼채	a twelve-beat rhythm cycle comfortable for working, dancing or walking
seefut	屎忽	literally poop-butt, ass (C)
sei malou	死馬騮	dead monkey (C)
seonsaengnim	선생님	Mr.; teacher
sesangeh*	세상에?	What in the world?

sifu	師父 (사부)	master of skill, e.g., martial arts teacher (C & K)
sikkeureo	시끄러!	too noisy, i.e. shut up
soju	소주	distilled spirit made of rice, wheat, barley or potato, etc.
ssibal/ ssibal nom	씨발/ 씨발놈	oh, fuck/ motherfucker
ssuk	쑥	mugwort
sugo	수고	trouble, hardship, great effort
sundubu	순두부	spicy stew of beancake, seafood and vegetables
tai tai/ -tai	太太 & 太	Mrs.; one's wife (C)
taquería		taco shop (S – Mexico)
tatay		papa, father, informal (T)
tontería		the fact of being stupid; stupid thing, something of no value (S – slang)
vato		dude, homeboy (S – Mexico, U.S.)
wa	嘩!	Wow! (C)
yaah*	야!	Hey you! Oh my!
-yah/ iyah	-아/-야	suffix makes name diminutive and calls that person's attention
yangban	양반	lord, nobleman; aristocratic class
yeh*	예	yes
yeoboseyo	여보세요	hello, used at start of phone calls
yo	요	mattress for sleeping on floor
yomogi	ヨモギ	mugwort (J)
yukgaejang	육개장	spicy shredded beef soup
yut	윷	four-stick game, often played at New Year's

ACKNOWLEDGMENTS

Blessed are eldercare workers: for they will be shown mercy and comfort. *Salamat, doh jie, gracias* and straight up thanks! to Bay Area Community Services (BACS) at North Oakland Senior Center, Grand Lake Gardens, The Avenue, the nursing aides of Lawton and Grove skilled nursing facilities in San Francisco, the Emergency Departments of Highland Hospital and UCSF Medical Center, and Oakland Kaiser Hospital's Palliative Care Unit of Internal Medicine, for skill and steady hands, creativity and compassion. To National Network of Career Nursing Assistants, National Association of Health Care Assistants, and Service Employees International Union's United Healthcare Workers, for organizing America's underpaid and underappreciated caregivers and amplifying their voices. To National Domestic Workers Alliance, Chinese Staff and Workers Association, Asian Immigrant Women Advocates, Fuerza Unida, Koreatown Immigrant Workers Alliance, La Mujer Obrera, and Chinese Progressive Association, for supporting homecare and all workers in the fight for dignity and living wages. To family eldercare specialist siblings Matthew, Ernest, and Beth, and their families, Kelly, Annalisa, Antonio, and Antonio, for love during wailing wall nights and open mike memorials. To Ching, Yoon, Toy-Louie and Chan cousins for sharing tales while tending oldsters of fire.

Blessed are angel editors, proofers and production crew: for they weave joy into the warp and woof of story. To Valerie Haynes Perry, editor, coach, and author, for tucks and tailoring, flagging fork-in-the-road decisions and emboldening artists of color by her example. To Luz Guerra, grammar and punctuation queen, writer and running buddy, for red pen wisdom and delighting in Oakland's stew of dialects. To Jai Arun Ravine, book designer, web wizard, and nimble author of daring dreamscapes, for unleashing sword dance artistry and raven wing magic during Rabbit Roar's first leap into the wild. To Kristianna Lee and Grace Nam, bilingual Korean teacher supermoms for glossary duty and love of the mother tongue. To Helen Louie and Patrick Chew for riffs on Cantonese, David Maduli and Hari Alluri for Tagalog meditations, and Luz Guerra for savoring Spanish in its spicy permutations. To Shirin Yim Bridges for early indie advice. To Shasta Grosbier, Kitty Grigsby, Tim Taylor and the printers at Worzalla Press for care, precision and pride in their craft.

Blessed are master mentors: for theirs is the Kingdom of Heaven. Shout out to Voices of Our Nations Arts (VONA) and its founders Elmaz Abinader, Diem Jones, Junot Díaz, and Victor Díaz—and to teachers Suheir Hammad, Chris Abani, Willie Perdomo, David Mura, ZZ Packer, Chitra Divakaruni, and Jimmy Santiago Baca for training generations of novice supplicants. To Kearny Street Workshop for injecting iron into the bloodlines of Asian Pacific American insurrectionist art, foiling eviction and erasure, and aiding and abetting survivors.

Blessed are fellow writers who hunger and thirst for righteousness: for they shall be fed by phat works of their own. To Sara Campos for that close read during days of white flag surrender. To our workshop sisters Linda González, Dorothy Lazard, and Meeta Kaur for generously sharing tales and tools. To Sweat Lodge poetheads David Maduli, Hari Alluri, Cynthia Dewi Oka and Sevé Torres for mouth-puckering chili truths.

Blessed are girlfriend prophets: for they enjoy the healing power of laughter. To *comadres* Myesha Jenkins, Linda Burnham, Letisha Wadsworth, Roma Guy, Diane Jones, Giuliana Milanese, Viola Casares, Petra Mata, Derethia Duval, Margo Okazawa-Rey, Margaret Benson Thompson, and Mina Karimabadi for X-ray vision and unstinting encouragement.

Blessed are musicians who dance through sun and storm: for they are keepers of the fire. To Korean Youth Cultural Center, Jamae Sori/Sister Sound and Ieumsae, Oaktown's village beat bands. To Korea Education and Exposure Program, Nodutol, and Hella Organized Bay Area Koreans/ HOBAK for *buk* barrel drum courage.

Blessed be my bodhisattva family: for they possess the creative power of love. Bear hugs to my daughter Nguyen Louie for freeing the spirits to sing through her illustrations. For her brave new children's tales. For her editor's eye and mama wisdom as the rabbit inside the roar. Appreciation to Nguyen's partner David and kids Lazlo and Siena for lending her to this project. High fives, fist bumps and affection to my son Lung San Louie, family nurse practitioner and sci-fi writer, for timely Buddha/ Tao advice and support during teeth-gnashing times. Finally, love supreme to my man Belvin, videographer, story ware-houseman, and techno-electro-mecánico for sharing eldercare and adventures with writer-the-grouch; without Belvin's fix-it strategies, tiger strength and Scorpio passion all would be ash.

Peace, love and gratitude to all.

Miriam Ching Yoon Louie is a third generation Korean Chinese American writer whose fiction and poetry tickles the bellies of characters until they giggle—or bite. Her non-fiction works, *Sweatshop Warriors and Women's Education in the Global Economy*, feature the voices of immigrant and women of color leaders and movements. Louie was a founding member of the Women of Color Resource Center and served as media coordinator for the women worker organizations Asian Immigrant Women Advocates and Fuerza Unida. She trained in fiction and poetry with Voices of Our Nations Arts. See miriamchingyoonlouie. com. While tending to her ailing family members, Louie met nursing angels who coaxed miracles from their elderly patients. This is her first novel.

Illustrations: **Nguyen Louie** is a third and fourth generation Chinese Korean American political cartoonist and children's book illustrator. Born and raised in Oakland, she now lives in San Francisco with her husband David Wegman, son Lazlo, and daughter Siena. She spent most of her life coping with dyslexia and overcoming the stigma of being labeled dumb or slow. Her brain is hardwired differently. She loves hearing multifaceted narratives and telling stories with pictures. Check out her latest musings at nguyenlouie.blogspot.com.